Zo's Quest

Zo's Quest

— BOOK ONE —

Abigail Ortiz

First paperback edition May 2023

www.AbigailOrtiz.com

ISBN 979-8-9880111-0-1 (paperback)
ISBN 979-8-9880111-1-8 (ebook)

Published by KMAO

DEDICATION

For Quest,
for all my Mahdi's,
for Pahana,
for my only Augur,
for my company,
for the Three,

"There is no fear in love…"
(1 John, chapter 4, verse 18)

PROLOGUE

Zo wakes, startled and blinded by an intense light flooding her room.

She blinks and covers her eyes, but the light is all-consuming.

What is this? Quest better not be pranking me, he knows how I feel about my sleep. She takes a deep breath and sits up, motionless in the penetrating awe of it. *No. There's no way he'd do this, at least not now. He was so messed up last night—*

"Quest!"

She gets up and fumbles for the door.

"QUEST?"

There is no door.

CHAPTER 1

*S*he frantically feels around, *Where's my pillow?
And blanket? Where's the bed?*
The bright light still permeates her vision. She continues reaching out for—anything, and finally loses her balance and falls.

She crosses her legs and sits still, defeated, unable to escape the light, and rubs the necklace charm of her family's crest between her thumb and her fingers.

"Quest," she whispers, then yells, "Quest! Where are you?"

"Quest," squawks an unfamiliar voice, "Quest? Quest! QUEST!"

What? Who the heck? Who talks like that?

The distant voice is coming closer, "You are on a quest, you say? HUMPH." (It's nearer) "We're all on a quest! How rude of you to assume you're the only one."

As she listens, her eyes begin to adjust.

"Why, life itself is a quest."

Squinting, a dark form emerges through the light.

"A quest for purpose!"

It's a bit clearer now.

"A quest for understanding!"

The figure stops in front of her.

"For knowledge. Peace!"

All around, things are taking shape.

"Quest, indeed. HUMPH."

She can now make out the large, yellow eyes glaring down at her.

"Stop sniveling! It's not becoming—and frankly rather distracting. Get up! GET UP!" It flaps massive wings at her. "Continue on your quest."

The oversized bird leans down and is now face-to-face with Zo. He's at least the size of an average man. His feathers are the kind of deep, dark black that reflects blue when the light hits it just right. He wears a satchel slung over his wing and resting against his belly. His only distinguishable facial features—apart from a broad and shiny beak—are those huge, piercing yellow eyes.

"HMM? Come now! On your feet. You're just short of the crossroad. Up, up! Be on your way. Pick your path and find your quest. Settlement ought never be an option. Come now! Up, up, up!" As he speaks, his wings beat about and his head twists and turns side-to-side, up and down and even upside-down.

Eyes wide and unbelieving, Zo finds herself in the middle of a vast forest.

"How? Where—how did I get here?"

"How? HOW? You find your own answers on your quest! HUMPH. You've come this far, aye? Surely only you know how you've traveled until now. No one can walk your journey for you, only you can choose your path. Come now, keep going. If you stop, you'll just be like any other of these nameless travelers." He looks around. "Pathetic forest. Time wasted. Cursed Wanderlands." Then returning his attention to her, he adds, feathers fluttering in fury, "On your way, now! On your way! The crossroad is just beyond that pass." The bird points.

Zo stands up. Her breath stops short as her surroundings settle into vision.

Travelers are everywhere.

Some are clearly people, but many of these travelers are creatures. Most of them carry packs of supplies. Others bear literal mounds, like shells garnishing snails, their life's possessions are stowed in the mass on their backs. But a scattered few hold little more than their clothing. There are several pacing to and fro, like they can't find their way.

For every one in motion, more are resting. At first glance, some seem to be engaged in conversation, but it soon becomes quite obvious that no one is listening to anyone else. Zo is an audience of one to a world of ongoing monologues, each engrossed in retelling of their story.

"So I's said, I's had 'nough! I's not goin`…"

"Then thems left. Jus` up an` gone. And now I'ms alone 'cause thems…"

"I DON'T CARE NO MORE!"

"Happy rights here. Comfortable. Er`thing me want's me gots here…"

"I coulda been an Other, but thems Others held me back. Thems knew I was better…"

"I's the greatest! No one's best me record still! I's the best then and now— YOUS HEAR?"

On and on and on in endless ramble.

Still there are a scattered few who appear quite comfortable, occupying the land as though they've found security amidst the babbling white noise.

But by and large, the majority have simply settled down, creating makeshift shelters out of the supplies they possess and the natural resources provided by the woods.

And these settled are becoming part of the very land which they reside. Limbs grow indistinguishable from rocks and trees, seamlessly transitioning from individual to nature as flawlessly as a trunk becomes roots and roots become grounded.

The sweet, familiar scents of pine, eucalyptus and cedar flood Zo, and she's overcome by a strange dread and a cold shiver crawls up her spine—

What if all the trees in this forest were once like these who are settled down? Is that what the bird meant? Did they all get so stuck in their places that they could no longer separate themselves from the land they camped on—they grew into it?

Rubbing her arms to hush her standing hairs, she mutters, "I must be dreaming."

"HUMPH."

The bird's head reappears in her vision, his wings are fastened to his hips. "I knew it. You were thinking of settling, weren't you? I KNEW it!" He throws his pinions in the air. "Why do I continue to try?"

He turns away, still talking to himself, and feathers flustered, gestures as wildly as he did before. "Every time I tell myself, 'It's just going to suck time away from my own quest.' And every time, I ignore myself, only to prove myself correct— every time! HUMPH. Not anymore! Never again, I say! That's what I say! But then again that is what I always say…"

Zo takes a deep breath and looks around. *Nothing makes sense.* She looks back at the kooky, big bird getting farther and farther away. *At least he has some handle on whatever's going on here, wherever here is.*

"Hey, uh, excuse me!" She hurries after. "What's your name?"

Still rambling to himself, he doesn't realize she's in tow.

She raises her voice, "AHEM. Please? Pardon me, but I don't know your name?"

Without slowing his stride, he turns his head over his wing and peers sideways at Zo with one large, yellow eye. "Nice to see you've decided to continue your quest. We'll see how long it is before you settle." He looks back ahead and his feathers calm. "My name is Mahdi. And you are?"

"Mahdi, it's a pleasure to meet you." She keeps pace. "Please, I don't know how I got here. And I don't know where my brother is. I was sleeping, and I left him in the living room, and I woke up to this incredibly bright light, and I called for him—Quest is my brother's name actually—and then you came, and the light faded, and now here we are."

Mahdi makes no attempt to acknowledge her.

She bites her lip, speeds up, and cuts him off. Placing her hand on his wing, the bird halts mid-stride.

"Please? Please, you seem to know something about this place. At least you have some sort of direction, and you were kind enough to stop and try to help me along. Please, would you help me find my brother?" A tear swells. Struggling to hold it back, she desperately searches Mahdi's sharp eyes.

"OH!" His feathers fluff and he crosses his wings. "Humph. I am a soft bird for sad eyes."

She lets out a small laugh, but holds his gaze.

"Alright. Alright!" He flaps himself free from her touch. "But the only way I can help you is to help you along YOUR quest for as long as our paths meet. That's all I know how to do. I haven't found anyone along my quest except for those I have met on the journey. But I have seen that nothing good comes to those who go looking for another who isn't on their own path. Your quest MUST be your OWN. Humph. You cannot simply follow another. We may journey together for a time, but we will go our own ways eventually, and if you choose to follow me, it may prove to be fatal for you—or me! HUMPH."

His feathers ruffle again, and he uses his wings to brush them smooth. "I will help you along your quest, until our paths go separate ways. Keep up. Pay attention. Come now!"

CHAPTER 2

As they walk, the forest thins and the ground hardens. A clearing reveals an immense mountain stretching across the horizon as far as the eye can see, and so tall its peak stands somewhere beyond the clouds.

A wide, beaten road is stretched out before them. It's as though many roads—trampled out by centuries of trailblazers traveling from every direction, all headed to the same destination—merged their paths into one. It spans the breadth of an industrial freeway, and its destination is a makeshift metropolis where mud huts and skinned tents stand, and goods, supplies and food are sold and bartered.

"The Crossroads at last," Mahdi whispers.

"'Crossroads'?" Zo looks around. "This is a market—like an entire city sized bazaar. I don't see a crossroad. It looks like every road lead here."

"The Marketplace, yes. The Market may help us along the quest. Look," he spreads out his wings, "the wide road continues on, around the great mountain. Most travelers take this road. It is the easy road to take."

Then he lifts a single feather.

"But there, just beyond the large tree at the foot of the mountain where the bright river passes, over beyond those tents, do you see? It is the beginning of the narrow path that leads over the mountain. Look, see? There are other trees too that align it, not far from the great tree." He puts both wings on his hips and straightens. "Few take the narrow road—a very few. It's quite difficult."

He drops his voice again and leans forward as he gazes toward the walking trail, "That's the road I'm taking."

The sight of the tree (even at this distance) is enough to steal Zo's breath.

It's an imposing mass that very well appears as wide as it is tall. Its bark is a brilliant white, but also glistens with flicks of silver. Its leaves bear every color, as though it is entering an autumn change, but more colorful with brilliant pinks and purples, rich greens and blues accenting the vibrant reds, oranges and yellows and even gold. Its branches sway ever so gently and its leaves shimmer like dancing rainbows in the breeze, yet never shed.

It is quite apparent that this tree is not experiencing a death of seasons; rather, it stands proud and in its very prime—even though its size assumes it is an ancient wonder.

The tree is grounded in the midst of, and stretches across the river itself. Massive roots reach out of the water from the far bank where the narrow road begins, across to the near side where the wide road intercepts it. This natural bridge is itself the very site of the crossroad.

The river glows in the late afternoon light, as though a hidden source of brightness lies beneath its depths.

The narrow road isn't nearly as distinguishable. Save for the trees marking the trail's head, it seems to vanish into the shadow of the ominous mountain. Zo can't make out a single traveler moving that way.

"Why would anyone take that road?" she wonders aloud as the noise and bustle draws her attention back to the wide road.

"Come now!" Mahdi ignores her. "I need sustenance."

But Zo doesn't move.

Look at all these—well, they're not all people.

She's taken by the variety of travelers. Many, like Mahdi, are familiar beasts. There are other oversized birds of assorted colors, profiles and plumes. And there are many other animals that stand and walk upright. Even giant insects roam about.

But also the trees are alive. They're personified, like those she encountered when she woke up. Except these are not grounded. Here they slither silently atop the earth, their roots gliding and tumbling like knots of snakes.

All travelers dress in their own unusual garb, but everyone's clothing seems to be made by hand, reminding her of pictures she's seen in history books. *Wait—what am I wearing?* She looks down to find she too is dressed in unfamiliar clothes.

The brutal shock of awakening in the light is finally fading in comparison to the overwhelming discomfort she feels in the midst of this alien commotion.

What is this place? How did I get here? Where is Quest? Is this a dream? Why doesn't this feel like my dreams?

Mahdi has continued on.

Sniffing the air, he catches a scent that brings the beginnings of a smile to his staunch beak. "Yes." He exaggerates his breathing. "Yes, very good." And taking another deep breath, he points a feather. "Come now, this way!"

Looking over his shoulder, he beckons his new companion along, only to realize just how far behind she is.

"Maddening! MADDENING, I say!" He marches back to where Zo stands still in the middle of the wide road, and grabs her shoulder. "Are you with me?"

She gazes through him for an extended moment.

Then the blue tint shining through his feathers lit by the setting sun brings her back to herself. "Mahdi! Yes! I'm sorry. It's all just so... odd and unfamiliar. I—"

"HUMPH." He crosses his wings. "You're sorry it's odd? Or that it's unfamiliar?"

Her eyebrows furrow as she stares at her companion. *What is that supposed to mean—* "No! That—no, that's not what I meant." She gently places her hand on his crossed wings. "I'm sorry I got distracted. I've never been anywhere like this before. I won't let it happen again."

"Well, then humph. I suppose you won't be opposed to buying us some eats?" He holds his head high and slightly angled, and peers down at her with one almost closed eye.

"It would be my honor, Mahdi, but I don't know if I even have any money."

"HUMPH! Of course I find the helpless traveler who's without coin. too!" He throws his wings into the air. "Come now, I need food! And you could do for some eats too, I've no doubt. Come, come!"

He leads her into the market, to a stand exuding a repugnant odor, like heavy, burnt frying oil mixed with something she's not familiar with, and lots of steam.

"I want the biggest one you have." He sits at an open stool. "And she'll take—humph, what size grub do you want?"

She's still adjusting to the stench. "What size what?"

"Your grub!"

"What's a 'grub'?"

The nearness of stating his hunger makes him more impatient by the second. Signaling the merchant, he turns to enlighten his acquaintance. "Grub," his beak is clenched, "G-R-U-B. Grub. Only the most succulent, mouthwatering, tender, delicious, deep-fried, protein packed, larva there is!"

"Larva?"

"Yes, larva!" Her blank stare exacerbates him. "Maggot. Squishy little bug baby! You don't know what larva is?"

Her eyes narrow on what she had only assumed to be large balls of dough being dropped in vats of hot grease. *Those are humongous maggots?* "I— I—" She leans in to whisper, "Mahdi. I don't think I can eat that."

"WHAT?" He looks as though he's going to molt. "They're delectable! Why, you won't find food like this—"

Her eyes plead as she continues whispering, "Please, Mahdi. Please don't make me eat that."

"HUMPH. Well why don't you go find something more pleasing to YOUR palate than? I'm staying right here." He reaches into his satchel and hands Zo a few tiny chips of precious stones. "Take this for exchange. They'll buy whatever your stomach fancies."

"Order up!"

A mammoth, deep-fried maggot with both ends hanging over the plate is dropped in front of Mahdi. His eyes open wide, examining his feast. A true smile breaks his beak for the first time since she's met him. He uses both wings to raise the colossal bug like an oversized sub, and slowly expands his salivating beak.

Zo quickly turns away and begins her search for something more... edible.

CHAPTER 3

*S*couring the market for where actual people gather, she can't help but be drawn to a rowdy crowd, moving synchronously like a mob, back and forth, while randomly bursting out in laughter.

Local entertainment?

Trying to peek over and through gaps in the horde, she finally elbows her way in to get a look at what's happening.

A blindfolded man wearing a hooded cape is stumbling about as his spectators yell out haphazard directions, leading him to run into or fall over something.

The crowd cannot get enough.

She rolls her eyes. *I can't.*

No sooner does she turn to elbow back through the thronged buffoonery, the blindfolded man falls against her, and the hoard erupts in another jovial roar.

"Hey!" Her face is tense and nostrils flared.

"Apologies, Miss." The man grins, making great use of his long arms and legs to exaggerate every gesture, prompting greater laughter. "Enjoy the show!" He turns back to the eager mass.

She snaps, "You ought to be ashamed of yourself!"

He freezes and turns back. "Why?"

But she's already shoving her way back through the swarm of mindless laughter.

She finds a covered booth with large crates stacked for tables and chairs. This eatery serves a skewered mystery meat with a smokey, grilled aroma, and comes with an assortment of sauces. And there is beer. *There's always beer.*

She orders a few sticks of meat, a sampler of sauces, and a pint.

The meat is tastier than she could have hoped. It's dark, thick-cut and perfectly juicy. It doesn't really need any sauce, but the sauces have unique perks, adding a nice variation every few bites. The beer has a heavy foam with a thick, rich flavor that hints at molasses and a subtle spice that makes Zo wonder if she's drinking a kind of hard ginger ale. It pairs perfectly with the meat.

Putting in for a second order, she decides to people-watch while waiting.

The evening sun is almost hidden beyond the horizon but she hardly notices, enchanted by the nearer brightness of the river running along the outskirts of the market. The white light from the waters below casts a beautiful glow upon the huge tree. Despite the constant stir of the Marketplace, she's entranced by it.

She tinkers with her family crest. Something about the way the lighted water causes the great tree to glisten gives her a sense of peace in spite of her own confusion and the surrounding chaos. *I wonder what that water tastes like? I bet it's cool and refreshing. That light is so strange, but it makes the great tree look beautiful. I want to feel the strength of the tre—*

"Ere yous get ya shine?" The server drops the second order in front of her, snapping her attention back into the eatery.

Zo grins as the robust scent of sizzling meat inundates. "I'm sorry, what?"

The server points. "That thing 'round ya neck," placing her change on the table, she adds, "I's seen it before." And in the same breath, she turns back to her work.

"My crest?"

Amidst all the novelty, it takes Zo a moment to process.

This is our family crest, it's Father's unique design. There's no way she saw it before. Unless—

She stands up and calls, "You've seen it? WHERE? WHEN? Have you seen..." her voice trails as the server vanishes behind a crowd of patrons.

She sits back down with a sigh. *I'll catch her on the next run.* Taking a large bite, she looks toward the river crossing again.

Where did they come from? Three travelers stand on the narrow path near a large boulder on the far side.

But a group with an over-packed carriage walks directly through Zo's line of sight. When they finally pass, the three on the far bank are gone.

She continues observing the bazaar while finishing her meal. Although she keeps an attentive eye, that server doesn't return. As her plates are cleared, a loud group of hungry travelers wait nearby to take her table.

I guess her shift ended. She picks up her change and returns to find her guide.

Approaching the putrid tent, she can hear Mahdi drinking and laughing.

With three empty plates piled in front of him and his fourth holding a mostly-eaten grub, the bird is in a jolly state and welcomes her back with a hardy one-winged hug. "I didn't thinks I'd see yous again!" He laughs, then hiccups.

"Thank you for dinner." She burps.

His face squints in disgust.

Really? My burp is ruder than his drunkenness? Ugh, typical. Ignoring him, she continues, "I think I'm ready to begin the narrow path. My serve—"

"Oh, you think yous ready, aye?" His eyes narrow. "Well," he slaps the bar and a small plume of dust shoots back toward the bartender, "I think I needs a good rest."

He hiccups again and shoves what's left of his food in his beak, then tips the merchant.

"Come now!" He stumbles as he turns. "Do please catch me."

She puts his wing around her shoulder, steadying him.

"Come! Let us away! To the resting place!" He looks back at the merchant, who points out the way to go. Then he swings back around, leaning heavily on Zo, and extends his wing to mirror the direction.

"Away!"

The resting place is a secured area with rows of cots stacked four bunks high. Zo finds a bed at the edge of a row where she can see the bright river and the large tree. She assists Mahdi into the bottom bunk, then climbs onto the second.

The bird is quickly asleep.

But Zo stirs, anxious to begin the path, to taste the lighted water and feel the great tree. She finds herself gazing longingly at them for what feels like eternity.

After some time, she spots three travelers near the large boulder again. *Just like before. What is it about them?*

Without another thought, she leaves Mahdi behind and finds herself rushing to meet them.

No sooner is she within a decent distance, the three vanish again. She pauses but feels a strange urgency as she looks for them.

Finally turning back, she bites her lip.

Where is Quest? How will I find him here? When will I wake up?

CHAPTER 4

"*W*ake up."

Zo moans, but doesn't move.

Mahdi's whisper is urgent, "Awake, girl. We must rise before the rest if we are to make it to the other side."

When did I fall asleep? How did I get back here? I remember—did I really see those three again? Was that just a dream?

Her body aches as she rolls over. "That wasn't even a good sleep. Please? I just need a few more minutes."

"AWAKE," he is sharp. "I leave now. If not now, I will get caught again." The bird paces. "One must leave before the temptations are awoken. I go to the narrow path now. If you must stay, then here we depart."

Curiosity surges like adrenaline, and she is now fully awake and scrambling to get out of bed. "What do you mean, 'leave before the temptations are awoken'?"

But he's already left.

The sun has yet to even hint at rising, and the Market is barren at this late (or perhaps early) hour. The few about are obviously lost to intoxications, and far more have passed out along the roads.

Zo yawns, stretching as she staggers behind. *I bet everyone normal is enjoying their unconscious bliss. Then again, there's not much normal about this place.*

The merchant tents appear deserted. There are faint sounds of music, laughter and indistinguishable voices coming from another end of the Market, but that direction is the opposite way from the narrow path, and she needs to pick up her pace to catch up with her companion.

UMPH. Zo falls to the ground. "HEY!"

His smile is broad as he reaches out to help her up. "Oh yes, I know that, 'Hey!'"

It's the blindfolded man, still wearing his blindfold.

"Honestly!" She refuses his assistance. "What is wrong with you?"

His grin doesn't fade. "I'd say I'm blind, but I'm assuming you can see—"

"I don't think it's funny. Your—whatever it is you're doing. It's not funny."

"Yes, I believe you said I ought to be ashamed. Why?"

She looks after her ever-withdrawing guide. "I don't have time for this. If you can't figure out that making fun of a disability is not funny at all, then you belong right where you've placed yourself, at the center of everyone's joke."

She turns to run after Mahdi.

"Where are you going?" He calls after her, "What's your name?"

But she doesn't stop.

Meanwhile, Mahdi hasn't lessened his pace.

Catching up, her adrenaline is waned, and it's all Zo can do to keep stride with this bird on a mission.

Passing the wretched stench of the grub tent, Mahdi abruptly halts. He inhales deeply, and sighs with a faint smile. Then he reengages his focus and continues in his dogged stride.

The moments he paused were enough for Zo to notice a short line of cloaked travelers behind the grub tent, each carrying a bundle or two and obviously involved in some sort of sketchy transaction. *What's going on—OH!*

Mahdi has already continued, and she is determined to stay by his side.

"At dinner last night," she catches her breath, "my server mentioned something about my family's crest."

"Come now," Mahdi still doesn't slow, "much time ahead for talking. No time here to waste."

CHAPTER 5

*L*eaving the Marketplace, the view of the bright waters highlighting the ancient tree with the colossal, dark mountain backdrop is finally an unobstructed sight. A dewy morning mist hangs over the river and lofts gently onto its banks.

Zo gasps, stopping, as her wide eyes take in the magnificent sight.

Finally content to slow his pace, Mahdi observes her awe and smirks, giving her time to take it in. "Glorious, isn't it?"

She breathes, and manages to whisper, "Absolutely, yes. Glorious indeed."

Careful not to block her view, he walks beside her, and points out, "The river is, Maisha Maji, the waters of life. The tree, Maisha Mti, the tree of life. The great mountain is called, Kubwa Hatima Njia, the path of great destiny.

"The mountain is vast and incomprehensible. It will try us. It will break us. No one who travels here can be unchanged, not even those who turn back to the wide road. The river and the tree will help us along our journeys." He reaches toward her. "Come now, I will show you."

Still captivated by the beauty, she takes his wing, and the two stroll down the bank.

"Maisha Maji, the waters, will show you yourselves—listen now—humph," he pauses. The intensity of his eyes command her full attention. "Your truest SELVES."

He continues, "At first glance, the river will show the reflection of the 'you' you are meant to be, that is the 'you' only you CAN become. It is always beautiful. The who you CAN be is always your most handsome self."

His eyes narrow again. "But be aware, you will long for the water's reflection. You will desire to be your mirrored self so much that a craving will quicken, a thirst only quenched by a taste of the waters. And you must taste them or you will never be sated. Humph. And taste them you should! It is living water—the purest, most delicious waters! There is nothing like it. You MUST taste it, indeed, for it will quench your thirst for a time beyond time.

"But," he looks at her with the admonishing side-eye of a master attending his apprentice, "you cannot stay at the water. You may desire to reside here, but the water will not allow it. Once it satisfies your thirst, the light of the water inside you will reflect the 'you' you presently are, the who you ARE right now."

He tucks his beak into his chest. "Humph. The disparity between the two is enough to make anyone flee in horror and shame."

Zo furrows her eyebrows and closes her eyes. *This is all too weird to be real. I don't understand anything he's saying. Wake up. Wake up, Zo!*

Observing her face, Mahdi clarifies, "After you taste the water, the light within it will be in you. It is the light that magnifies your flaws. You will not like who you see—you will be repulsed, because the light brings your innermost ugly into view. You may not believe that it is true, but indeed you must know the waters ARE truth. The waters cannot lie, as much as light cannot bear darkness. I tell you this because this truth causes may to turn and flee, but you must not fear it."

He watches her closely to ensure he again has her full attention.

"I said Kubwa Hatima Njia will change you—and it will —but the great mountain can only provide the tests to challenge the who you already are. It is the waters that hold the potential to CHANGE you as you face every challenge along the path. The waters empower you. Enable the best you." He holds up a feather and points from the river, "But once the waters are inside you," to Zo, "you govern their authority."

And spreading out his wings, he adds, "That is why you must drink! Yes, your thirst will be squelched and you will thirst for nothing else, but the more of it is, YOU WILL FINALLY BE IN CONTROL of you. The waters GIVE life—not just sustain it. The very command of one's own life is bequeathed in Maisha Maji."

Dropping to a solemn whisper, he adds, "The Waters of Life."

Zo takes some time to take it all in.

Then she crosses her arms. "So this river of life will show me my most beautiful self, then when I drink it it will show me my worst self, but that's okay because I need to drink it if I am to make the journey over the mountain and become my best self?"

Eyebrow raised, she looks sideways at her guide, making no to attempt to hide her skepticism.

"Go," he gestures. "See for yourself."

CHAPTER 6

*J*ust short of the water's edge, she stops to take a deep breath and clutches her crest.

Where are you, Quest? I miss you so much! Father, and Ma, and you too, Bro, but I'm lost without Quest...

Forgetting the waters before her, tears fill her eyes and she rubs her crest between her thumb and pointer-finger. Her insides reel and her legs give way. She drops to her knees and buries her face in her hands, weeping.

Mahdi remains silent, observing. He remembers his first time at these bright waters. *The deepest pains, the darkest places that one strives to ignore or push away come full force at this boundary. No word of caution can encapsulate it, and no heed can suppress its impact. It's a vastly differing and deeply personal experience for all who dare approach these waters. Warning, young one, is utterly futile.*

This water's edge is a natural hurdle—a very initiating trial to the narrow path! If you cannot pass here, here we must part.

He knows this.

But he also knows she need not face it alone.

He carefully approaches, and sitting beside her, lays one wing softly on her shoulder. Her body shutters beneath her companion's gentle touch, and her muffled weeping lets loose to a deep, abandoned wail.

Rocking back and forth, she aches to be with her family again.

After some time, her energy drains and her moans soften to sniffles. Her eyes are swollen and her cheeks are hot.

She looks at the blue edges of Mahdi's feathers. *He's kind. Even if he tries to hide it. And he's soft. Oh, geez—he must think I'm such a wreck! He doesn't even know me, and here I am weeping on his shoulder. This is not your normal, girl, get it together. He must regret inviting me to tag along.*

She sits up and buries her face in her tunic, then peeks through her hand and bent arm to see if the bird also feels out of place.

Wing still resting on her shoulder, he greets her timid glance with a kind smile and tender eyes. He is neither surprised nor uncomfortable by her display.

She returns his smile, then again covers her face with her clothes. Rubbing her eyes, her discomfort fades. "Does this happen a lot?"

He shrugs. "It is different for everyone who comes this way, but most experience a similar encounter."

"Encounter?" *That's an odd description.*

"Humph." He nods. "Yes. Yes, you are encountering Maisha Maji."

"You say that like the waters are alive."

"Indeed they are," he stares at the river. "The Waters of Life."

She bites her lip. *This is awkward. But I guess it makes sense to be uncomfortable. An oversized, talking bird in a strange world just rocked me through a random crisis of emotion, and is now personifying water. This isn't normal. But his words and his company are calming.*

"Well," she shrugs, "I do feel better. I guess I really haven't given myself a chance to grieve."

"Grieve?" Mahdi's head tweaks at this word, but he pulls it back into his plum.

"You may feel better," his voice is flat as he gazes at the water, "yes, but you lack control. Yes. You may feel well, but you are not yet IN control."

"I'm fine, Mahdi, really. I just—"

"You still cannot conceive it, but you will." Smirking, he points. "You have yet to peer into the waters."

She frowns. "Yeah well, I'm sure I'll look my best." She touches her face. "Ugh, my eyes are puffy and my skin is hot and clammy. I doubt even this 'water of life' can help me now." She smirks and looks up at her feathered friend and chuckles, *I can't believe I feel a particularly deep connection with a bird!* She smiles at him. *This is so weird.*

He returns an empathetic grin.

If I'm not going to wake up, I may as well press on. Raising her head to the sky, she takes a deep breath. "Okay." She glances at Mahdi again, who again is looking at the waters. She takes another deep breath before she stands. "Okay."

Pausing once more, she holds her crest and suddenly remembers the group she saw on the other side of the bank just hours before. *Or at least I thought I saw them.* She looks over and finds the boulder where they stood. *They just… disappeared.* She searches the mountainside. *Where are they now? Did I imagine them? I suppose it could have been a dream.*

Her eyes settle back on the waters. Tapping her family crest beneath her shirt, she whispers, "For Quest."

She approaches the edge of the river. Before looking down into the water, she peers up again at the magnitude of the mountain, and takes one more deep breath.

Then looks down.

CHAPTER 7

*I*t takes a moment to adjust to the light the river emits.

Wait—there's no spotlights or even LEDs under the water. How is this even possible? Light's not an attribute of water, but the water and the light are the same? Like water is wet, and somehow this water glows. Which isn't possible. So this must be a dream. And if I can't wake up, I'll just ride it out until I do.

As her eyes focus, Zo's reflection begins to take shape. Now she sees herself, her best self, and she is stunning.

She's never given much thought to her looks. She's honest enough to consider herself average and simply hasn't sought to adjust that perception for herself nor anyone else. She's comfortable in her skin, and being comfortable is comfortable. But her reflection here is a marvel to behold.

Her eyes shine with maturity, a warm kindness and humble grace, and yet remain fiercely strong. A keen sense of wit glimmers through with just the hint of an unbridled spirit. Reminding her of many happy summers spent playing on the soccer field and splashing in pools and rivers, her rosy cheeks beautifully accent the laugh lines beside her eyes and at the tips of her smile.

She never gave much thought to wrinkles before either, but here in this reflection she sees happiness, sustained joy, hope and a bit of adventure in those perfectly imperfect lines. They speak the unspoken story of their suitor. And for the slightest moment, she feels a sense of sadness for the world that demands ways to evade these gleeful markers of life well lived.

Then she sees her smile. It's still crooked, but she has a new and profound appreciation for that goofy grin. Of the very little that she knows about her biological mother, she does know she was born prematurely. She learned earlier this semester, her lopsided grin is the result of an underdeveloped facial muscle; it never caught up. She touches the lower side with her fingertips and for the first time, feels love for it. It is also a reminder. Had there been even the slightest shift in circumstance, her life would have been lost before she ever took her first breath. Her crooked smile is a souvenir worthy of pride and gratitude.

Admiring the softness and radiance of her complexion, her skin appears to glow increasingly brighter. As her image fuses with the light, she realizes how dry her mouth is and how weak her body has become. Her mind quickens to what now feels like a distant memory of the sorrow she had known only minutes ago.

Her thirst is ravenous.

She plunges her hands and face into the water and drinks unabashed.

As she lifts her head to breathe, her eyes are closed. The air is fresh, clean, as though in the few moments she's taken to drink, a new rainfall filtered the world all around.

The water tastes sweet, crisp and pure, and refreshes her unlike anything she could have dreamed. She feels it move through her, down her throat and from her stomach out, tingling into every muscle, like all the while her body has been cut off from its circulation and these waters are now surging life back into every cell. It doesn't hurt like pins and needles, though, it's a sensation similar to the warmth of adrenaline, but without apprehension. It's an awakening to part of her she never knew was sleeping.

"Woah." She smiles as she exhales. "Woah."

She wipes excess droplets from her eyes and smiles again before looking down for her reflection. She's confident the beautiful change she feels inside has further affected her outside.

As the waters still and her reflection again takes shape, her eager anticipation sours. *Wait—what? What's?* She gasps. *No.*

She tenses, not recognizing who she sees. The eyes that beamed with grace and strength now show anger, fear, cowardliness and the weary spirit of a beaten and longing soul. Her skin is pale, matte and sickly.

With a clinched fist, she splashes the water and turns away.

Sitting with her back to the river, Zo cannot find any words. She looks to Mahdi for understanding.

"Things aren't always as they seem." He sits beside her. "But these waters do not lie. They cannot. You must accept the truth of your present you if you are to become your best you, the you the narrow path can help you be."

He pulls a worn bota bag from his satchel and turns to look at himself in the waters. He smiles, and a tear fills his eye. Gazing at his reflection, he remembers his first time on the path. He drinks and washes his face, then turns his head away as he fills his water sac.

Zo sits in silence with her back to the river, contemplating all the waters revealed, the ugly and the beautiful.

As the sun rises, it stretches over the wide path. The Marketplace is awaking, and a scattered few are already moving to and fro. Within minutes smoke begins to rise from the various eateries and voices call out to sell their wares. The scattered few quickly becomes a crowded bazaar.

Quest, where are you?

She takes out her crest and presses it into her lower lip. Then she takes a deep breath. Enchanting aromas of freshly prepared breads and meats compel her. "I could eat."

Mahdi looks over his wing toward the Marketplace. "The temptations are awoken!" He jumps to his feet. "We must leave now, or be drawn in and undone." He stomps quickly toward the great tree.

"But I'm hungry, Mahdi. Can't we just get a bite and come right back?"

"If here our paths must part, then part they must. I will not turn back now. And if you knew, you ought not, too."

Inhaling the enticing aromas one last time, she punches the ground, jumps to her feet, and jogs to catch up.

"Well, I'm going to need food soon." She looks back over her shoulder. "I don't run on air. This tank needs gas." Smiling to herself, she recalls the joke she kept with her brother.

Quest!

"Mahdi, yesterday at dinner a server recognized my charm!"

He continues his stride. "Charm? Charm? You ought not consider yourself too highly amongst those you pay for service. Humph. That is precisely how—"

She intercepts him. "No. Not like charming kind of charm." She holds out her necklace. "See? This is my family's crest. Our father designed it. It's perfectly unique to our family, but the server said she'd seen it before."

He glowers beyond his captor, offering only an impatient reply, "And what of it?"

"Well, if my server has seen another, then it has to mean Quest is here, too."

His eyes remain fixed beyond her. "Yes, the quest is here, and if you would get out of my way, I may continue—"

"No, Mahdi. Not 'the quest.' My brother. Quest is his name. He's here."

His head twists around. "Where?"

She sighs. "I don't know. My server went back to work before I made the connection and I didn't—"

"Then you must continue YOUR quest, young one." He rests his wings on her shoulders and turns an eye to look in hers. "You cannot find another if you yourself are not found." And without missing a beat, he steps around her, continuing on toward the tree.

She sighs as she looks back at the Marketplace. *For Quest.* Then she tucks her necklace safely beneath her top and hurries after the bird.

CHAPTER 8

"Wow." Taking in the marvel of the magnificent tree, Zo repeats in whisper, "Wow."

Mahdi, too, beholds the sight. "Impressive, is it not?"

Breathe, woman, don't forget to breathe. There's no way— I've never seen a tree this big! I didn't realize how far away it actually was. It's HUGE!

They stop in front of the grounding of a massive root, the diameter of which dwarfs the span of Zo's outstretched arms. Mahdi also stretches his impressive wingspan, which still barely covers half of the root's circumference.

Zo admires how the trunk squats and bends from the opposite bank, over almost the entire width of the river. The water itself runs both through and around its roots on the Marketplace side. *This tree is its own mini-mountain—a hovering hill! Its roots kick into the water like a playful kid splashing, knees-deep. But the tree hunches across the water, too, like an old man leaning into his cane.*

Zo raises her head, and her eyes and mouth gape. "This tree is an eclipse."

She takes to studying it. Ma's green thumb and love for vegetation was not lost on Zo. This tree has endured not only the test of time, but also has obviously weathered many stormy seasons and misfortune. It is bulky throughout, bent, twisted and misshapen, as though it sustained seasons of drought and perhaps some violent turbulence in its youth.

I can't imagine this tree lacking water, unless it sprouted before the river formed. Ooo, maybe it held through a tornado— THAT would be cool!

There are sealed collars (Ma always called them "scars") where branches might have been torn away.

"That's odd." She points. "So much of it is submerged in the water, but there's no moss or lichens attached upriver." She walks around to the downstream side. "No trace of algae either."

Curiosity draws her closer. The bark is a pure, matte white and smooth to touch, but also curls out, peeling away from the tree like cinnamon. Beneath this outer layer, metallic-like glints catch her attention. Pulling the exterior, she finds this deeper layer as reflective as refined silver.

"How peculiar," she mumbles.

Mahdi stands at a distance, observing his companion's curiosity. "Ah, the vascular cambium. That layer is where a tree may be graf—"

"Grafted in," she unintentionally finishes his thought. "Yes, I know." Still considering the coloring and texture, her voice drifts with her mind, "Father taught us how to graft…"

Tending to the garden was a family affair. Just a few weeks after they had moved in, Father and Bro showed the siblings how to graft scions, young shoots they'd collected from Amma's favorite pear tree at the orchard, onto the pear tree in their yard that was yielding less favorable fruit.

...Recalling Father's instruction, Zo parrots her memory, "'It's a fusing of the living tissues.'"

Pointing out the silver, she looks up at Mahdi. "But I've never seen anything like this before."

She continues moving around the bank, taking in the tree. Nearly every fork is in fact a graft union, and yet (apart from the dramatic differentiation between foliage from limb to limb) the rootstock remains true throughout. The variety of buds and mature fruits also range from branch to branch. Only the oldest branches bare golden leaves, as though dipped and plated.

She smiles. "This tree is remarkable."

"Humph. Yes, indeed. Do keep some bark for yourself. You'll find Maisha Mti quite satisfying to an empty stomach. Tastier than you'd imagine, too. Just a bit fills you up."

"Wait," she tries to contain her amusement. "You're saying to eat the bark, when this tree is full of all kinds of incredible fruit? You're kidding. Right?"

"The fruits are delicious, it's true." Pausing, he leans in, one-eyed, closer to his naive companion. "But the source of the fruit is the tree. The fruit can only give you what it takes from the tree. Better to get what you need from the source. And Maisha Mti is the Tree of Life." He smiles. "Get a good chunk, here I'll slice you off a bit."

Until now, Zo hadn't noticed what large and obviously sharp talons Mahdi has.

"You want it with the cambium attached—like this, see? The cambium is the meat of it. The bark itself will do in a pinch, but the cambium is what you want to chew. We'll wet some leaves in the river, that will help it keep. We should collect some sap, too —yes, that'll keep nicely. It heals what ails..." Mahdi continues rambling to himself as he reaches up and pulls off a few leaves and, after soaking and wringing them out, presses them onto the underside of the bark.

He turns back to her. "Here keep this in—humph. You have no satchel, mm? Of course you have no satchel! Humph. HUMPH. I suppose I must…" Grumbling, he shoves the extra bark into his bag.

She smirks. *He is right, I have no bag, no supplies. No funds. I only have this quirky companion. And I am grateful for him.*

He's still mumbling when she reaches out and takes hold of his wing. He falls silent, and awkwardly glances from his surrendered appendage to its captor.

Looking him straight in his uncertain eye, she speaks with all sincerity, "Mahdi, thank you for being willing to help show me the way. I have nothing but gratitude, but I hope to make it up to you."

He grins and turns his head into his wing, trying to hide his unexpected self-consciousness. "You are welcome." He pauses —still awkward—then gives her hand a gentle tug. "You are still hungry, hmm? We will nibble a bit on the other shore. Come now, let's cross. And we'll check the tap for sap."

He hops on a monstrous root and begins his perfectly balanced walk over the water's edge toward the trunk.

"Mahdi?" She's right behind him, though her pace is more cautious across the water-soaked root. "Why don't you fly? Wouldn't it be—"

"Easier? Hmm? Yes. Easier, indeed, but," he stretches out his wings revealing clipped feathers. "Even still," he assures, "the narrow path cannot be shortcut. It is not simply about the destination, young one. It is the process that matters. That is the quest! There is nothing to be gained in merely flying to the end. No chance for change if you choose mere convenience—"

He continues talking all the way over the natural bridge, but his words remind her of her family. She pauses and repeats in a low murmur, "'No chance for change if you merely choose convenience'..."

Zo always knew Ma was going to garden when she began to hum sweetly to herself. She would put on her apron and sun hat, and grab her old metal watering can just before entering the backyard.

She ignored Father's insistence to install sprinklers, and only finally agreed to let him put up a misting system to stop his nagging.

"Plants deserve attention," Ma would say. "Water is just a basic need, but it is a need that demands my attention. I cannot shortchange them out of petty convenience. I don't want my plants simply to grow, I want them to thrive! To be happy. And they need to know they are loved to do that. They need my company, my attention, my voice. When they are happy, I'm happy. The time I give to these wonderful creatures helps them thrive, and I'm the better for it, too."

...Zo smirks. *I miss you, Ma. And I remember.*

"—why I should stay lost on the wide road if that were the case." Mahdi is still talking as they reach the trunk. "Careful around now. There's a lightly beaten path if you watch closely to your feet. Look too far ahead and you will stumble, and if you stumble, you will fall fast into the strong waters below, and our paths will certainly be parted. You need to only see your next step. Keep your eyes to your feet now."

He continues his way around the trunk. "It should be just around— Yes! The tap remains!" He leans against the trunk revealing a lidded bucket, hooked to a spile, hanging off the tree.

He pulls a small glass dropper bottle out from his pack. "Here now, let's fill this." Slumping down against the tree, he holds the flask to the spout. Drip by drop, it fills with a clear fluid.

"As I mentioned, the sap from Maisha Mti has healing properties. A drop will do on any wound. And you take a drop—" he holds the syringe over his open beak "—if you are not well."

Waiting for the bottle to be full, Zo scans the next shore and spots the boulder where she first saw the three travelers the night before. *That was just last night? It feels so long ago. I feel so different. Surely it's been more than a few hours?*

"There we have it." Mahdi screws the dropper back onto the bottle. "Let us away!"

As they continue on around the trunk, Zo can't help but notice the tree has no shoot suckers. *Not even the tiniest water sprout? Truly remarkable.*

The morning sun is now proudly on display and yet the light from Maisha Maji has not lost its luster.

Stepping onto the far bank at the head of the narrow path, Mahdi's restlessness finally dissolves. He breathes deep relief and giggles to himself as he extends his wings. "At last! At last! I am free to the narrow path!"

He turns to Zo, wings still outstretched and a twinkle in his eye. "And now, my hungry traveling buddy, we eat."

CHAPTER 9

The companions sit beside the large boulder.

Mahdi makes grandiose gestures, pulling the bark out of his satchel, unwrapping it from the newly moistened leaves, and breaking off two bite-sized pieces. He holds one over his beak and extends the other to Zo. Then he drops the morsel into his mouth and snaps his beak like he's giving small applause.

"Ahh." He preens his wingtip and pats his belly as he continues to chew. "Delicious. Mmm. Mm! Yes, absolutely divine." Leaning back against the boulder, he closes his eyes.

Holding the small piece of bark in her still outstretched hand, she stares at the bird. *He's so goofy, acting like he just consumed a feast. Like he really needs some time and space to digest that itty bit.*

After a few moments of silence between them, she smiles. "You're funny." Examining the bark, she adds, "This can't be all," she looks back at him. "Is this it?"

He smirks.

She glances back and forth between her companion and the wood chip. *If he is joking, he's not letting on.* She smells it. *Minty. Citrus. And, maybe lavender? There's a sweetness, but a kick of spice, too.* She looks again at her companion, and catches a speck of yellow peeking through a very nearly closed eyelid.

"Go on." He's still smirking.

She takes a deep breath, and studies the wood one final time. *When in Rome*— She tosses it into her mouth.

Her nose has not deceived. The flavors she picked up are definitely present, and there is an unfamiliar, nutty richness to it.

"Hm…" She plays with the texture. *I thought it would splinter, but it feels solid like meat.* She moves the chip to her back teeth and begins to chew. *Yes, it's very meaty, like a perfect filet. And super juicy, too! Every bite bursts like a ripe grape. Mmm. Yeah, it's a heavy flavor—rich, maybe? I don't know how it seems like the more I chew the more there is. Wait—*

Nearing to swallow, the bark toughens to a consistency favoring dried meat. Finally consuming it, she peers with wonder at the happily digesting bird. "Delicious, and somehow completely filling. How is that possible?"

Far too comfortable, Mahdi doesn't move. "Maisha Mti, the Tree of Life." He smiles. "A little bit goes a long way."

"Yeah," she smiles back, "yeah, I get that."

She closes her eyes and leans back against her elbows as the sunlight warms her face. Then hearing a strange, muffled whistle, she opens her eyes once more to find her bird friend snoring.

Lying on the ground, Zo's mind wanders back through the day's oddities. She thinks of the bright light that brought her to this strange place, and the light the waters release, *Are they all connected?*

She thinks over the different foods, from the bark of the Tree of Life, to the scrumptious meat at the Marketplace, and that dastardly grub Mahdi swooned over (she shutters). She thinks about all the peculiar travelers she's observed, then remembers the three beside the boulder and wonders why she felt so connected to them—

The boulder.

She sits straight up. "The boulder. The boulder! Mahdi! Mahdi, this is THE boulder! They were RIGHT HERE!"

But the snoring bird gives no indication of rousing.

She gets up to explore.

The boulder stands as high as her nose and spreads wider than tall.

Her hand grazes it as she walks around, like a child letting her fingers pass along a fence. She guesses where the three stood when she first noticed them and positions herself there. Then looking over the bright water, she tries to find where she was in the Marketplace. *I can't even make out the resting place from here, how could I have possibly seen them?* She surveys the surrounding area. *There's no way. I must have been daydreaming.*

She turns, leaning her back against the rock, head up, arms dangling. She taps the boulder, making up a beat, when her fingers find an odd dip that catches her attention.

Motionless, mouth agape and wide-eyed, Zo stares at the stone.

"M—Mahdi," she breathlessly manages to whisper. "Mahdi. Mahdi!" She leans around the boulder. "MAHDI. MAHDI, WAKE UP!"

The bird scrambles to his feet. "What! W—wh—WHAT IS IT?" Looking about, he finds his companion peeking out from around the backside. "What is it, young one?"

As he approaches, her stasis stare draws his attention to the odd dip she's discovered.

It's an engraving. And it's fresh.

"Humph." His head twists sideways. "Why is that vaguely familiar?"

"It's our crest." She holds her charm in one hand and outlines the stone etching with the other. "It's, it's impossible." *Unless...* She covers her mouth. *Unless Quest was one of those three!*

"Of course there is a simple explanation," Mahdi begins, "your charm is simply not original."

"No." She scoffs at the absurdity of it. "No, that's not right. Father created our crest. He told me it was his design. He even has the original mold. He wouldn't lie. And why lie about that? It doesn't make sense. He was an honest man. No, this— something else is…"

The bird glares at her, waiting, but she is silent, comparing the two crests.

"Yes?" The mystery of her rapture has piqued his interest. "'Is'?"

She can't help ignoring him. *This is different. This shouldn't be here.* She touches the stone. A subtle variation is etched in the copy within the empty space of the crest. *It's not right, but it's not a mistake. It was added. But why would an arrow be…* She follows the direction it points.

A thicket grows against the boulder there. And beyond that, the narrow road continues.

"Mahdi, look," she points out the arrow.

He examines it closely and lifts his head to look beyond the bush. "Well it would appear that someone wants you on the narrow path, my dear. Perhaps your brother—" Realizing he is again being ignored, he crosses his wings. "Humph."

Zo has pulled back branches and is both arms inside the thicket. And now she's up to her shoulders and going deeper still.

"Here!" She twists and pulls herself free. "I found it!" She's covered in leaves and twigs and has more than a few scratches, but she has pulled out a rugged, leather rucksack. "They left it for me!"

"'They'?" Mahdi's yellow eyes expand in curiosity. "Whom are 'they'?"

"I don't know, but I saw them standing here while I ate in the Market and again at the resting place—at least I think it wasn't a dream. But I felt this connection, and here, I find our crest right here where I saw them. And the crest pointed me to this bag. Mahdi, it was THEM."

"Humph." His suspicions are high. "I've much yet to tell you about the path. And I'm certain there's much more I have yet to know."

She releases the straps and unrolls the top. It contains a small vial of sap and a leaf-wrapped chunk of bark from Maisha Mti, a canteen with water from Maisha Maji, a beautifully woven, hooded poncho, a small fixed blade in leather scabbard and a long rope. Within the loop of the rope, a folded note rests.

A gentle gasp escapes her as she reads:

Know that I love you and I am proud of you...
Always

Her mouth hangs.

She looks up at her friend with big, watery eyes. "This, this is," she shakes her head. "It can't be." *But the handwriting is unmistakable!* "Mahdi, Father wrote this."

"Father?" He cocks his head side to side. "You hadn't mentioned a father. How long has he traveled the path?"

"No, Mahdi, he's..." she's lost in thought again.

He rotates his head around in several directions. Annoyed with her continuously dropped speech, he screeches, "'HE's'?"

She looks up and startles. Her companion is rather twisted.

A gentle smile crosses her lips before she returns her attention to the note. "He—" a sob steals her breath. "He's dead. This—it can't be from him. But it's HIS handwriting, and HIS words. But it can't—unless…"

She grasps the bird by both wings and leans in close. "Mahdi, are we dead?"

He flaps himself free and looks with concern and doubt at his now frightened companion. "'DEAD'? I'm certainly as alive as you, and you as alive as I! No deader than when we met I'd suppose, and even more alive now than before I'll wager. Dead?" He gently places both wings on her shoulders and looks her square in the eye. "Young one, you have only just begun to live."

Zo leans against the boulder, and sinks down to the dirt, still examining the note. "Then how can this be? This is from Father. But how is it possible?"

I really must be dreaming.

Mahdi intently watches his traveling buddy. He's already grown fond of her. *She is naive to this land. I want to help her find her way.* He crouches down beside her. "Young one. Listen now. There remains much to teach you about the narrow path, and I've still myself much more to learn. And all the more, I believe there's even much, much more beyond either of our knowing yet ahead.

"But I am certain I am where I'm supposed to be right now for this moment. And I believe you are, as well. Why, you have a goodie bag and a love letter from your father as proof!"

She chuckles. "This is without a doubt the wildest dream I've ever had. But I'm glad to be dreaming with you."

Then she re-stuffs her bag, and stands up and extends a hand. "Are you ready, sir?"

"One more thing." He opens his satchel and takes out the extra bark he cut off for her. "Take this. You don't know how long we may journey together, nor how long our journeys may last, nor whom else you may encounter along the way." He hands it to her, "Keep it. Humph, I've at least roughed this trail a time before."

"Thank you, friend." She stows it.

He smirks, then springs to his feet. "Let us away!"

CHAPTER 10

*T*he narrow path ascends gradually. The landscape is mostly tall grass covered in large patches of vibrant wildflowers.

It's so beautiful out here. Zo walks with zeal. *Every step forward gives just a subtle change in perspective.* She looks over her shoulder. *And yet I've already covered so much ground. I LOVE being outside!* She looks up at the mountain before her. *I'm going to destroy this path!*

From this side of the river, it doesn't seem as daunting. Its peak remains well-hidden beyond the clouds, but Zo is more confident in the journey ahead than any of the strange circumstances that led her here. *I was made for this—my body is built for conquest! This path better be ready for me.* She picks up her pace, practically bounding up the hillside.

Observing his companion's enthusiasm, Mahdi smiles. *I remember how excited I felt my first time on the narrow path. How eager and ambitious I was. Her drive is contagious.* And he, too, picks up his step.

But before long, a fresher memory consumes him. He steadies his pace as his mind replays him losing his way and returning in defeat to the wide road. He is sobered, yet and still he appreciates Zo's fervor.

"This is so beautiful, Mahdi," she calls back to him. "The colors here are—I don't know, more! And the air is somehow fresher, almost," she slows down and inhales deeply, "ahh, sweet. Which is crazy because we're as much outside here as we were on the other side of the river. But it's different here. Peaceful and perfect. Why do so few come this way?"

She waits for him to catch up.

"It is exactly as it ought to be, young one. Of those who come, even fewer remain steadfast to the course. The beginning is a delight. Kubwa Hatima Njia is The Path of Great Destiny. But do not forget we attempt to travel the mountain, it will try you and it will break you. The narrow path is narrow because only few pass, after all."

She shrugs. *That doesn't make sense. Right now, it's all too beautiful. It's incredible—surreal! Why wouldn't more want to travel here?* "I'm sure if people only knew what it's like, I mean, you can't nearly appreciate it from the other side."

"True enough." He tucks his beak to his chest. "It is available to all who would seek it. And few do."

"But do they KNOW, Mahdi? Why would they come unless they've been told? Don't those who make it over the narrow path return to tell them?"

Sighing deeply, he pauses. "Very few return, and of those who do, most are too defeated or enraged to remember the beauty."

"'Enraged'?" —*what?* "Why?"

He tenderly pats her head with soft, gentle feathers. "There is still much ahead we have yet to know."

They continue quietly for some time.

The sun peaks and eventually descends low in the sky. The companions decide to make camp.

While Mahdi preens, Zo wraps herself in her poncho and fluffs her rucksack to use as a pillow.

After some time staring at the fire and listening to nature settling in, a strange feeling creeps over her and she cuts her eyes to their farthest corners.

As the evening bows quietly to the night, her discomfort grows. "Ever get the feeling someone's watching you?" She laughs awkwardly.

Mahdi answers without hesitation, "Indeed I have, and indeed we are."

Well that's terrifying. But he's so calm about it, like he's obviously expecting it, which means it can't be a big deal, right? She lets herself relax just enough to initiate conversion.

"Where I'm from, all the animals and birds are smaller and, well, wild like the ones we've seen and heard along the path today. Mahdi, why," she pauses. "What makes you—and the others in the Marketplace—" She bites her lip, not wanting to offend him. "How?"

Not riled by her question, he receives her sincere interest as a welcomed invitation and he leans close, eager to enlighten.

"There is a difference between 'natural' and 'wild'. There is a natural order, a singular one that functions in accordance with its intention. Then there are those many of the unnatural, and as such, dysfunctional. THESE are the wild kind."

Seeing the uncertainty in her face, he changes his approach.

"I was not always the bird you see before you, young one. Temptations and settlement revealed my wild kind. But now I believe I am in my natural state—or rather I am becoming my intention. I am not the wild I once was, but I am not yet the full nature of my intention." He smirks. Then he turns to stare at the fire in pensive thought, as though chastising himself for revealing too much.

He takes a deep breath. "The dysfunctional and unnatural has so crept into and overtaken our world that what is wild has become mistaken and even accepted as natural. Perhaps this too is a problem where you are from?"

Zo sits up and thinks. "That's, really deep, Mahdi." Leaning back, she adds, "I just thought you Evolved—"

"HUMPH," he stops her short. "'Evolved' you say? HUMPH." His feathers are ruffled. "There is a legend, ancient lore explaining our inception, but I don't follow such nonsense."

And as though a second thought raptures him, his demeanor softens and he speaks slowly, unaware he is uttering his contemplations, "I was different before. I have of course evolved throughout my life. But this path, it's changed me."

He turns to focus on Zo. "Young one, this I have observed, this one thing of the path I know, you cannot leave unchanged. Neither by commission nor by will. This path and only this path will Evolve you."

His stare returns to the fire as he continues, "I have bore witness to the devolution, the degeneration, the degradation of existence apart from the narrow path. You grow throughout life's span—yes, yes!—but as one piece of you evolves another withers, as the mind grows the body shrivels. And decay lends to decay, which decays beyond life's passing."

He sits in silence. His attention is still fixed in the fire's light, lost to the wanderings of his thought.

Zo also gazes into the fire.

Considering his take on the wild, she remembers her neighbor, Mr. Harper's cat, Mr. Whiskers, a very friendly feline who would often visit their family as they tended to the garden or engaged in various outdoor activities.

She adored that cat. His purrs and affection calmed her through many difficult seasons in her young life. She would pet him as he sat on her lap, and together they would watch the birds in the yard bouncing from branch to branch and chasing each other in flight. It was her refuge…

While gardening one day, she noticed the birds came to an abrupt silence, followed by the familiar sound of Mr. Whiskers jumping over the fence.

Bending down to greet him, she was mortified to see he was carrying one of her beloved sparrows between his teeth. He dropped it in front of her, and proudly sat beside its broken and bloodied body as it struggled to take its final breaths.

Shocked, she stared at the defeated bird. First sorrow weakened her, then rage activated her. She looked up at Mr. Whiskers and yelled, "HOW COULD YOU?"

The cat jumped back a few feet. Then almost as quickly, his eyes fixed back to his bounty, tail twitching.

Meanwhile, Zo had picked up a few stones from the garden.

With tears streaming down her face, she threw one after another at the fleeing feline.

From inside their home, Father had heard her yell and ran out in time to catch the last rock hit the fence and Mr. Whiskers narrowly escape.

He looked at his daughter, who dropped to her knees and was crying over the dead bird, and quickly discerned the situation. He held her, shielding her view from her lifeless friend.

She wept on Father's shoulder.

In her youth, she couldn't understand how the sweet cat she adored could kill one of her beloved birds. She was devastated by this betrayal.

With his daughter in such grief, Father also teared. "I know the fondness you have for Mr. Whiskers, and the joy birdwatching gives you. You must feel miserable and conflicted. I'm so sorry." Holding her, he cried with her.

After a few minutes, he lifted her chin and spoke softly, "Inside even the tamest animal is a wild nature. Don't hate Mr. Whiskers. He was trying to give you a gift. He can't understand how he hurt you."

...The odd but familiar snore of her companion pulls Zo back to the present.

She rubs her eyes to adjust from the bright fire, and peers into the darkness around. She can't make out anything or anyone watching, but she can't shake her discomfort either.

Shivering a bit, she returns her gaze to the hypnotic dance of the flames. She snuggles in tight beneath her poncho, and closes her eyes.

Her eyes open wide.

The moon is still high, but something's jolted her from her rest. The fire's dance has long settled to still, glowing embers. The world around appears asleep. Mahdi continues his careless slumber.

Zo takes a deep breath. Then yawning, she stretches and relaxes her muscles. *Geez, I must really be wound up— THERE!* She freezes. *There it is again!*

A sure sound of movement is nearby, like leaves rustling beneath someone's feet.

Someone or something is very close. "Mahdi," she whispers sharply through closed teeth, "Mahdi!"

But the sleeping bird sleeps.

The noise again, only longer this time, it's as though someone is trying to get her attention.

Her eyes grow, pupils adjusting to the odd lighting of the moon from above and the embers beside. She slowly turns her head toward the shaking behind her. There's no form apart from a young tree. Not so much as a shadow of anything peculiar, only leaves and branches and a narrow trunk.

Mahdi's traveled this way before and he's sleeping soundly. It's not bothering him, so maybe it shouldn't bother me. It's probably just a squirrel, or more likely an owl. We ARE outside. No reason to make it into anything bigger, like lions or tigers or bears—JUST ignore it. Mahdi isn't phased, so it's fine. It's not the boogieman, Zo. It's fine. Besides, sudden movements wouldn't make anything better if it was—NO. No. It's fine. It's fine. But what if it's—

She sits up, looking intently into the tall grass that surrounds their camp—

"Quest?"

But only stillness answers her call. The noise has stopped.

She rolls back slowly and snuggles again in place. Breathing deeply, she watches the shrinking glow of the cooling embers.

CHAPTER 11

*T*he sweet medley of songbirds dancing in the dawn blissfully calls Zo to wake.

Mahdi is already sitting up with his eyes closed, meditating or perhaps simply basking in the beauty of their surroundings. There is a subtle mist that gives the morning air a crisp, clean scent. Zo happily stretches away her stiffness.

"Good morning, Mahdi." She sprawls out.

The bird doesn't move, but offers a muffled, "Mmhm."

She smiles and sits up, turning toward the rising sunlight, and watches the songbirds playfully flutter and chipmunks scurry about their morning duties. *It's like being in the yard back home.* She closes her eyes, grinning as she lays back down.

"Come now, child," Mahdi breaks her muse. "You mustn't spend all day taking in the sun. Much path is before us, and we've but fleeing hours to conquer it."

He moves beside her and opens his satchel, then gestures for her to follow suite. He pulls out his bark and water and breaks off yet another tiny bite to eat, then sips one simple sip from his bota bag. He takes just a moment to enjoy his tiny feast before returning everything to his bag, then stands up, ready to move on.

All the while Zo watches him, still holding her grin.

He crosses his wings and taps one talon. "Your watchful eyes slow our progress, child. We mustn't dawdle." Then the warmth of the rising sun on his gently misted feathers lifts his gaze toward the sky. And for a quiet moment, he lets himself again soak in the morning.

Zo sits up, pulling her meal from her bag. "I'd argue that watchful eyes prevent a recession in one's progress. Kind of like digging deeper to build higher." She smiles a cheeky grin, then consumes her bit and takes a sip with all the revel her still sleepy consciousness can muster.

Leering at her with one eye, he does his best to hide his smirk. Indeed, with each revelation of increasing comfort between them, he is growing fonder of his traveling buddy.

Again they are off. Wayfaring by day, campfires by night.

Still, Zo can't shake the feeling that they're being watched. But as time passes, she allows herself to become desensitized to the random noises of rustling brush that pursue them.

The path becomes higher and steeper with every passing day, and the vegetation thins as the terrain grows harder.

Zo shares stories from her childhood, growing up as orphans with Quest, and being found by their forever family. She also shares many of the dominating dreams she's dreamt since she could remember, and how her dreams are always somehow sibylline with her life.

Mahdi occasionally asks a question, usually seeking clarification on things she takes for granted that do not correlate in this world. Overall, he proves to be an excellent listener—so long as they're moving.

Summiting a rather rocky stretch, where the path is only recognizable by a narrow smoothing along the rough ground, Zo finds a fragmented line of resting travelers and bushes and boulders all murmuring to themselves ahead.

Not knowing what to do, she stops and calls back, "Mahdi, what's going on here? It's like there's a line."

"At last," he sings, "At last we're nearing!"

With the vastness of the path still before them, her face balls up in confusion. "Nearing what? This isn't the end."

"The end? No, young one, we have barely begun. We are near the Gathering Place."

The bird catches up and passes Zo, and without so much as a hint of hesitation, steps around the first babbling boulder.

"Carry on, now, we carry on. Ignore these settlers along the path. They have given up their quests. We travel onward." He steps over a small, mumbling bramble bush and around a chattering person whose clothing and even body appear to be becoming one, settling in with the sediment beneath.

The settlers all seem entranced by their own words, like those she first woke to by the bright light in this world. It's been some time since she thought back to that transition, and considering it now, she remembers Quest and longs for her family.

Everything here has to be connected. At least it seems to be connected. Climbing this mountain is almost like riding a rollercoaster, I can feel it all pulling me up this mountain. It has to be leading me to Quest. I will find you, bro. Her hands ball into tight fists, and she steps around the chattering rock and between two arguing shrubs to follow after her feathered friend.

She does her best to go around, over and generally avoid stepping on any part of the minefield of settlers. Mahdi is less careful, and quickly disappears around a rocky bend.

Unable to keep pace, Zo bites her lip as she looks after him. *This is the fastest that bird has moved since we met!*

"OUCH." She stubs her foot against a boulder.

"Watch it!" the rock sneers.

Her eyes move from her aching toes to the sullen stone. "Sorry." Looking up she realizes, *He's continued on without me!*

She pauses, surveying the settler-speckled path, and sees that it leads to a low opening cut in a very high and very sheer cliffside. *I don't see a way around that ledge, and I'm definitely not going to try to climb over it. Mahdi's nowhere in sight, so best guess is he went in the hole. Okay. Creepy, small cave it is.*

Still doing her best to politely navigate through, she hurries to catch up.

Entering the cave, a cool gust makes her stop and catch her breath. Her eyes, too, need to adjust to the diminished light.

A vast lair at the bottom of a small hill is laid out before her.

Settlers thicken along the way here, and are a throng in the valley below. Inside the cave they take the form of wet, ever-growing, ever-gabbing stalagmites.

Tents are speckled throughout the cavern below, similar to the Marketplace, and in the center a quad is carved out like a small town square. Beyond the chamber on the far side is another, higher hill, and at its top a speck of light shines in.

The path must carry on there.

Not far ahead, Mahdi stands, wings fastened to his hips and head turned sideways, awaiting his traveling buddy.

He smiles as Zo nears and spreads his wings wide. "Welcome to the Gathering Place."

CHAPTER 12

The Gathering Place is not as busy as the Market. Almost all the tents here are residences.

Approaching the square, one voice rises over everything and the pair find a crowd intently listening to an enthusiastic speech.

They observe from outskirts until the sermon ends. As the audience withdraws, Mahdi finds an opening and, grabbing Zo's hand, heads toward the center.

A large, reddish-brown mountain lion is pacing, smiling and offering gestures of gratitude to the few still lingering.

Mahdi catches the lion's eye and the two exchange mutual sparks of recognition and affection. The lion graciously excuses himself from the final stragglers, and beaming, turns and reaches out.

"My friend." He embraces Mahdi. "Your return is a most welcomed surprise!"

Zo cocks her head. *Mahdi's never even hinted at having a friend. This IS a most welcomed surprise!* She smiles, arms crossed, watching her buddy greet his buddy.

The two hold each other, arm and wing, exchanging salutations. Then Mahdi turns back and spreads his free pinion.

"This, Yakov, this is my dear traveling buddy, Zo."

Recognizing a twinkle of pride in Mahdi's eye, Zo tucks her chin to hide her smile. *Father used to look at us that way.*

Mahdi continues, "She is no ordinary traveler, Yakov. No settlement here, no! She is like Jael, the mountain goat—an overcomer! Able to conquer where others dare not tread. And mark my words," he points a single feather, "she will see what others cannot imagine."

Zo blushes and a gentle scoff escapes her lips before she can stop herself. She looks to the lion and manages an embarrassed smile.

Yakov smiles kindly. "You have found favor with my friend here, child. Not a simple task. You must indeed be set apart." With one paw still grasping Mahdi's wing, Yakov extends the other toward her. "Come, rest. You are welcome as my personal guests for as long as you need. Come, come. We have much to catch up!"

Inside a nearby tent, large floor cushions are heaped in mounds and spread throughout. Several scattered groups are lounging and sharing conversations. The trio finds rest on a pile of pillows near the entrance.

While Mahdi and Yakov visit, Zo does her best to digest the surprise of meeting a friend to her friend. *What else is my traveling buddy keeping from me? A bird and a lion walk into a cave—HA! Who would have thought? And they're old friends at that! Yakov is obviously a leader here. If the crowd was any indication, he seems to be well liked and respected.*

As the trio begins to unwind, a tree-person—skin raised and cracked like bark, arms and legs hung long as branches with fingers narrow and delicate, and long weeping hair as the vines of a willow—enters and quickly approaches them.

"Pardon me, Yakov, and welcome esteemed guests." She bows her head, the vines of her hair sweep over her face. Then she quickly straightens. "But supplies are critically low and your arrival may prove the perfect timing. If I may be so bold, have you any sap from Maisha Mti?"

Yakov clears his throat. "Yes, Pahana, you are welcome." He turns to his guests. "Please excuse our informalities, we are all family here." Then looking at Zo, he adds, "Our principal work is in caring for the wounded, newly arrived or returned, as well as tending to those who have settled. Pahana herself came here as one in need and now helps others as she once received. And she is quite right, your arrival may very well be the fulfillment of our hope. So few travel the path."

Zo stands up and grabs her rucksack. "I was studying to be a nurse back home. I'm happy to help. I've been curious to see what the sap does." She looks to Mahdi, who returns an approving nod.

Then as an afterthought, he beckons her to his side and whispers, "Whatever you do, refrain yourself from the waters here."

"I assumed Maisha Maji flowed through the great mountain? Is the water different here?"

"It is very different to take the waters directly from its living stream." He pulls her close and lowers his voice, "The waters here, although born from the river, do not flow with the river. The Gathering Place does not consider the plight to dig up the freshwater worth the effort in comparison to the works already being done here. The waters you may find here are out of context and so polluted."

Zo raises an eyebrow. "Oh." *I guess that makes sense?* "Okay."

She smiles as she excuses herself, and follows the tree.

CHAPTER 13

*P*ahana leads Zo from one settler to another.

She's so patient. I guess that makes sense. Trees are rooted in the ground, watching the world go by, so that kind of implies patience. But she's a living tree—like, really alive. Talking, thinking, walking!

Her direct care is exceptional, and she does seem sincere. She's really listening to everyone's story. All. The. Stories. There's so many of them and everyone has something to say. And somehow she's present and patient with each settler. Like there isn't anything more important than who she's with right now.

Broden was like that. I've never met anyone who could make you feel like you were really important, not like Broden could. Until now.

Each settler quiets after sharing their tale. Pahana's patient presence draws them out of their monologued trances. She then explains the purpose of the Gathering Place and asks if they are willing to share their supplies with the community. Then she leans back and lets Zo examine them. Pahana showed her how to administer the sap.

A drop applied as salve bubbles throughout a wound like hydrogen peroxide, then fizzes down, coating the abrasion, and after a few moments is completely absorbed by it. The injury shows improvement almost immediately. Within minutes, all that remains (if anything at all) is a scar. Of course broken bones take longer than flesh wounds, and a gash longer than a scratch, but every visible injury heals in kind.

Occasionally (and only when their story tells of anger and offense toward the narrow path itself), Pahana encourages the traveler to receive their drop of sap orally. Many refuse. These she warmly embraces with a sigh, and moves on.

The few who accept respond in one of two ways: Some perk up, as though waking from a restful slumber, a glimmer of light in their eyes and bright glow rejuvenating their skin. But others reject the sap, gagging, coughing and spitting it out. They often sneer at Zo and Pahana, and always send them away.

The rays of outside light filtered throughout the cave dwindle as the day draws to a close. Throughout the settlement lanterns are being lit.

Pahana lifts her head. "Tomorrow's light will reveal more wounds." She turns to Zo and smiles. "It's time you return to your friends."

They gather their collection of supplies and head back to the center of the village.

"Pahana," Zo asks, "I don't understand why some refuse the sap? And why does it heal, but also make others sick and angry?"

The tree plants herself and looks over the vast settlement before closing her eyes and taking a deep breath. "Not everyone who hurts wants to be healed. I suppose the healing can often hurt more or differently than the pain they are accustomed to. Healing the soul is not as simple as healing the body. Giving voice to your pain and having someone listen—truly, simply listen—are the first steps toward that healing, but they are not the last. Many do not wish to go further."

She uproots, and they continue their way.

She's so much like Broden. He listened to everything. He even listened to cars! He could always diagnose an engine just by listening to the sounds it made. He could fix anything with those ears, and he'd listen to anyone, even grumpy Mr. Harper...

Zo and Broden used to play catch in the front yard. She preferred to play with him because Quest couldn't be bothered to throw ball for more than a few minutes, and Bro threw harder and faster than Abe.

One day, she accidentally deflected a pitch with the edge of her glove, and the hardball went high and came down on their elderly neighbor's mailbox with a THUD, before landing in the surrounding bush. She jogged over to get it, and no sooner had she reached down to grab it, Mr. Harper flung open his front door and wobbled down his walkway as quickly as his cane and crooked leg would let him.

"YOU GET OUT OF THERE!" He scowled. "I SAID GET!"

Zo looked at him sideways. "Excuse me?"

Her heart began to race as he approached. She froze.

Come on, Zo, move! COME ON! Her eyes were wide and locked in on the fire she saw behind his. *If my legs aren't going to help, I have to hold my ground. I can do this. I can do this. I'll kick his cane out from under him. If he tries to hit me with it, I'll shove him before he has the chance. Oh god—oh god!* She had only ever fought to defend her brother or someone else in need. *Breathe, breathe. I got this. I'm faster than him. This old man is messing with the wrong kid!*

He was only a couple hobbles away. As Zo clenched her fists, Broden appeared between them holding up both hands.

"Mr. Harper, good afternoon, hello." He reached out to shake hands. "Is something wrong?" Broden looked into his neighbor's eyes with respect and compassion.

"I'LL TELL YOU WHAT'S WRONG!" Mr. Harper waved his crooked finger in the air, as though he were trying to smack a fly. "EVER SINCE ABE AND AMMA TOOK IN THESE TWO LITTLE DEVILS, MY AZALEAS KEEP GOING MISSING!"

"WHAa?" Zo scoffed. Her face scrunched and her ears got hot. "No one wants your dumb—"

But Bro stopped her. "Mr. Harper, I can assure you my SIBLINGS are not to blame."

She grumbled, "This old man must be blind."

Bro gently signaled her to quiet, then reached back to hold his little sister's hand. He took a deep breath.

"Mr. Harper, you know our parents. We've lived here since before I was born. You know how Ma and Father raise us. Please, sir, what exactly has happened?"

"It's not worth it, Bro," Zo whispered. "Let's just go."

But he held fast to his sister's hand and pulled her to his side, placing his arm around her shoulder.

Mr. Harper's fierce eyes moved from Broden's determined peace, down to Zo.

She was fighting back tears.

He took a deep breath.

"It's just, this was the Misses favorite flower bush. She loved azaleas. She planted it. She kept it. And now ever since she passed it's just dying right along with her."

Broden shook his head. "I'm so sorry, Mr. Harper. Mrs. Harper was a beautiful, dignified lady." He sighed and looked at Zo. "I'll tell you what, I stand by my assurance that my siblings are not to blame." He squeezed her hand and turned back to Mr. Harper. "And my siblings and I will come here on the weekends to help you keep your yard, because that's what neighbors do."

Zo turned sharply to her brother, but his gaze was fixed with Mr. Harper's, and the two shook hands.

Returning to their yard, Zo whispered harshly, "WHAT? BRO! WHYyy? We should've just left. It wasn't my fault!"

Broden put his hands on her shoulders and got down on one knee to look into her eyes. "Sometimes, sis, what's important is taking the time to listen. You don't want to go through life passing everything by just because it's not your fault. We never would have known that Mr. Harper needed help if we didn't listen. And he would have just been angry for no good reason. But listening gave us what we needed to help. And it'll help us, too. Quest could use some sun on his pale skin and we could always spend more time together."

He smiled and shuffled her curly hair, then picked up his mitt and jogged back to his position to catch.

I could have taken him, Zo remembers mumbling as she pounded the ball into her mit.

…She smiles to herself and shakes her head. "I get it now, Bro."

"Pardon?" Pahana asks.

Stopping in her tracks, Zo stares at her.

"I didn't catch that." The tree tilts.

"I—I didn't mean to say that out loud." Zo turns red. "Sorry."

Pahana smiles. "So you talk to yourself. Any other quirks I should be aware of?"

Zo snickers. *The tree can hold her own. Okay, okay! I hadn't realized now much I've missed a descent sense of humor traveling with my ever-quiet, speak-only-when-speaking-is-necessary traveling buddy. I like Pahana. She's comfortable, familiar, like getting to know an old friend.*

They stop at one of the large tents that borders the town's square to drop off the supplies. Guards are posted here, and they aren't allowed inside. *What all is in there?* But before long, they're chatting again, on their way to where they left Mahdi and Yakov.

One large tent remains between them and their destination. "Mmm," Zo sniffs the air. "It smells like fresh baked bread."

"It is." Pahana smiles. "This is where our bread is prepared and our beer housed."

Zo flinches. *That doesn't make sense. Since we crossed the river, we only eat a bit of bark and drank a sip of water every morning. That's it. I thought that was normal, but they have bread and beer here?*

Pahana continues, "You are fortunate to have arrived today. The bread is only made fresh every few days."

"Are there fields nearby? What grains do you use for your bread?" Sniffing the air again, Zo stops. "Something smells so familiar."

"Aren't you perceptive?" Pahana smirks. "Here I'll show you." She holds open the tent.

The walls inside are lined, floor to ceiling, with rows of kegs used to divide several stations, all set up like an assembly line. There are workers keeping a close eye as the bread bakes in pans over open fire pits. Some are kneading dough, while others mix ingredients. Still more sit around large, depressed milling stones and use softball sized rocks to grind the oversized grain down to flour (each berry is similar in shape and size to a rugby ball).

"Our grain grows wild and is harvested from the hillside just above where the narrow path continues, beyond the far end."

Pahana points back in the direction they were working. "We gather it over several days, and grind it here on the stones." She leads Zo along in succession. "Mix it with beer here, and over here we knead in one very special, very 'familiar' ingredient."

Smiling, she points out a single piece of bark from Maisha Mti that is being divided between several mixing bowls.

"And we use the remaining grain berries to ferment and brew into beer. Our water is stagnant, and on its own could prove very harmful, but the fermenting process purifies it."

Wait— WHAT? They're diluting everything! Zo says nothing, but her face speaks frankly.

Pahana tilts her head. "I know this is not what you are accustomed to, but the bark is not common here. With so many settlers, we HAVE to spread it out. When we knead it in with the dough, a small bit can feed many, not just one."

"But that dilutes it." Zo shakes her head. *The bark has sustained me every day I've traveled, but only enough for each day. It can't be possible to live off a fragment of a bit. At least not to travel. You can't help them and withhold what they need.* "I don't mean to impose, it's just—"

"Life here is different than traveling along the path," Pahana's tone has changed. "The settled cannot handle a pure bit."

"And what of those who don't want to settle? How can they be strong enough to return if—"

Her vines wilt and her voice becomes soft and sad, "Few do." She clears her throat. "Very few."

Then taking a deep breath, she perks up. "And that is why we remain. Our path ends here, in service to those who will not go on. We provide what they need to stay alive on the path, even though most choose not to continue along it."

After a few moments, she nods with a smile. "Now to return you to your friends.

CHAPTER 14

*M*ahdi raises his wing to welcome them.

Zo smiles and quickly sits next to her traveling buddy. *Ah, there's my friend. I enjoyed some space, and even hanging out with her. But you, you get me.*

Yakov stands to greet them and quietly checks in with Pahana. Then he smiles at Zo as he sits back down. "Our healer tells me you were of great service today."

Pahana and Zo exchange courteous smiles. Then Pahana bows her head and excuses herself.

"Oh," Zo's surprised. "Must you go?"

Pahana stands still, but her eyes glance to Yakov.

Yakov stares at Zo, and after an awkward silence, insists, "Yes, of course! Please, Pahana, join us before you retire."

She slowly sits down.

The lion doesn't waste a breath, "You were very useful today, Zo, thank you for your service."

"I'm grateful I was able to help. Pahana would make an incredible nurse! She's great with—"

"She is well-trained, yes. We do pride ourselves on the excellent service we give to the travelers here." Grinning, Yakov carries on, going into great detail about the wonderful aid and amenities the Gathering Place provides.

Rude. And arrogant much? This cat does not stop. Zo glances at Pahana, who is looking down. *Let's see if we can have some fun without the chatty-cat catching on.* She twitches her foot until Pahana looks up. Zo makes a face. Pahana hides a laugh and returns an understanding smirk. Both continue exchanging silly faces whenever Yakov and Mahdi aren't looking.

A tray of fresh bread and beer are brought to them.

Pahana stands to pour the beer and serve the bread.

"Please, my friends," Yakov's smile peels his lips too far back, revealing an unsettling amount of teeth and gums, "this meal we share in your honor. Please, please enjoy!"

Zo looks to Mahdi, who gives an assuring nod.

The bread has a hard crust that cracks and crumbles when pulled apart. Once open, the dough steams and the familiar scent of Maisha Mti is released.

Zo takes a moment to breathe it in.

She pulls a chunk of dough out of the crust and balls it up between her hands, then tosses it in the air, and catches it in her mouth. She closes her eyes, savoring the familiar taste wrapped in the sweet warmth and soft texture—until she realizes all eyes are fixed on her.

Looking around, mouth full, she smiles uncomfortably.

"You certainly have a different way of eating," Yakov teases. "It's peculiar. But a pleasure to witness."

"Uh, thanks." Her cheeks flush. She tries to clear her throat. "This bread is interesting, too." *It's sweeter than it smells, and I can taste the flavor of the bark, but it's very subtle. Way too diluted to be helpful—OH. They're still staring at me.* "I, uh, like how doughy it is." She smiles and reaches for the beer.

Wow. This is way too bubbly. She scrunches her nose and sips it. *Ugh, and it's dry and bitter and bland.* She puts down, but after swallowing another large lump of dough, needs to chug something to clear her throat. When she can freely breathe again, she belts out a burp.

Mahdi and Yakov both stare with pursed frowns.

Pahana giggles.

Eyes wide and hands covering her mouth, Zo attempts to apologize but can't control her laughter.

When all have had their fill, Pahana stands again. "Thank you for welcoming me to sup with you. Now if I may be pardoned, I have field duty at sunrise."

"'Field duty'?" Zo asks.

"Yes." Pahana nods. "I will be harves—"

Yakov cuts in, "Ah, yes, harvesting the grain." (Zo and Pahana exchange glances.) "It would be good of you to welcome our young guest to join you in the harvest."

Zo, Pahana and Mahdi all exchange stares, not saying a word.

Pahana finally speaks, "O—of course, you are welcome. Though you should rest soon if you choose to join, sunrise is not far."

"Go, Zo." Yakov shows another wide, toothy grin. "Pahana will show you where to rest."

Zo looks to Mahdi, who is looking sideways at Yakov before realizing he's being observed.

He doesn't seem too impressed with his old buddy now. She tilts her head. "I could stay?"

Mahdi straightens and kindly turns to his traveling buddy. "It is well, Zo. Anyway, you ought to rest. As must I." He stands. "I take my leave, Yakov, good night. Pahana, please, if you would be so kind?"

"Of course." She bows. "Please follow me."

"Good night, my friends!" Yakov laughs as they leave.

Zo rubs her neck. *I don't know about him...*

CHAPTER 15

*P*ahana wakes Zo before the sunrise and gives her something new.

"What is this?" Zo takes it. "A fancy hula-hoop? It's so little. Or maybe a really big dreamcatcher? And I'm digging the arm-stitch, rope knitting, but what's it for?" She stands inside the cording and pulls the hoop up to her waist. "It's stretchy."

"I don't know what a hula-hoop or dreamcatcher are," Pahana smiles, "but we use these to collect the harvest. The circle is made of young cane from the fields. It is light, sturdy and large enough to carry on your back, like this." She puts her arms through it like a backpack. "And the net is strong and expands for the grain."

They walk quietly through the sleeping cavern and continue up the far, steep hill along the narrow path. There are fewer settlers on this side of the Gathering Place. As the morning twilight gleams into the brilliant pinks of daybreak, they exit the cave.

The narrow path descends into a large valley and then up again along the far mountainside. But today's task takes them above the cave, to the grain field growing along this hillside. It's rocky terrain, but not difficult to navigate.

The mature grain stocks wear a lovely shade of pale purple and stand about as tall as a door. They are thick and strong, very similar to a heavy, stunted bamboo. Like corn, the plant stands on top of brace roots. No more than three of the rugby kernels grow on each stalk.

Pahana leads Zo up the hill and to the far right.

"We rotate sections every day. Only take the berries that drop when you shake the stalk, like this." She gives one a swift, sharp jolt, but no grain falls. She moves on. "Leave what sticks, it shall be harvested another day." She points. "What's already on the ground will be collected by the Others."

Zo raises an eyebrow. "Others?"

Pahana tilts her head, searching Zo with soft eyes. "Have you not heard their sounds? Felt their presence as you have traveled?"

That first night, I thought it could be Quest. That rustling has followed us along. 'The Others'? I guess I just got used to it. Zo nods. "I have."

A large cloud shades the morning light, and as it passes the narrow path is revealed below. Zo's eyes follow the path. *How is it that we've traveled so far, but this mountain looks bigger now than when we first started? And why doesn't anyone travel this side of the Gathering Place? This journey is way bigger than I could possibly have imagined.*

Returning her attention to the chore, she notices the long shadows cast by the still climbing light. Then she sees Pahana among them. The stalk silhouettes fall like bars stretched over her.

She does seem caged.

Pahana turns, catching her gaze. "Is everything alright?"

"Uh, yes. I'm sorry. You mentioned 'the Others'? Who are they?"

Pahana shrugs and continues harvesting. "I don't like to speak of them."

"Why?"

She stops and turns back to Zo, silently listening for something.

Then she finally speaks in a hushed whisper, "Those who despise the narrow path. They surround it, but will not follow it. They use fear, mockery, deception and manipulation to sway the traveler, and so hope to destroy the path. A path that is not traveled too soon will be lost. So few travel anymore. I, I fear— No, I'll say no more." She returns to her work.

'Fear' what? I guess they can be unnerving, but not frightening. Is she trying to get me to ask more questions? No. No, she's really working, definitely not interested. Ugh. She's really just going to kill the conversion like that? Why is everyone here so weird?

Before long, there is a rustling nearby.

That sounds close. Way closer than usual. And we're not exactly on the path up here.

Growing up in and out of residential facilities and foster care placements, facing crisis early and often, Zo honed an exceptional deadpan expression and instinctively poker-faces whenever her nerve kicks in. Scoping the area, she doesn't notice Pahana is now observing her.

The noise frightens Pahana, and she turns ready to run, but freezes, seeing her companion's calm demeanor. "You aren't frightened by the Others?"

Zo smiles her crooked grin. *Yeah, no, that definitely spooked me. But I'm not saying so.* She shrugs and returns to the harvest.

Pahana smiles in kind and also returns to work.

The stalks are often reluctant to share their grain. The heat of the day has come and gone, and as the light begins to crouch low in the sky, the two each collect enough grain to almost fill their nets.

Pahana reminds Zo how to carry the full sack on her back, putting their arms into either side of the hoop and through the netting holes. They carefully trot back through the Gathering Place, then leave their yield at the baking tent.

Again, they meet up with Mahdi and Yakov before turning in for the night.

The following days carry on very much like the first, going out to help heal and comfort the settled. At the end of the fourth day, Mahdi pulls Zo to speak privately.

"You are happy here?" he asks.

She smiles. "I'm enjoying my company, yes."

Mahdi's eyes search her own. "And you are learning much?"

She tilts her head. "I have."

"It is well. Very good, yes. Indeed, it is good."

What's are these questions? What are you up to? Looking up at her traveling buddy, her expression communicates what she hesitates to say out loud.

"Yakov and I have discussed it. You are of great help here. At tomorrow's dawn, I will continue along the path. Tonight you must decide if you are to accompany me or if your path ends here."

Oh. Woah. I wasn't expecting that. I mean, I guess we've been here a while. I didn't think we'd stay here this long actually, but now that we're here, this feels kind of rushed. She looks at Mahdi, then glances over to Pahana.

He follows her gaze. "You may wish to stay. The work here is good. Your work here is good."

She fixes her eyes back on him. "But Quest—"

"My young traveling buddy, you mustn't forget, you first must find your own quest."

He can't still be confused by Quest's name. She smiles. *I know he's not. I need to find him, though, I ant to. But he is a wise bird. Figuring out my own way may not be a bad idea. But he's my brother! He could be lost. Or he could have found a great traveling buddy, like me. Or he could be looking for me.*

She nods, silencing her internal debate. "I'll see you in the morning."

He smiles and gently rests his wings on her shoulders. "Before the dawn."

Zo lies awake in bed.

I want to journey on with Mahdi. I miss my brother. And I love the work I do here. It feels good to help, to be part of something that impacts lives. I feel important here. And my heart aches for Quest…

She tosses and turns almost as frequently as her mind.

"Zo?" A soft, familiar voice disrupts her deliberation. "Are you awake?"

Rolling over, she's slightly startled to find Pahana kneeling so close. "Yeah. Uh, what's up?"

"I am frightened. May I sleep with you?"

"Um—" *Weird.* "—sure." She scoots over. "What happened? Why are you afraid?"

Pahana lies down facing Zo, and whispers, "It's the Others. I fear them."

But we're not outside. "We're safe here, though, right?"

Pahana takes a shaky breath. "At night, alone in the dark, I can think of nothing else. I cannot rest, my mind is overcome." She hushes, "You were so brave in the fields the other day, as though they could not scare you. I was ready to run, but your company comforted me. Forgive me, friend, but I am not afraid when I'm with you."

Zo lies on her back. *What has this tree endured? What brought her here? Yakov said something about her needing help— what happened? That has to be why she fears the Others so much. They are eerie, sure, but at least they seem harmless and their sounds have become so common, I stopped really noticing them a while ago. I'm sure she'll tell me if I—*

She turns back to ask about it, but Pahana is already fast asleep.

This is the first time I've see her so peaceful. She smiles. *I feel badly for you, friend. You need to be protected, and I don't really trust Yakov to do it. He seems okay, but also off, like he's only nice as a courtesy when he needs something. I used to be so protective of Quest. He was a skinny nerd, and he was my brother, and I'd fight anyone who came at him! Geez, he never appreciated it, though. He did NOT like me helping him, not at all.*

I guess I get it though. Skinny big brother defended by chubby little sister probably didn't help with the bully situation. Oh, who was that one bully at school? The last time he messed with Quest was the day we met the Salvador's. Abe, Amma and Broden, our forever family. I miss our family. I miss all of us.

Before long Zo is dreaming…

A dancing fog floats along the narrow path.

As it moves, it begins to divide and take the shape of three separate pillars. They hover, shifting, becoming distinctly human.

And they glide off.

The farther they go, the more they appear to be calling, beckoning her to join them.

She reaches out to them, but can't move.

Something is holding her back.

…She bolts upright.

It's still and dark all around, but there's a rustling nearby.

The Others.

Her heart's already racing from her dream, and now her pulse seems to beat against her eardrums. She clenches her fists, but Pahana moans through her sleep.

They are holding hands.

Taking a deep breath, Zo tries to relax.

Footsteps.

Her heart leaps. A cold sweat pours over her. She jumps out of bed, but her hand will not release Pahana's. Leaning down close, she can feel small growths from Pahana's palm are attached to her own.

The footsteps stop, and she twirls around.

"Zo?" Mahdi whispers, "Zo?"

She exhales relief. "I'm up."

He is quiet.

"Mahdi, I—" *I what? I'm stuck? I want to go but I also want to stay? I still haven't decided, but I know I don't want to wake Pahana—*

He embraces her in the soft warmth of his down. "I am proud of you and so grateful our paths crossed." He holds her close.

This stupid hand! I can't even give him a proper hug. She holds him as well as she can, and whispers through tears, "Thank you."

He takes a deep breath and pulls her back at wing's length. "Until we meet again, my young traveling buddy." He squeezes her shoulders, turns abruptly and starts away.

"Until we meet again, my friend," she calls after him, wiping her face with her collar.

She stands silently in the dark until his soft steps are no longer heard.

Then she sits beside Pahana.

The faint light of dawn begins to break through the cavern. When it's just bright enough, she turns and gets to work freeing her hand.

It hurts.

CHAPTER 16

*P*ahana wakes well-rested for the first time in a very long while. She smiles and sits up to stretch, swaying as though gently moved by a breeze.

Then she turns around to find Zo still drooling, hair stuck to her face and snoring through a deep, deep sleep.

Trying to muffle a giggle, Pahana covers her mouth and notices the palm of her hand is covered in broken shoots. She looks again at Zo and sees her hand wrapped in bloodied dressings. She reaches toward her to examine the wounds.

"Pahana! Pahana? Oh, Pahana. What are you doing here? You're late for your duties." Another worker has come to summon her.

"I was just about to waken—"

"You've no time," the worker rushes her. "Besides, Yakov has other plans for her. Come, come."

Pahana looks once more at Zo, then bows her head and obediently follows.

———

Around midday, Zo wakes up and rubs her tear-crusted eyes and pulls back the random locks of hair matted to her face.

She stretches big and deep, and collapses back into her sleeping mat. She sprawls out, then rolls over, sits up and reaches for her rucksack.

For the first time since arriving at the Gathering Place, she begins her day with a bit of bark and a sip from her canteen.

After savoring her tiny meal, she pulls out her bottle of sap and unwraps her hand. The shoots from Pahana were so strong that her skin tore when she picked and pulled off the suckers. She lets one drop of sap fall into her palm and closes her fingers over it, rubbing it in.

It stings at first, but the more she rubs, the more it soothes. Finally opening her fingers, no traces of injury remain. Admiring her restored skin, she takes a deep breath. *Ain't nothing like the real thing, baby!* She sings to herself, putting her supplies away and tidying up a bit.

She finds Yakov in the center of the cavern.

Okay, Zo, you've got this. Just don't let him talk first, and don't let him talk over you. Good morning, Yakov, where can I find Pahana? Polite and to the point. Just please don't talk over me. She catches his eye, but the lion pounces before she has the chance to open her mouth.

"Zo! Welcome! You are awake at last. I am glad to find you chose to stay here with us."

"Hi, Yakov, thank you. I overslep—"

"You were tired after a long night of deliberation and departure from your friend, I quite understand, no need for apology."

"Yeah. Uh, I wasn't—"

"Yes, please, come with me. I have something to discuss with you before the day grows too old." Placing his paw on the small of her back, he leads her to the familiar stack of pillows in the resting tent. They sit facing each other.

"Zo, Mahdi has the conviction that you are not a settler. I trust Mahdi. He is a good bird, a noble bird, tried often and found quite true." He falls unusually silent.

After a few disquieting moments, he leans forward and his eyes narrow.

Why is he looking at me like that? He almost looks hungry. He is a mountain lion after all. Oh god. Am I assuming the worst because he's a mountain lion? Am I making him into a predator? But he could leap at me. What if he does? And I get cornered, and the last thing I see are his dead, hungry eyes, and his shiny, too many teeth before—

"Zo, I would like you to apprentice me."

Her head tilts. "Come again?"

"I wish for you to come under—" Stopping short, he smiles to himself. "—I want you to come under my wing, if you will, and let me teach you—"

"Wait." She holds up her hands. "Yakov, thank you. I hear you. I just, need time. To process."

"Of course. Of course! Take all the time you need. For now, you may continue your good work beside Pahana."

"Yes! Thank you. Please, do you know where she is?"

He leans back against his pillows. "She is on field duty today."

"Field duty?" A surge of adrenaline rushes through her. *She must be terrified out there alone!* "I'll be off to work then, Yakov. Thank you."

He nods.

She runs to the fields.

"Pahana!" She searches for her friend, but hears no reply. "PAHANA?"

"I'm here," she answers quietly.

Heading toward her voice, Zo breathes deep to steady her panic. "Are you okay?"

"Yes." Pahana sounds doleful. "Is your hand well?"

Zo stops and looks down at her hand, recalling the pain she endured to free it. "Yeah, it's fine." She continues to make her way through the field. "How about yours?" She finally finds her sitting among the stalks, gazing out over the path. "Pahana?"

"Hm?"

"Is everything okay? Is your hand okay?"

Lifting her hand, she smiles. "All better. The shoots have shed."

"What happened?" Zo sits beside her, placing her hand palm-side up next to Pahana's.

"I'm not certain, but it would appear I've grown attached to you."

They both laugh.

Zo wipes a joyful tear from her eye. "That really wasn't that funny."

Pahana shrugs. "I guess we both needed to laugh."

They relax, basking in the warmth and light of the early afternoon, free of the Gathering Place. They talk for hours before remembering their duty. Then they work quickly and cram Pahana's berry net. Together they carry the overloaded bulk back into the cave.

Days pass slowly as every second together feels worthy of imprint.

Zo lives submerged in a happy haze of the present. The constant pace of chores keeps her mind occupied, and following routines alongside her willow friend makes Zo content. The two are practically inseparable.

I really like being with Pahana. Geez, how long has it been? Wait—how long HAS it been? I've lost track of time. It must be months since Mahdi left? Months! That's crazy! Can it really be that long? I miss my traveling buddy. I adore Pahana, and I enjoy our work together, but I still don't feel quite comfortable here at the Gathering Place. I miss Quest. I can't give up on finding him.

Her dreams seem to beckon her back to the narrow path, often waking her in the middle of the night where she continues to find her hand or hair attached to Pahana.

With every passing night, her internal conflict to stay or return to the path becomes increasingly unbearable and, although she tries to hide it, it begins to wear on her throughout each day.

Lying quietly, late one evening, Pahana sighs. "You must leave."

But Zo is so lost in thought that, although she heard her friend, she didn't hear what she said. "Excuse me?"

"You're not happy here, you should go."

"But I AM happy. That's my problem. I am perfectly happy here. And I am torn. I miss Quest."

"Happiness isn't a problem, Zo."

"That's not what I meant. One thing my father used to say was, 'If the goal of life is to be happy, then a life well-lived is an unfortunate deed.'"

"That doesn't make any sense."

"Right? That's exactly what I used to say! But he insisted, he'd say, 'What makes me happy might not make someone else happy, it might even harm them. If I only live to appease my happiness, I'd be hurting a whole lot of folks. Happiness should never be your goal—a welcomed byproduct, of course, but only if you set your goals to helping and giving. For us Salvadors, it's about saving.'"

"Well then, if you are not content with the work we do, you should go."

"But I COULD be. I can see myself living happily through the end of my days here with you." *Yeah, yeah, I think I could.*

Pahana rolls away.

Zo scoots nearer.

"You should go." A tear escapes Pahana's closed eyes.

Well, now I'm not going anywhere. Zo says nothing, but resolves to stay with her friend. She envisions them working together, listening and healing, laughing and sharing well beyond their years.

And for the first time in a while, she falls asleep happy…

"Zo. Zo."

Opening her eyes, a fog has filled the cave.

"Zo." The far off voice is so familiar, soft and kind. "Zo, my darling."

Where is that coming from?

"You must remember who you are," it continues.

As the haze gathers into a cloud, and pulls further into the distance, it takes the familiar shape of the three pillars.

It's just a dream.

"My darling, you must remember who you are."

An unbridled need compels her to get up and follow the pillars, but once more she's unable to move.

She looks down at herself and realizes she has settled with Pahana. Her skin is cracking like bark. Her body grows both one with her friend, and the two together with the ground. Looking up at the still fading mists, she begins to wallow in her shame.

I'm being consumed alive by a shallow grave. Oh no, settlement, I am not the one!

She struggles to break free, pulling, ripping and tearing through the pain. Her fingers dig into the earth around her, grasping for anything that might help free her. She screams out. But there is only a distant whisper in reply,

"Remember who you are."

...Her eyes open wide.

It's still dark.

She is laying on her side, sweating. Her heart races. She's out of breath.

Pahana stirs.

Zo tries to sit up, but can hardly move. Pahana's arm is wrapped tight around her waist. She tries to lift it, but Pahana's suckers are attached from her fingertips throughout her arm and back behind.

Zo turns her head, but it too is restrained. She attempts to pull her legs out, but they are numb. Her eyes widen as realization sinks in,

My dream, it's really happening!

Only one arm remains completely her own. As she reaches for her rucksack, Pahana moans and shifts. Zo pauses, and tries to look back at her friend, but can't.

I'm sorry, Pahana. She furrows her eyebrows and bites her lip. *I don't mean to rouse you, but I need to get free. My bag is way over there, so I need to stretch and that's going to pull you.* She takes a breath. *And it's really going to hurt.*

The farther she reaches, the more Pahana stirs and moans. Finally a few suckers hooked into her shoulder snap.

"Ow!" Pahana is groggy, but awake. "What's—OW!"

Zo pulls harder through the pain. She can almost reach it.

Snap, snap!

Pahana is completely alert now. "Zo, you're hurting me."

Snap! Snap!

Zo's fingers feel the leather, but she can't quite grasp it.

SNAP

"Please? Stop, Zo," she whimpers. "It hurts."

"Just a little more." Zo pulls hard.

SNAP

She has the bag.

Pahana is crying.

"I'm sorry." Zo scrambles to open it with her free hand and feels inside for the blade. "I'm so sorry, my friend. You were right, I have to leave."

Pahana has done her best to keep quiet, but the news of her protector's departure stings deeper than her severed shoots. Muffled sobs overtake her, and she weeps.

"I'm so sorry. I'm so, so sorry." Zo holds her unsheathed knife. "This is going to hurt."

"Please?" Pahana manages between sobs, "Please don't. Please?"

Zo reaches behind her back with the blade and begins to saw through the suckers until she can freely move her shoulders. She then works to free the arm trapped beneath her.

Taking deep breaths, feeling every cut, Pahana regains control and bears the remaining pain with great resolve.

Zo cuts her arm free from her waist. Pahana begins to break the remaining suckers between their torsos, and Zo moves to their legs. Finally their hair is all that binds them.

They sit up, two wounded friends facing each other.

My arms are exhausted! My muscles feel like wet noodles. She looks up at Pahana. *But she's enduring way more pain than I am. Let me take a break for both our sakes.*

They sit motionless for a while, both bleeding, both spent.

Pahana takes the blade. Assuming the responsibility to free her protector, she winces through each severed strand.

Zo swallows hard.

I've hurt my friend—the one I'm supposed to be protecting, and now she is taking it on herself to endure more pain to let me go. She lifts her head high to contain the wells filling her eyes, but a single tear escapes as her shaken voice whispers, "Thank you."

Pahana returns the knife.

Zo cleans and sheaths it, and puts it back in her bag. She takes out her vile of sap and offers it first to her injured friend.

"No." Pahana holds herself tight. "I cannot endure the sap while you are here, knowing you must leave."

Zo bites her lip. "Then I'll leave it with you." She holds out the bottle. "Here, please take it?"

But Pahana refuses, "You may need it for what is ahead."

"You need it now." She puts the vial in her hand. "And, here, please take this, too." She removes the extra bark from her bag and gives it to her.

Pahana receives both under one condition. "You must take a drop before you leave. And you must leave now, right away."

That makes sense. I get that that's right. But damn that hurts. I have to leave right now? Pack your bags, Zo, rejection has caught you once again. She turns away, busying herself in readying her things. Finally, she turns back. "May I hug you goodbye?"

Pahana looks down. "I fear my shoots may latch."

Zo bits her lip hard and nods. She eats a bit of bark and takes one sip from her canteen before putting her bag on her back. "I'm ready."

Pahana holds out the dropper.

"Until we meet again, my friend." Zo searches her face for a glimpse of hope.

But Pahana is silent in word and expression.

Zo tastes the sap.

It makes her gag and her stomach instantly wretches, convulsing to spew it out. But remembering the radical effects it had on the settlers, she swallows hard, and turns and runs away.

CHAPTER 17

*T*he brightness of the clear, starlit sky stuns her. Zo stops at the cave's opening, leans against the threshold and looks ahead along the silver-cast path. Then she gazes back into the darkness of the Gathering Place. Her legs and feet are tingling with pins and needles. She reaches to massage them, then rests her head against the cold stone and takes time to breathe the fresh outside air.

I feel new. She checks her arms and legs. *The wounds have vanished—that's so cool! And my back doesn't sting anymore.*

Securing the rucksack, she looks once more into the cave. Then, taking another cleansing breath, she jogs down into the valley.

The hollow is covered in a tall grass that grazes against her hips. The night is calm, and the air lends a cool, crisp breeze as she cuts through its stillness.

In, two, three, four. Out, two, three four. Deep, controlled breaths. In, two, three, four. Out, two, three, four. You got it. Yes! Man, I've missed this. That's right legs, you love to run! She releases a jubilant laugh, and picks up her pace. *Faster now—*

RUSTLE

GEEZ! That scared the crap out of me! Deep breath. What was that? She turns her head, maintaining her stride.

RUSTLE

Okay, now it's coming from the other side.

RUSTLE RUSTLE

And behind too? It sounds even closer. The Others. She runs a bit faster.

RUSTLE RUSTLE

They're gaining! She looks ahead, *About centerfield to a touchline left,* and breaks into a full sprint.

Her heart pounds. Whatever was behind is now advancing around. She hits the slope of the far side and bounds up the rocky hill.

The noises hold to the grassy valley below.

Looking back over her shoulder, she trips on a half-buried stone and falls with a hard thud on the unyielding ground. She rolls to her side and recoils in pain.

Voices call up from the hollow, "Does she believe she is special?"

"Who do you think you are?"

"How could she just abandon her like that?"

"She has no idea where the path will take her. No idea how it all will end."

"Betrayer."

"You are not ready."

"This is not safe."

"No idea what lies ahead."

Trying to ignore them, she checks her hands and knees, then rolls onto her back. *Just scratches and bruises. I'm fine.*

But the voices are relentless, and as she catches her breath, she can't help but hear them.

Why won't they shut up? They speak like they know me. They don't know me! They don't know... I just miss Quest. I don't know if this path will even bring me to him. I should be looking for him. Should I be looking for him? What's the point? Why am I doing this?

The chatter of the Others causes doubt to seep into her thoughts, and her questions give way to confusion. And just as confusion begins to morph into fear, the light of dawn breaks the night, and the voices below cease.

Amidst their muzzling, Zo feels the growing warmth of the rising sun, and her mind too is hushed.

Exhausted, she closes her eyes and falls fast asleep.

It's late morning when she finally wakes.

Sitting up, she looks back over the valley to the distant hillside with the cave and fields that mark the Gathering Place.

It's farther away than I realized. She brushes herself off. *I hope Pahana is okay. Geez, I already miss her.*

She turns ahead and gasps at the inordinate magnitude that still stands over her.

I want to go back to her.

But bearing in mind the bitter taste of the sap and the pain they endured separating, she swallows her desire and again sets out on the narrow path.

CHAPTER 18

*T*he terrain up this side of the valley is more barren and markedly rougher to tread. But even in its sterility, the path still holds an inescapable beauty that strengthens Zo's resolve with every step.

She sets camp late in the afternoons, just as she learned to do with Mahdi. Enjoying the sounds of nighttime, she rests peacefully beneath her poncho and snuggles into her bag under the open starlit sky. Her morning bit of bark and sip of water invigorates and sustains her well throughout every day.

She still thinks of Pahana, but gratitude outshines the longing.

She needed me. I've always needed someone to need me, because I've always felt rejected. Wow. I've always felt rejected. And if someone needs me they won't reject me. Pahana never rejected me, not even in our separation. I guess maybe she didn't need me after all?

She chose what was best for me because she genuinely loved me. She saved me. I don't think anyone else would have freed me from myself, despite themself. That's real. I miss you, my friend. We made a mess out of us, but our friendship was true. I wish you well.

As each day passes, Zo finds herself to be increasingly pleasant company, and she grows stronger, more confident and determined.

I can do this. I may be alone, but I know me better now. And I got this.

Nearing another summit, the slope is steeper than any she's yet encountered and she has to lean forward to use all fours. But she likes the challenge and enjoys engaging her arms in conquest.

She looks up. *About twenty feet more. Oh look! There's bushes peeking over the edge. It's been so barren this way, it's nice to see the green.* The higher she climbs, the thicker and taller they grow, until she summits.

"These are not bushes." She dusts off her hands.

Before her stands a very old, very dense forest.

The afternoon is still young, but the tree canopy already casts heavy shadows. Surveying the darkness, she decides to make camp outside the timberline. *Rest now. Tomorrow will provide a full day of light to travel through that dark wood.*

Old, dry kindling and fallen branches are easy enough to come by without venturing too far, so she gathers as much as she can and makes camp midway between the peak's edge and the tree line. It's been quite some time since she's had enough wood to make a decent fire, so taking full advantage of the situation, she builds a magnificent bonfire.

Playing with her hair, she gazes into the heart of the roaring light, marveling at the hypnotic dance of flames. Entranced by its fierce beauty and intoxicating aroma, she loses track of time, and dusk sinks into starry night. Before too long, the fuel is consumed and the blaze dwindles. She falls asleep blissfully watching the embers glow and smoke rise.

In her own company and surrounded by the wonder of nature, the path has become a delightful endeavor.

Rising with the dawn, Zo stifles the remaining smolders with handfuls of pebbled dirt, then tramples though it herself, *Just to be safe.*

She savors her morning meal to the sweet wafting scents of residual smoke and early morning breezes cleansed by the dew. Refreshed and ready for the new day, she packs up and heads toward the forest.

The thickness of the canopy still spreads a gloomy shade, but rays of light stretch toward her, breaking through all around. *It's a complete juxtaposition to the shadows that the fields cast over Pahana. It's like Jedi light sabers, the Force, rather than prison bars. Instead of uncertainty and the dread of captivity, I feel free here.*

Crossing into the woodland, her eyes take time to adjust.

Even with the prominent overshadow, the air is thick with humidity and warmth. She pulls up her wild locks, rolls her sleeves back and takes a minute to look around.

She welcomes the dramatic shift beneath this canopy with a smile. Woodland creatures chase one another, birds dart to and fro, playfully and protectively, insects move together like fluttering clouds and miniature regiments.

Life is teeming everywhere.

But this hub of vitality makes the path much more difficult to follow.

"You adorable little bastards. You've all crossed the path in a billion different places and beat out your own paths all over it. Look at this. How am I supposed to follow this?"

Doing her best to stay the course, the deeper she travels the more confusing it becomes. The rays of light that gave her hope when she entered this forest, are now growing short.

"It has to be nearing midday." She stops and looks around. Surrounded by wood, she can no longer tell from which direction she came. Her heart leaps, and fear creeps in.

Patience, Zo. Take deep breaths. You don't control this, but you CAN do this. Yes, this sucks. And being patient sucks, but just be patient. There's nothing else you can do. Breathe. Go ahead and watch the cute animals ruin the path. It's entertaining, right? Take a second to enjoy the moment, and just breathe.

After some time, the light begins to creep long again and her muscles finally loosen. "The rays fell toward me when I came in, so—" She faces the direction the light now grows toward. "Onward!"

She continues with a swifter stride, remembering from yesterday's summit how early the light fades here.

CHAPTER 19

"Dammit, don't disappear!"

She hadn't noticed the shadows slowly consuming the light. Now, as what's left of the rays floats up the trees, she's still too deep in the woods to see a way out.

Time to change my approach.

She finds a tree about 10 feet away with a dimming ray rising steadily up its trunk and heads straight for it, goes around it, and finds another tree with a similarly climbing beam ahead. She goes to it, around it, and continues in kind as quickly as she can, racing against the growing darkness.

No! I never gave myself a chance to find a safe place to make camp. All these old branches are sure to impale me.

Hands reaching through the darkness, she makes her way to the next tree just as the last speck of light is totally eclipsed. "WOAH!" She trips, but the familiar roughness of thick bark catches her before she falls. Leaning her back against the tree, she sinks to the ground.

"Crud."

As her body rests, her mind again races. She breathes a deep sigh—then sits straight up. *Is that smoke?*

Turning side to side, trying to catch another whiff, she can't help but recall all the strange ways Mahdi would contort his neck. She smiles. *Aw, my traveling buddy, I miss y—*

"THERE." She's caught the scent again.

Sniff, sniff, sniff

"There it is." SNIFF

She stands up. SNIFF

Turns toward it. SNIFF

Holds out her arms. SNIFF

And is once again tracking through the woodland.

After tripping several more times, bumping into two low hanging branches and getting snagged by a few bushes, she smirks. "There you are." A speck of light is now visible in the distance. "Smoke means fire, and fire means people." *Or death.* She bites her lip and shrugs.

Her pace quickens and she sees the fire burning inside a small clearing (no bigger than her dorm room). And sitting there beside, the silhouette of a traveler facing the flames.

"Hello?" She steps out of the dark.

He jumps. "AAAAAH!"

Zo jumps, too. "AAAH!"

His hand steadies his heaving chest. "What's wrong with you? You scared me!"

"You scared ME!" She laughs.

He stands and faces her.

Why is he staring at me?

"It's YOU," he finally speaks.

She snaps her neck back. "Who?"

He smirks. "I know you."

Her body pulls into itself. "You do?"

The oversized hood covering his face gently billows as he walks toward her. "I'd know that sassy voice anywhere."

She arches her back. "Excuse me?"

"I've been following you."

And she shrinks. "Excuse me?"

"Well, I suppose I've become lost in this blasted wood, but I left everything behind to follow you."

"Uh-huh." *The knife is buried in my bag, but there's a stick right here.* She squats to reach for it.

"You don't remember—" He trips over a root and falls flat on the ground.

Zo crosses her arms and stands. "I'd ask if you're okay, but you just told me you've been following me."

He laughs.

THAT laugh. "Oh, no."

Finding her realization more humorous than her reservation, wildlife scurry into flight as uncontrolled laughter thrusts his hood backward, revealing his face.

It IS him. She scoffs. "Why would YOU follow me? You had such a good thing going, making fun of blind people."

He brushes himself off as he stands, then extends a hand. "Please, join me?"

With no better option, Zo passes his hand and sits beside the fire. The two are silent, each staring into the fire until—

POP!

"AAAH!" He jumps again.

Zo laughs.

"Oh, so now it's okay to laugh at the blind guy?"

"Wait—" *No way!* "You're not ACTUALLY blind?"

"No?" He shakes his head, frowning. "What, the blind guy couldn't have followed you all the way out here?"

"That would explain how you ended up ahead of me," she mumbles.

"Says the lady who doesn't appreciate making fun of the blind."

She shrinks.

"My hearing is excellent, thank you. Likely better than yours. A collateral perk to the whole not being able to see thing."

They're silent again.

He sighs. "Anyway, what do you mean ahead of you?"

"Well, I think you're ahead of me. It's dark here now, and I seem to have lost my way—"

"Quite possible since it's so dark and all."

"—BUT, I caught wind of your fire and here I am."

"Good thing the blind man can build a fire."

"Hey! I've always advocated for—" *What am I saying? Am I a total hypocrite? Wait. Why am I even explaining myself to this guy?*

"'For'?" His eyebrows are raised. So is his smile.

She shrugs. "You know what I mean. You're the one who tricked me, let's not get it twisted."

"Did I?"

"Yes, you took advantage of your own disability and made me believe you were making a mockery—"

"Well, it would seem now that you are the one disabled, my lady. What with it being so dark and all."

Touché. She takes a deep breath and sighs. "I'm sorry. I wasn't trying to be offensive. And yes, I definitely have a disadvantage here. So thank you for letting—"

"You're welcome," he quips with a grin. Then softens and adds, "And I forgive you."

Sighing again, she rolls her eyes. "So what's your name?"

"Nah-ah-ah. I asked you first."

"What? When?"

"At the Market when you so very rudely and quite mysteriously dismissed me. Why else would I have followed you?"

She shrugs. "My name's Zo."

"'Zo.' Is that short for Zohra, Zoé, Zoel, or—am I close?"

"Nope. None of the above. Just Zo."

"Okay, Zo." He extends his hand again. "My name is Augur, and after following you all this way, it is my very sincere pleasure to formally meet you. How do you do?"

Smirking, she shakes his hand. "Hello, Augur. How do you do?"

"I'm glad you asked. I'm a bit out of sorts, actually. I met this lady who dared to challenge everything I am, only to leave me to my own questionable devices when I dared to question her intent."

She smirks again and shakes her head.

"So what's a clueless guy like me do?"

"I can't imagine." *And I can't stop smiling.*

"Well I'll tell you, I took off after her."

"Yes, I picked up on that, but—"

"Wait, it gets better. You see, I left everything, my heckling family, my heckling friends, my lucrative heckling entrepreneurship—everything—to follow you." He falls silent.

And? After an extended moment, she bites. "So, why?"

"I don't know." He sighs. "You're the first person to question me, to challenge my choices. I don't know why others haven't. Maybe they pity my eyes and so they don't doubt my lifestyle. Maybe they just don't care. I don't know. But you—you're different. You're bold, confronting, decisive. You're honest. And perhaps a bit cutthroat, but I like that. And I guess I've needed it. I know following you is perhaps a bit unorthodox—"

"To say the least, you don't even know me."

"—BUT, although I may not be able to see, I DO have vision. And I follow that, and THAT led me here, to you."

"But that's ludicrous!" She gawks. "I mean, I guess it's romantic—"

"Thank you."

"—BUT far from realistic or even reasonable. I mean, please excuse my expression, but you can't just blindly follow someone you don't know, who you've barely even met!"

He lifts his hands. "Yet here we are."

"And expect— What?" Her eyes reflect the meddling of her mind. "What DO you expect?"

He shrugs. "I don't know. I just know I needed to go."

She scoffs. Then falls silent.

After some time, Augur clears his throat. "I realize that everyone sees me as the blind village idiot, and I understand that I'm the one who created that image. But I can tell you with certainty, all blundering and joking aside, sometimes seeing can be the very thing that blinds you."

Her crooked smile fills her face as she considers his words. "Father used to say, 'If you don't see it before you see it you're never going to see it.'"

"YES. Exactly! That's it." He taps the side of his head. "Some things have to be seen first in here. You master THAT vision and whatever your IT is," he sighs, "it's yours."

She raises an eyebrow. "So what's your 'It,' Mr. Augur?"

He smiles. "I don't know. But it brought me here."

Leaning back, she admires his grin. *He is quite handsome when he's not making a fool of himself.*

"You know, I may be blind but I can tell when someone's staring at me."

A rush of adrenaline bursts from her chest, setting fire to her cheeks. *I'm staring? Duh, yes, I'm staring. And he can tell? Oh geez, that's awkward!* She runs her fingers through her hair. *Wait. What is this?*

She lets her hair down, and begins picking through the strands.

"Have I been too forward?" He's still smiling.

"What? Oh, uh, no. I just…" Sifting through her hair, she finds it. "Ahha."

He leans forward. "What is it?"

A small vine is tangled with her hair. She pulls at it. "Nothing I just—ouch." But it's knotted in. She starts unraveling it. "I just have something—OUCH." She traces the vine back through her hair, then gasps.

"Are you okay?"

"I, uhh." *No, I'm not okay! A vine is rooted in my scalp! A vine, IN. MY. SCALP. How in the—* She gulps. *Pahana.* Shame overwhelms her, and she quickly pulls her hair back up. "I—I'm fine. Sorry."

"No need to apologize." He tilts his head. "But you're well? You're sure?"

"Yeah. Yeah, no, I'm good. Thanks."

He leans back. "Okay. Well, you know why I'm out here, but you haven't said anything about why you are?"

"Oh, uh," she catches herself fidgeting with the vine. "That's a strange and complicated story."

"Strange and complicated stories around a campfire. Sounds like we have what we need for a beautiful evening."

She smiles. "Okay…"

And she goes on to tell of Father's recent passing and how hard it's been on her and Quest. How she buried herself in duty, and her brother drowned himself with booze. How even in their differences, they were always together. Then backtracks to growing up as orphans, she and her brother always had to fight for everything. Until finally getting adopted by the Salvador's. Then Ma and Bro's passing, reemphasizing how difficult it was to lose their forever family. Fast-forwards to her mourning getting cut short by the bright light, and meeting Mahdi, and on and on. She shares every important detail she can think of.

And Augur listens and laughs (appropriately) and asks questions, following along as though her story is the most incredible he's ever heard.

Then he shares about his upbringing. How despite his attempts, his obvious differences made it difficult for him to ever really fit in. How he just wants to be treated like everyone else. And how he finally gave up trying to be like them and exploited his difference to manipulate their likeness to his advantage.

He sighs. "We're not so different, you and I."

She looks at him sideways. "Oh yeah? How's that?"

"Well, I mean aside from all the many, many obvious differences, we're both different."

"We're not so different because we're different?"

"Precisely. And there is the account of you following an unknown someone—a bird, actually, out here to the middle of nowhere, which feels strikingly familiar to something I recently did."

"No way! I followed Mahdi because he at least seemed to know what he was doing."

"There you have it." He smiles. "We're both following someone who knows what they're doing, at least more than we do and certainly more than those we were around."

She laughs. "Well, YOU are different, I'll give you that."

"Thank you, madame." He bows his head. "And with you I share the same affinity."

A twig breaks.

Augur turns. "Something's close."

"The Others," Zo whispers.

"What—" He stops short to listen.

snap snap

Ignoring the noise, he leans in and whispers, "How do YOU know about—"

Snap

"Don't worry," she cuts in. "They don't like—"

Snap SNAP

"—the light."

SNAP

Augur tilts his head. "Well they—"

SNAP SNAP

"—sound close."

SNAP SNAP SNAP

Silence.

Zo inhales slowly and whispers, "I see it."

A large shadowy figure stands just beyond their clearing.

"Well? Humph. Are you going to invite me to join you?"

Laughing, Zo jumps up with her arms wide open. "Mahdi!" She embraces her friend. "Come, join us. Mahdi, this is Augur."

"Humph. Yes, the village idiot from the Marketplace. I see."

"My reputation precedes me." Augur picks up a walking stick and bows low.

"Your actions proceed you. HUMPH." Then he whispers to his traveling buddy, "What are you doing here with this buffoon?"

"Warming herself by my fire." Augur grins. "As you are."

"Ahem." Zo positions herself as a barrier between them. "I got lost in the darkness and followed the scent of the fire, and found Augur here."

Mahdi frowns. "HUMPH." And again he whispers to her, "Yes, well, we—YOU and I—clearly have much to discuss."

Mahdi and Zo both wake with the dawn.

Subtle pink rays slice through the thick canopy. The fire pit still smolders, and Augur is snoring as loudly as he has all night long.

They pull out their breakfasts, and Mahdi motions for Zo to come near. She grabs her rucksack and sits beside her friend. He mumbles thanks over his meal and eats. She follows in kind. But Mahdi doesn't waste a second, "What is this moron doing here with you?"

Zo smiles and glances at her new acquaintance. Running her fingers through her hair—*The vine!*—she shrinks back.

"What?" Mahdi leans nearer. "What's that?" Then he sits back and looks down. He says nothing, but his feathers heave a heavy sigh.

"I—" *What do I tell him?*

His head is low.

He knows. Just say it. She swallows and sighs deep. "Mahdi, I settled." Her eyes search her friend. He doesn't move. He says nothing. *Even his 'Humph' would be a welcomed relief, but nothing?* Her jaw is tight as she fights back tears. "Mahdi, I—"

"Settled. Yes, I heard." He remains motionless. "You settled."

Then lifting his head, he looks squarely in the eye of his traveling buddy. "You settled. And yet here you are. You settled, but that does not define you. Listen, young one, you must NOT let that define you. You did not stay there, and there is still much ahead of you. You overcame, Zo."

Tears burst, rushing streamlines of cool relief down her warm cheeks. *He doesn't hate me.* She breathes. And smiles.

"Now, getting back to the fool at hand." Mahdi tilts his head toward Augur, who still snores in blissful slumber.

Zo looks again, and notices a smirk draw in the corner of his otherwise motionless lips. *He does have good hearing.*

"I found him here, not long before you arrived. Or, maybe he found me? I don't know what I would have done if I hadn't caught wind of his fire. He followed us all the way from the Marketplace, Mahdi. And he really is blind."

Crossing his wings, he leans back. "Humph."

There it is. She smiles.

Augur stretches and yawns in obnoxious exaggeration. "Come now." He leaps to his feet. "We're wasting precious sunlight." He bends down and picks up his bag and walking stick.

Smiling as he passes Zo, he taps Mahdi's feet with his stick. "Do try to keep up." Continuing on, he calls back, "And snuff out those cinders, please!"

Zo chuckles.

Mahdi isn't impressed.

They get up together, but Mahdi insists on stifling the fire pit himself. "You are a lady, humph."

And once again, together they set off.

CHAPTER 20

*A*ugur leads the way.
His pace is consistent, despite a few shameless attempts to show off his agility.

Mahdi maintains a steady distance (and steadier disinterest).

Zo keeps pace between them.

Augur is a goof. He's quick on his feet, and he has zero shame. He has to know he's annoying Mahdi, he humphs every time he does something silly. It's amusing how they keep at each other. They banter like sitcom siblings. At least it's entertaining in this endless forest, and it's nice to have company again. It feels weird that we're still wandering here, but I have to admit it is beautiful.

"The darkness is already upon us, boy! Humph. We must set camp."

"Does the darkness frighten you?" Augur grins.

Zo cuts between them. "Mahdi and I are at a disadvantage here."

He grins and opens his mouth to counter, but simply nods. Then stopping mid-stride, he squats low, hands flared and head tilted. His ears are set to something.

Zo and Mahdi stand tense and silent. *What did he hear? What is he doing?*

Augur takes a deep breath, cracks his neck and drags a single finger to his lips. "Hushhh." He leans forward.

The two hold their breath.

But he over-leans and rolls into a somersault. Now, lying flat on his back, he laughs hysterically.

"HUMPH. Come now, Zo. This imbecile has taken more of our time than he's worth." Mahdi storms off into the darkness.

"Wait!" She starts after him, but stops short and turns back. "Augur, seriously! How has this path not changed you?" And she leaves him to catch up with her traveling buddy.

Augur stands up alone, mouth agape, hands extended. *That was absolutely brilliant. Not to mention daring! I could have rolled right into a tree or a large stone—* "I very well could have impaled myself!" he calls after her, then shakes his head. "Not so much as a chuckle? What is it with these two?"

He hurries after them.

Zo can hear Mahdi plowing ahead, but his footsteps are increasingly distant as she fumbles through the dark. "Slow down, Mahdi!" she calls after him. But the pats of his feet are fainter still.

Come on! Ugh, I don't even know if Augur's behind me. It's dark. I'm tired. I keep almost falling over everything. And these bull-headed boys are behaving like a couple of real jerks! Why won't they just tolerate each other? Pretend to be cordial for all our sakes! Act like they have some dang manners! UGH. And what am I doing running after them? They're not going to change.

Why should I try to fix this? I— She strains to listen. *Great. I can't even hear him anymore.*

She finds a tree and sits down.

"They need to work out their—OUCH." *Something bit me!*

She moves her hand across her chest to shoo away whatever bug is attempting to make her its evening feast. *What's this?* A small, thin stick, has pricked her just below the collarbone. She plucks it out and holds it up, but feels suddenly woozy.

"What isss thhisssss?"

The slow drawl of her speech takes her by surprise. Her head starts to spin, and she has the feeling she's falling. She flails, but can't feel the ground beneath her. *What's happening?*

"We found her." Someone is near.

"She thought she could escape." Another.

"She had no idea what lay ahead."

Who? I know those voices.

"She's a settler."

"You should just give in."

"Settle."

She keeps grasping about, but can't find anything to ground her. She doesn't even realize she's lying on her back.

"Settle, Zo."

"You already have."

"You already are."

Shadows lean in, but her vision doesn't hold long enough to see clear.

"Look at her hair," they persist.

"Settler."

"Clear markings."

"You've settled."

"Give in."

"Let go."

Their taunting continues.

She is paralyzed.

What's going on? I can't speak. I don't feel anything. Damn this dark! It's like there's something here, over me. A weighted presence. Yuck, it's heavy. I feel violated. AND I CAN'T MOVE! What's going on? Why am I so dizzy? It's like falling, but also being crushed. I feel sick.

"Settle. Settle. Settle."

The voices meld into a disorienting dance.

Opening her eyes only increases the vertigo. She closes them tight.

"Settle. Settle. Settle."

No. No, I will not. I did NOT settle! I am ON the path.

"Settle. Settle. Settle."

No. No! NO!

"Settle. Settle—"

"nooo," a soft moan finally lifts the weight of her tongue. *YES!*

There is a moment of respite, as though the sounding of her will surprised the Others. But they are quick to regroup. "Settle. Settle."

Come on, again, "Nooo." Her moan is stronger.

"Settle. Settle."

Louder, Zo! "Nooo! NO!"

Silence.

Her fingertips twitch. Then her hand can move.

Slowly, she tucks her head into her knees and wraps her arms around her legs. *You're okay. You're okay.* She listens for something—anything, but the eerie silence remains.

Something grazes her ear. Reaching to rub it, she accidentally swats something to the ground. *What now?*

She grabs it and sits up. *Small. Furry. Wiggling. A mouse?*

"Let me go!" it screams.

She screams and drops it. *That voice.*

The Others resume their chant as their co-critter scurries to safety.

"That voice? WAIT." She laughs. "You, you're nothing more than filthy little varmint?"

Silence.

"Oh, oooh! I've got you. Ha! The Others are just dirty rodents. That's why you're always hiding in the dark, you're just scared little mice! Haha! You better not mess with me anymore. Run away, you pests! And don't bother me again, or I'll—"

"But you're so fun to bother."

"Augur!" Zo laughs relief. "Did you see them? Did you see the Others?"

"I can't see, Zo, so no. But my hearing is fine, and apparently so is your voice."

"Okay, then did you hear them running away?"

"No. But that's not surprising. The Others are only heard when they want to be. How did you get rid of them?"

"I caught one. I didn't mean to—it was on my ear!—but I think I stunned it when I knocked it down. I grabbed it. Augur, it was TINY! Like a mouse. And I think they poisoned me. There was this tiny spear—"

"Uhhuh. Okay, time to go. Let's find the bird before they do."

"It's fine. Mahdi's not afraid of them."

"Of course he's not, all the more reason to find him. Come, my lady." He takes her hand and helps her up. "You're a bit wobbly." He adjusts his hold to her arm. "Something really did happen, aye?"

Oh, now you're concerned? She frowns. "I told you what happened."

"Here," he places her hands on his shoulders. "Stay close and don't let go, you got me?"

"Yeah, I got you." She smirks. "Just don't drop into a somersault or flip into a handspring."

Mahdi has almost made it to the edge of the canopy, but the woods are still too thick and the darkness too heavy to tell any difference. He presses on, though, undaunted.

But this dark woodland is not kind to those who try to leave.

The forest begins to whisper, "Where are you going?"

"We know you, black bird. Yes! We remember you."

"Don't leave!"

"Not again."

"It's beautiful here. Only despair out there."

"Humph," Mahdi snorts. "It's pitch black in here, and the days are far too short."

"Only the nights are dark. Nights are supposed to be dark."

"Better sleeping in the dark."

"Better rest."

Mahdi flaps a wing. "Yes, well, too much rest is not conducive to my quest."

"He's on the path."

"We're on the path."

"You keep stumbling, you must be tired."

"Yes, sleep. You've journeyed far."

"You've journeyed long."

"You really should rest."

"Humph, I've already been adrift in your confounded wood far too long. You've never spoken before. Yet now you speak in verbose, insisting I resign myself to you. HUMPH. Not I, you wandering wood. In your rambling I believe I've discovered your dark secret."

"Secret, secret."

"Black bird, what do you see?"

"We see you, black bird."

"We see your secrets."

He holds his beak. *I must keep pressing on through this dark. I'll break free. They cannot stop me if I do not stop.*

———

"Augur, I think I—"

"Shh," he raises a hand. "I hear something."

Silence.

Zo exhales. "I don't hear anything, but—"

"Hush."

Silence.

"Augur, stop. I see something."

"Light?"

"Yeah, I mean I think so. It has to have light to see it. It's over that way," she taps his shoulder, "but maybe it's moving?"

"I heard voices."

"Mahdi?"

Silence.

He whispers, "I don't know, maybe. It's coming from over there." He moves her hand to his opposite shoulder.

"Well I definitely see something over here." She turns him in the direction. "Are you sure you're hearing Mahdi?"

He turns back. "No. Maybe? It's far off. You can't hear anything?"

Silence.

"Nope, nothing." She turns him back again. "But whatever I'm seeing is moving away. I think we should follow it."

"But what if I AM hearing Mahdi?"

"Well, what if I'M seeing him?"

Augur sighs.

"Let's go check out the light. Your ears are way better than mine. If it's a bust, you can use your superpower to lead us back."

Silence

He slumps. "It's stopped."

"The voices?"

"Yeah. Yeah, it's all gone." He sighs again. "Lead the way."

She shifts his hands to her shoulders and starts out. "Whatever it is, it's moving, but I don't think it's moving away." The closer they get, the clearer it becomes. "No, I was wrong, the light's not moving. It looks like there might be people moving around it?"

"The Others?"

"No way. These things are way too big."

"Where are you going?" A third voice halts the two. "Don't you like it here? Isn't it beautiful?"

"Yes." Another. "It's beautiful here. Everything you could want is right here. Don't go."

The movement ahead stops. Then shadows begin to grow between the backlit objects.

"Whatever they are," Zo whispers, "I think they're coming closer."

Augur also speaks in a hush, "Can you still see the light?"

"It's dwindling."

"Keep moving toward it."

"Why would you leave?" The voice sends a chill down Zo's spine. "What else could you possibly desire?"

They continue, "You are on the path right here with us. Why go? You don't know what's ahead. It will destroy you."

"Stay. You are safe here. Rest."

"Yes, rest. You'll feel better in the morning."

But the two keep moving toward the narrowing light ahead.

Zo gasps. *It's the trees!* She whispers sharply, "Augur, the trees are moving!" A heavy dread creeps through her as she realizes, *It's the trees speaking—they must shift every night! That's why we can't get out. They're keeping us in!* "They're blocking out the light!"

"The light is not true." The trees are listening. "It deceives you."

"You're tired. Rest now."

"Stay."

A tree-lined wall stands before them, growing wider from the bottom up. The gaps between are closing in.

"We have to climb." Zo steps on a root, but it jerks away and she falls back onto Augur. "You twitchy tree! Okay, Augur, lock your fingers and bend your knees. Yeah, good. I'm going to step into your hands to—"

"Just GO!" With a sudden heave, he hoists her high enough that a twisting branch slugs her in the gut.

It knocks the wind out of her, but she manages to catch a solid grip on the limb and raises her leg over it. The tree fights back, flailing about like a bull battling for freedom from its saddle. But Zo hugs tight, and straddles back until her rear is snug against the trunk.

"Alright, grab my arms."

Walking stick between his teeth, he takes hold of her forearms and pulls himself up with the ease and grace of an acrobat. The tree still thrashes, and he's nearly tossed out, but as a master of fall and recovery, he catches himself and, holding tight, scoots toward her.

Meanwhile, Zo's managed to turn around and is hugging the trunk. She can feel it steadily widening between her arms and legs. She stands up and looks down. *They're zipping up from the bottom. This has to be the way out!*

"We need to get to the other side NOW. We're going to have to jump between them. There's a branch on the left, so go around to the right. We're about maybe 8 feet up—"

"Go, go, go!" Augur pats her shoulder.

She takes a deep breath and jumps.

"OMPH. I'm oka—"

"Get out of my waaaaay!" Already airborne, Augur's right side scrapes the tree closing in, yet somehow he lands safely on his feet, barely missing Zo.

Still on her back, she watches as the swelling trees seal in the darkness.

CHAPTER 21

*I*t's night and there's a dense fog, but for the first time since they entered the dark forest, the soft glow of the moonlight greets them.

"It's amazing." Augur's nostrils flare as he sucks in the air. "I didn't even realize how humid it was in there."

"You're right." Zo stretches out. "It's like a heaviness has lifted." She takes a deep breath. "Ah! It's good to breathe again!"

Augur sits down and opens his bag. He pulls out a familiar leaf wrapping and eats a morsel.

"Wait—" she double takes. "You?"

He chuckles. "Of course! I'm on the path, too, you know."

She smirks and turns her attention back to the trees. Her smile fades. *Mahdi, I'd only just found you—*

"Aye, Zo!" Augur calls, "You mind describing this to me?"

He's already a distance away, leaning over something.

She starts toward him. *What's the fog doing there? It looks like it's getting sucked—*

It clicks.

"Augur, step back. Step back NOW!"

She tugs his cloak. He steps backward. She grabs him and pulls him nearer.

The thick fog discreetly rolls over a sheer cliff. The ledge stretches as far as she can see along along either side. In the diminished light, it's impossible to find a safe way down.

"Death drop?" Augur asks.

"Yeah, pretty sure."

"Of course. Any idea how deep?"

"It's too dark."

"Find me a heavy stone."

She gives him one, and he lets it drop over the edge. Leaning forward to listen, he clocks the passing seconds with his fingers, *One, two, three, four, five.* "Crap." He sucks his teeth.

"What?"

"More than five seconds."

"And?"

"It doesn't really work after five seconds."

"Well, what's five seconds?"

"Just over 100 meters."

"Meters, meters…" *So at least the length of a football field, but down.* She lets that sink in. "Woah."

"Let's call it a night?" Augur suggests.

Zo sighs. "Yeah."

The fog is still heavy in the morning, but now there's enough light to see the cliff isn't just a cliff, it's a canyon.

It's like the mountain was karate-chopped in two. There's no way across this. She picks up small stone and throws it over. *Looks like Augur's 'death drop' is about the width of a tennis court and the ground is higher over there. We can't jump it, even if we had motorcycles and ramps it would be suicide. And there's no bridge or anything to get us over. But that has to be where the path continues.*

She sucks her teeth. "I think the only way across is down."

"Perhaps I should add, 'See the blind man fall off a cliff,' to my act?"

"Well, it's down or back into the woods."

"I'll call it, 'Plight and Plummet,'" he flings out his arms, "my finale performance."

She ignores him. "We could go in and search for Mahdi."

"No," he is curt.

She responds in kind, "What?"

"No."

She inhales deep. *Change your approach, Zo.* She exhales. "But Mahdi—"

"You're forgetting what it took to get out of that devil forest!"

Her eye twitches. *Did he just use attitude to cut me off? Give him grace, Zo, he doesn't know you.* "I'm remembering my friend who's still in there!"

He softens, "We cannot go back."

"But he—"

"Think about it." Augur bites his thumb nail. "Take your feelings for the bird out, and just think. That forest was reacting to us. It was blocking us. It was intentional. We go back in, even if we did find the bird—which there's no telling—do you think it's going to let us out again?"

She holds tight fists. *All good points, but he's still my friend, I HAVE to do something.*

Augur continues, "He said himself, we each have our own path to follow, and not always together."

She sits, tense but quiet. *He's right. There's no way the dark wood lets us through a second time. And there's no way to know if we'll even find Mahdi, or even if he's still in there. He could have made it out, same as us. He would expect me to carry on. We have to move forward.*

She sighs. "Then there's no other choice, we have to go down."

Augur raises his eyebrows. "Yeah, right, my ultima magnam. No, thank you. There must be another way."

She stands. "Well, I'm not just going to sit here. Do you have any rope?"

Mahdi wakes.

He winces. *Aye, my eyes! My head is pounding.* He lifts his pinions to cover his head, but they move slowly. *I feel like a too thick grub.* He sits up and rubs his face beneath his wing. He's still surrounded by trees.

"Humph. Blasted, devil wood," he mumbles. "What's this? Have I been skewered?"

Reaching for the small stick poking out of his leg, he notices several more are stuck in his wing. He pulls them out and examines them. Each have unique carvings from end to end, and sharp, hallowed points.

"Poisoned!" He throws them down. "Blasted! The Others foiled my escape! HUMPH."

They have about 60 feet of rope between them.

I don't trust you, demon trees. But there's nothing else to use as an anchor.

Augur sits with his arms folded, nibbling his thumbnail. *Down can't be the only way forward. But I will not go back into that wood, and she is right, we can't just sit on this ledge. There has to be another way.*

He feels a warmth grow from the far side of the canyon. Turning toward it, he can sense a powerful light. *That's not the sun, it's midday. What is that?* Leaning toward it, he calls, "Zo. Zo! Do you see that?"

She turns back. "See what?"

"You don't see it?"

She looks in the direction he's facing. "See what?"

"An absurdly intense light. You don't SEE it?"

"The day isn't getting any younger, Augur. There's really no time for games."

He gets up and begins walking toward it.

"Augur," she warns, "that's not safe. Stop."

He ignores her.

"It's not funny! You're walking toward the cliff!"

But he's spellbound.

"STOP!" She runs and tackles him a few feet from the edge. "What is wrong with you!"

Still entranced, his face leans ahead. "You don't see them?"

"What? Who? This isn't funny, you can't see—"

"On the other side, there's three of them. They're surrounded by incredible light."

She rolls over to see, but the fog hasn't cleared.

"We need to go with them." His blind eyes are fixed.

Zo still searches. "I don't see anything or anyone. There's no new light."

"They're telling us to come." He gets up. "We have to go."

Still on the ground, she grabs him by his trousers. "You're crazy!"

But he pulls away.

She grabs his ankle.

"Zo, it's okay." His gaze never turns to her. "I trust them. Let me go."

"You're going to fall off the edge. There's nothing there!"

He shakes his head. "We don't know what's there. But we have to go." He nods. "It's time to go."

"Augur, this isn't funny—"

With one swift motion, he kicks his leg free and jumps over the ledge.

"NOOOOOOOOO!"

She is alone.

CHAPTER 22

S ilence.
No crying out. No thud (nor series of thuds).
Just silence.

Where are you, Augur? Where are you? Calm down, Zo, you're breathing too hard. She strains to listen, but as she holds her breath, her pulse pounds inside her head. *Calm down, Zo, CALM DOWN.* She's sweating and begins to cry and jump and pace altogether, uncontrollably.

"He went over! I can't—he, HE WENT OVER. I can't! I can't!"

Just breathe. Just concentrate on breathing. In, two, three, four. Out, two, three, four. Good. Again.

She ties one end of the rope around her waist, then gets down on all fours and with one outstretched hand, slowly crawls through the fog toward the ledge. When she reaches the drop, she sinks to her belly and drags herself just enough to peek over.

"Augur?" she's barely able to whisper. She clears her throat. "Augur? Augur!" His name echos throughout the canyon.

"Yes?"

She yelps, leaping back on all fours like a terrified cat.

"I'm here. I'm okay, Zo."

Oh dear—breathe, breathe! He's alive. He's okay. "Wha —what? Are you INSANE? What kind of sick, twisted— WAS THAT FUNNY TO YOU?"

"No. No, Zo. I'm sorry."

"You're sorry? You could have been killed! And I—I could have died trying to save you!"

"Zo, listen. I saw—"

"Where are you?" Her body is trembling with frustration.

"Just below you. There's another ledge. Here take my hand." He stretches up against the mountain's wall. "Reach down. Can you feel me?"

She crawls forward again and, ensuring that her weight is enough to safely anchor her, lets her arm down. "I can't feel you."

"Here, listen." He pats the rock.

Shifting slightly to the right, she reaches down again and feels his hand. "How much room is down there?"

He crouches to feel around. "I'd say about two meters from the face to the edge, and maybe three, maybe a little more across."

"Okay." She crawls back and sits up. "I'll figure a way to get you up here. I have the rope, I'll be your anchor—"

"Zo."

He sounds like he's smiling. How can he be smiling right now?

"You come here. You said yourself, we have to go down. This is the way."

She shakes her head. "But what's beneath you? If I go down there, how will we get back up?"

"We're not going back, remember?"

She looks up and sighs heavy. *There's no way.*

"If you wouldn't mind, my lady," his voice is playful. "Please be sure to bring me my bag and walking stick before you join me."

"I—I can't just jump down there like you did. I can't."

"You don't have to. I'm here. I'll help you."

Says the blind man. "Yeah, that's not as reassuring as you think."

"Come on. I'm right here." He taps the wall again. "I won't let you fall."

She gets up and collects their supplies. *I can't go down. But we can't stay here. I really don't have a choice. Breathe, Zo, breathe. I have to do it. But I hate heights, let alone fog-blinding death drops! Just trust the blind guy with your life—UGH. I don't have a choice. Breathe. I'm doing this. I have to. I'm doing it.*

She brings their things to the edge and hands them off. "Okay. I'm going to find something to tie this rope to—"

He snickers. "You're insulting me."

"I don't care, I don't want to die." She looks around. "There's nothing, Augur. Oh god, there's nothing to tie the rope to."

"Zo. I've got you." His voice is full of compassion and conviction.

I want to trust you, Augur. But you're blind. That's a legitimate reason not to trust you with this. Oh god, but I think I need to trust you. How am I supposed to trust you right now? You're blind! I'm going to die. Tears swell, and her heart returns to racing.

"I've got you, Zo."

She takes a deep breath, then forces herself to the ground. *Come on, legs. It's just like climbing over a fence. You're just climbing over a fence. You got this. You've climbed a ton of fences before. It's not a cliff, it's just a fence. Just move your legs over the fence.*

"There, I feel your feet. I've got you."

"Okay, okay, I feel you." She takes a few moments to steady her breathing. *You've got this. Roll over, Zo. Tummy down. It's just a fence.*

Augur's hands move to her calves. "I've got you."

"You sure you've got me?"

"Mmhm."

He's got you, Zo. He's pretty strong for being scrawny. He's got you. Go on then.

Slowly lowering herself, his grasp moves to her thighs, then hips. Once he has her by the waist, she lets go, and he eases her down. As soon as her feet touch the ground, they both sink against the ledge.

"There. That wasn't so bad, aye?" He chuckles. "You just followed a blind man over a cliff."

She lets out a laugh. "I think I hate you."

"That's better than the indifference you left me with at the Marketplace. I'll take it."

She takes some time to breathe and lets her fingers dig into the strength of the landing. *I'm alive. We're both alive. Thank you, rocky ledge.* She sighs. "Now what?"

"I guess that means the fog isn't any clearer down here?"

"It's thicker, actually. All I see is white. I can hardly see anything, not my hands, barely my shoulders."

He uses the walking stick to feel around. "There's something on this side. It's not big. It's like a step down. I'm going to take it."

"Wait—"

"It holds. Here's another one. Also solid. And here's one —no, this one is bigger. Here, take my hand."

She hesitates before reaching out. *This is crazy.*

The narrow path descends the ridge along the canyon's face. It's derelict, with occasional gaps where debris (more likely boulders) have crashed through, and the fog still casts a heavy shadow.

The two inch along, Augur's walking stick leading the way.

"The air feels different now." He pauses briefly to breathe. "Has the fog lifted?" And he continues along.

"Hmm. I don't think it's lifted. Maybe dissipated?" Zo searches through the dim. "It's gotten darker as we've descended. It's still gray above, but it's black all around. Below looks darker still."

"I did notice you are still holding tight to my bag—" he stops. "Wait. Hold here, this next gap is wide." He extends his rod as far as he can, then reaches back. "Take my hand please, anchor?" Holding tight, he leans out. "I think... I feel... Yep, there it—WOOP."

"What? What's that noise? Why'd you make that sound?"

"I, uh," his shoulders sag. "I lost my staff."

"WHAT? You're kidding? Please, Augur—right now is really not the time—but PLEASE tell me you're joking?"

Hands pressed into his face, he leans into the rock. "I wish I were."

Zo slides against the wall to the ground and lets her head fall back with a thud. "Ouch."

"It's okay, my lady. With my lean and the extension of my staff, I'd say it's just over a meter across, and almost half a meter down. We could easily make that."

"I really hate you." She exhales. "I can't do that, Augur. There's no way. In the dark? And how big is the landing? I—I can't do it. There's no way. No. I can't."

"We can't stay here."

She leans forward to examine the jump and immediately chastises herself for looking into the dark abyss. But then she squints. "Augur. I, I think I see something? A small, green, glowing something is over there."

"Is it the landing?"

"I don't know." She sighs. "It doesn't seem too far off. But I don't know."

"I'm going to try." He forces a short breath.

He's not joking. He's already proved he'll just jump of a ledge. "You can't see it, Augur! You're only guessing the distance from tapping it once!"

"Then you go," he dares.

"NO."

"Then I'm going." He stands up, readying himself to jump. "Okay. If I don't make it, Zo—"

"Wait. Let's just think—"

Leaping, he yells, "I love youuu!"

His voice echoes throughout the canyon and loose debris falls all around.

Zo coughs, trying to wave the dust away. "Are you okay?"

"WOOOOO HOOOOOOOOO!"

This time the canyon shakes. The edge where Zo's feet extend, falls out from beneath her, and her legs now dangle at the knees. Chased by more debris, it takes a little longer for the air to settle.

She hides her face in the collar of her shirt. "You IDIOT," she whispers as loud as she thinks is safe. "This entire canyon can collapse on top of us!"

He's doing his best to contain his laughter. "I'm sorry, I'm sorry. It was a RUSH. I mean, I leapt and I made it. AGAIN—ha! A blind man jumping off a cliff, what an act."

"Yeah, well, you made it a lot harder for me. Half of this side just fell into the abyss. How is it over there? Is there room for me?" Her eyes widen.

The green luminescence has grown. She can make out Augur's silhouette as he crawls, patting around at the ground. She stands up staring in silence as the glow spreads wherever he touches. She can now see the entire landing.

"I'm coming over!" She leaps.

And lands safely.

"You didn't even wait for me finish checking." His hands, knees and feet all glow. He's covered in it.

She smirks. *He looks like he's one of those glow-stick dancers at a club.* But there are more pressing matters, and Zo is now inspecting the luminescence. *Look at this. What is this—a juice? Yes, it must be from these little pods.* She picks one out of the clover-like ground covering, and smashes it in her hands. *Look at that! These berries make little chemical reactions. The juice glows. Perfect serendipity!*

She looks up. "I could see all around you. I knew where to jump, and I had enough room. This whole landing is covered with a plant, and when you squish its fruit, the juice glows!"

"What else can you see?"

"Nothing. Well, not a lot. Wherever I stand, the glow illuminates about a step's distance around—both of us, actually. But I guess you can't see that, so…"

Augur bows. "So you're taking the lead."

"It would appear that way, yes." She nods.

He tugs the front of his hood, as though tilting a hat. "Lead on, seer."

"Wait. Before we go, now that the path has crumbled around us, and since I still can't see what's ahead, let's step up our safety game?" One end of the rope is still tied around her waist. She pulls the rest out of her bag and secures the other end as a lifeline around Augur. Resting one hand against the cliff, she holds the line slack with the other. Augur keeps his left hand against her shoulder and firmly grasps the rope with his right.

She takes the first step out.

Fresh fruit squashes beneath her, igniting the glow. She takes another step, then the next. Squish, glow, step. Squish, glow, step, and step by step, on and on the two continue their descent.

"I'm hungry," Augur whines. "Are you hungry?"

"I hadn't thought of it." Zo exhales sharply. "I've been a bit busy trying to prevent us from plummeting to our doom."

"Well, it's all I can think about right now. I need to eat."

Zo sighs. "Okay. Just let me check to see how wide this ledge is... Hm. It's good here, actually. Enough room to even sleep in shifts."

"Madame, I'm impressed. Only this morning you were crying about me going over the edge, and now you're leaping drops, leading our parade through the darkness, and ready to fall asleep where the slightest subconscious shift could make you— what was it—'plummet to our doom.' That, my lady, is growth."

The sound of his smile and his sarcasm make her grin. *Did he really say, 'I love you,' before he leapt into the unknown? No. Don't go there. Now is not the time, Zo.* "To be fair," she resigns, "we don't really know if this has all been the same day."

"You're right. And I am both famished and exhausted."

They eat and relax, enjoying each other's company before taking shifts to rest.

While Augur snores, Zo studies the ground cover and looks back along the way they came. *How is it possible that the glow is still strong? I swear I can see as far back as we've covered. That thick patch back there has to be the landing.*

Holding her hands up, she measures the green descent about one and a quarter hand high. Watching for what feels like an eternity, the glow line only shrinks slightly, *Maybe?*

She bursts a pod between her fingers and counts, *One-thousand one, one-thousand two*, on and on until she reaches 10 minutes, and still the glow remains. She holds her hands up again and the path measures as long as before. And Augur's snoring is still just as strong.

'Love.' She scoffs. *What does he even know of love?*

She thinks about Mahdi, Pahana, Quest, and their family. *Love isn't self-seeking. Love sees the best in others. It's honest and patient and fiercely loyal. Loving someone is more than leaping, it's staying, and seeking, and saving.*

She recalls her dream, *"Remember who you are." I am a Salvador. A savior. But I feel like I'm failing. Everyone I've ever loved—Ma, Broden, Father, Quest, even Mahdi—every pillar in my life is either gone or lost. Like the very foundations of my being have all been swept away, and I'm left falling through nothingness. Bleak, suspended animation. Everyone is gone. What is this? Sorrow isn't strong enough to describe it. Anxious, absolutely and angry. Plus hopeless, destitute, and lonely. Trapped. Longing. And heavy. Very, very heavy.*

'Love.' She scoffs again looking down at her snoring companion. *He knows nothing of it.*

"Zo. Zo, wake up. Wake up, Zo. It's time to go. Ha! That rhymes!"

With an irritated yawn, she sits up.

"Did you catch it?"

She rolls her eyes.

"Zo, go. Yes? No?—OH. Ha! You get it?"

She sighs.

But he persists, "Zo—"

"I got it," she snaps.

Silence.

"Did," he's cautious in his question, "did I upset you? I was just trying to brighten up the place."

Silence.

"Come on—"

"It wasn't funny. And your persistence despite my blatant annoyance simply proves you condescending."

"'Condescending'?" He pulls into himself. "Me? I'm not the one with the superiority complex, my lady."

"What?" She squints hard, like his words are so ridiculous, they're painful.

"Ever since I met you you've been a snob."

She rolls her eyes. "Then why'd you follow me out here?"

"Because ever since I met you I knew I loved you."

She scoffs.

"You don't believe me? What else do I need to do? Why else would I be here?"

She crosses her arms. "You know nothing of love."

"What?" He raises his hands. "Who are you to tell me—"

She blurts out, "What have you lost?"

He falls silent.

She looks away and sees that the glowline has significantly dwindled. She sighs. "We should go."

Still silent.

Looking up into the distant gray, droplets begin to splatter on her face. "Of course rain." She holds out her hand and is surprised to find the glow doesn't easily wash away. *At least that's good news.*

She looks back at Augur and sighs again.

Thunder booms throughout the cavern, felling debris all around.

"Come on. We need to go."

Each picks up their bag, and they pull the life line snug.

The two continue their descent in deafening silence.

"Wait."

Zo stops, holding out her arms. "There's another drop off here. I can't tell how far away the next landing is."

Augur stoops down, sweeping the ground. "There are only pebbles here."

"Maybe, if I can get a handful," she throws them in the direction of the drop. "I can't see anything. There's no glow over there."

"I heard them hit."

"Me, too. But how far away is it? And what if that was just the sound of them hitting the wall?"

Augur breathes deep. "One of us needs to try."

"Right." Zo bites her lip.

Silence.

"I'll go," he volunteers. "Here, help me get this thing off."

"No. No way. That's the lifeline. I'm not just going to let you fall if you miss."

"If I miss, the weight of me falling will bring you down too." He's fidgeting with the rope. "There's nothing to brace you up here."

"No. No. Absolutely not." She pulls his hands apart. "I'm not losing you, too."

He snaps his wrists away. "I'm going."

"If you miss, chances are I'm going to miss, anyway. If we're bound, there's at least a chance for both of us."

"If I jump, there's definitely a chance for you." He continues with the rope.

He is really on some hero junk. Why do guys always have to prove themselves by doing something stupid? "I'm not going to let you go without the rope."

"There you go again!" He throws his hands in the air. "You always have to be right! You always have to be in control!"

"It's not about, Augur, it's about safety. You don't get to leap off to your death just because you're upset that your crush isn't equally obsessed with you."

"You think?" He scoffs. "Of course you do. I realize that this may not add up to you, Zo, but I'm not jumping because I'm mad. I'm jumping to protect you."

She scoffs.

He scoffs. "I'm going."

"Please take the rope." She puts it in his hand.

"Fine!" He grabs it, then stands at the edge, left foot forward. *You've got this, Augur-me-boy. Just like before.* He leans against his right leg and begins rocking back and forth, synchronizing his arms in motion—

Zo tightens her hold on the line and sits down, bracing herself against the cliff. *He's put himself at risk three times now. Given, the first time he was in a bit of a trance, but he did take the initiative to lead along the cliff. The second time he says he did it to protect me. Now here we are again. How would I behave if I loved someone? Probably exactly like this.*

Observing the awkward silhouette of his spindly arms and legs preparing to leap quite literally into death for her sake, she realizes, *Maybe he really does—*

—and he jumps.

THUD, THUD.

CHAPTER 23

*T*he lifeline is limp.

Zo pulls it up as fast as she can, but there's no weight.

He untied himself! "No. Oh, god, no! AUGUR?"

"I'm alright, my lady."

She startles.

And she breathes.

Then yells, "WHAT IS WRONG WITH YOU? I told you to keep the lifeline—"

"I held it, as you asked."

Why does he sound like he's smiling? Is this lunatic actually smiling right now? He's INSANE! He completely twisted my words for his intent! She takes a deep breath. "I CANNOT BELIEVE—"

"Zo! Zo, I didn't mean to drop it. I hit the wall hard. I think I blanked out for a second."

"Wait—" she tilts her head. "The wall? What wall?"

"I think we made it, Zo." His voice returns to a smile. "We're at the bottom."

"We made it?"

Standing beside the ledge, he grabs her ankle and pats it reassuringly. "We made it."

She refocuses. "That doesn't change the fact that you jumped without the rope."

"I jumped WITH the rope. I held it. It just wasn't tied to me."

"Then what's the point!" her words are soaked in frustration.

He shrugs. "To appease you."

"You're asinine! And again once, condescending."

She unties herself, shoves the rope into her sack, and grabs a few glow pods. In spite of Augur's extended hand, she hops off the ledge by herself and begins to walk away. But each step becomes more reluctant as she realizes just how dependent on the glow she's become. She stops. *Breathe, Zo. Just breathe.*

Augur hasn't moved. He listened as her angry steps become hesitant, then stopped altogether. *The way she breathes through her fear is precious.* He smiles. "It's a dark, dark world, Zo. For what it's worth, I'm glad to be in it with you."

She sighs. "Come on."

Searching for a way up the other side of the canyon, they move in opposite directions to cover more ground. So far, they've only met a cold, sheer face.

Zo squishes a pod and rubs its glow on the front of her shoes. *There. Yes—ha! I'll best you yet, you random boulders. I stub my toes no more!* But her feet sink in the pebbled terrain, hiding the glow.

"ZO!" Augur's voice echoes and debris sprinkles the gorge.

Shielding herself beneath her poncho, she rolls her eyes. *He'll never learn.*

"Sorry!" He whispers loudly, "Come over here!"

Lifting her feet slowly to ensure she doesn't stumble, she makes her way back. Getting closer, she hears soft murmuring. *Is he talking to himself? Wait, no. That's Augur's voice, but I don't recognize that one.* She's pauses. "Augur?"

"Zo," he exclaims, "I found someone! This is Aminah. She's a mole."

Zo lifts a foot to see, but loses balance amidst the shifting pebbles, and reburies it to keep from falling.

But she sees just enough to know that, like Mahdi, Aminah isn't just another wild animal scurrying along the path. "Pardon my clumsiness, Aminah. It's a pleasure to meet you."

"Quite alright. Quite alright. Thank you, very grateful you covered your light. My eyes are much too sensitive. Be sure to wipe that dreadful juice off your feet before entering."

"Entering?" Zo waits.

"Aminah says there are tunnels through the mountain. There's a way to the other side."

"Yes, yes, but why you would ever want to go there is beyond me. Dreadfully bright, awful place. Come now, rid yourself of that light or the tunnels will lose you."

Zo rubs her toes into the ground but the tiny stones are too loose to do much, so she spits into her hands and smudges out the rest.

The mole permits her to keep some glow in her palms, "But you must keep your hands closed until we arrive. Stay low now, stay close. The tunnels will lose you if you don't know the way. We built them that way, keeps out the Others, loses them should they follow. Here now, try. Will you fit this hole?"

Augur cringes. "The Others travel this far?"

"The Others are throughout. Vile critters, the lot of them. But we've got ways of dealing with them."

Zo squats and measures the hole. "I don't fit."

"Quite alright, dear, quite alright. That's what my paws are for." Aminah makes swift work of it. "The tunnels are much wider than this entrance. Plenty of room inside." The mole disappears into the hole.

Zo and Augur listen to her scratching.

"That should do it." She pops her head back out. "Stay low, stay close."

Augur follows Zo, and Zo follows the mole.

The entryway is low and narrow for a short stretch.

Zo sniffs. *What's that subtle, stale stink? Oh, gross! It's like that time a mouse decided to die inside our dorm room wall. Barf. That odor lingered forever.*

When the tunnel opens, there's enough room for the trio to stand and walk together. The stench increases as they journey, but before long their noses adjust.

Aminah leads them through twists and turns, uphill and down for what feels like a blind eternity.

"You said you have ways of dealing with the Others?" Augur asks.

"Indeed, one must. They're mindless dribble, every one of them, subjects to the Puppeteer."

"The 'Puppeteer'?" Zo pauses before whispering to Augur, "That sounds sensationalist."

"It's not," he replies. "The Puppeteer is one of the names for the boss at the Marketplace. Owns the whole thing. Also known as Tenebrae, Teivel—"

"You know him?" Zo asks.

"IT," Augur corrects. "I've heard tales. You don't just go up and introduce yourself to the Puppeteer. There's protocol. Security. I grew up believing It was a legend, just scary stories—"

"Stories?" Aminah cuts in, "Yes, the Puppeteer would rather you believed just that. Manipulation is a powerful weapon. Fear, its ally. It wields each with masterful precision. The Puppeteer is quite real, indeed. And quite dangerous, don't you be fooled. There's more truth to those tales than you or I would wish."

"So the Puppeteer runs the Marketplace and employs the Others, but the Others are here on the path?" Zo tries to make sense of it all.

"Yes, dear."

"Why?"

"The Puppeteer doesn't want any on the path. The Market catches the lot of them, but for those who make it beyond, the Others have a keen way of picking them off."

"But why?"

"'Why?' Why what, dear?"

"Why does this Puppeteer send the Others? I mean, so few actually travel the path. Why waste time on so few?"

"Who could say why?" Aminah shakes her head sadly. "One thing is apparent, the Puppeteer does not want anyone on the path. Why else would It construct so complex a web as the Marketplace right along the mountainside? Why blocking the very entrance to the path, no less!"

This IS interesting. "What do you mean?"

"The Market is built like a labyrinth, a great maze to steer you away from the path. Travelers enter and without understanding become dumb and lost within, led astray by alluring temptations, all the while subtly made subject to Its authority." Aminah sighs.

"Much easier to settle in and around the Marketplace than to climb the mountain. There's delicious foods, numbing drink, titillating entertainment, lots of travelers—all kinds! Most live their whole lives without stepping foot beyond the Market because they are blissfully deceived. Enticement baits them, and they unwittingly become ensnared, utterly dependent to their vices."

With a sad, soft huff, she adds, "Deception lends them to believe the purpose of the path is to reach the peak or to get to the other side of the mountain."

"Wait—" Zo cocks her head. "That isn't the purpose?"

"Oh, heavens no, dear!" Aminah waves her paws. "The purpose isn't the destination. Destination is bound. The purpose of the path IS the path. And I'd wager the Puppeteer knows it. That's why It does everything It can to keep travelers from stepping foot on it. And to those who dare, It sends the Others."

But we didn't have difficulty getting started. "We both left the Market without incident. There were no hinderances to find the path."

"Hm," Aminah pauses. "Had you yet awakened your temptation?"

"'Awakened my temptation'? I wouldn't know. Who is that?"

"Not 'who,' dear." The kindness in the mole's voice eases Zo's speculation. "The temptations aren't sirens singing you into their snare. The temptations are our own inclinations, individual to each of us and as a part of us as the very meat and hide that covers our own bones. But, though part of us, our temptations are not for us. Once you begin to feed it, your temptation will only increase in hunger and demand. There is no true sating the temptations, for the end of their appetite is the devouring of their host. What you feed will dominate."

I do remember Mahdi squawking, something about waking the temptations. She makes it sound like a virus. There's still so much that I don't understand here.

Aminah sniffs the air. "Come now, we're almost there." She scurries ahead.

Zo and Augur quietly follow behind, each considering her revelations.

"Oops. Careful not to step on me now, dear." Aminah has stopped at an opening.

"Welcome friends, to the Hermitage."

CHAPTER 24

Zo holds up her hand.

In this deep underground dark, the green glow spreads much farther than before, and a massive cavern opens before them, surrounded by tunnels and speckled with mud huts and countless moles.

The glow attracts the attention of the entire community. Some scatter to various tunnels or into their homes, but most are curious about the upright visitors.

Aminah leads them to her hut.

They have to duck to enter and remain crouching inside.

Her home is a single room, with furniture fashioned out of the ground. A little dirt couch (which can comfortably sit a few moles) is just the right size for Augur to squat on. Zo prefers to sit crosslegged on the ground.

The room fills with a small procession of curious moles and is quickly surrounded by the underground community, all hoping to learn about their above-ground tourists.

Zo and Augur field simple questions—What is your name? What news do you bring?—but are weary from the day and still distracted by questions of their own.

Abigail Ortiz

Catching on, Aminah shoos most away. "Come now, leave my guests to rest. They've traveled long and hard. Out, out, out! There you go. They're in no hurry to leave, let them rest now. Out, out!"

As the labour parts, she carefully selects a few to stay. "I've talked with our guests, and whether they know it or not, they have questions only we can answer. They intend to carry on, and we are obliged to inform them."

Those she's chosen sit in a semicircle before the two, waiting patiently.

Zo's eyes are big as she looks around. "So, um, where to begin?"

"What questions do you have, dear?" Aminah smiles. "These few are my trusted. You may ask us anything."

Taking a moment to consider, Zo's stomach rudely distracts her. "I'm terribly hungry, would you mind if," she motions near her mouth.

"Not at all, dear! Pardon my manners. Please, make yourself at home. Would you like a fresh beetle?"

"No! No." She swallows hard, remembering Mahdi's grub. "Thank you. We have our own provisions."

"Then eat, please do eat while we share. Whatever questions you have, please ask." The mole makes herself comfortable. "Now, we have discussed the Puppeteer and the temptations—"

"I'd like to know more about the Others," Augur requests.

"They are vile creatures," one mole says.

Zo can't resist, "Are they rodents?"

"They are many types," another speaks, "but most are small and all despise the path."

"Small?" Augur leans back. "I—I can't believe it."

"They are tricksters," the second continues. "Like the Puppeteer, the Others incite your own instincts against you. They are well-trained and use weapons to tap into and manipulate your natural fears."

The first speaks up, "They are limited in number and size. Too much credit given to them is like surrendering yourself. In reality, you are on the path. Why, that very fact—you traversing—that frightens them. The farther you travel, the closer to the Trailblazers you become, and the Others tremble at Their name."

"Don't be fooled," the third adds, "they are mere pests, when all is said and done."

The second chimes back in, "We have found the Others to be very much more intimidated by a traveler who is aware of their tricks. Without the aid of the traveler's own fear, there is very little more the Others can do than be of nuisance."

The first speaks again, "Tell me, dears, what do you know of the Trailblazers?"

Zo shakes her head.

Augur shrugs. "I hadn't heard the name before now."

"Like the Puppeteer, the Trailblazers have many names and many tales, but unlike Teivel, the Trailblazers set Kubwa Hatima Njia. It is said that They were the first to climb the great mountain—in fact, it was They Who pulled it out of the soil. And They divined the living river, routing it down the mountain so that all may access it. They planted and tend to the great tree, as well. Travelers often share stories of meeting the Trailblazers along the path in the form of Three."

"'Three'?" Zo asks. *Like the three by the boulder beside the tree. And the three pillars in my dreams at the Gathering Place.*

"Three..." Augur remembers, *There were three who called me to leap over the edge at the canyon.*

Aminah leans in. "You have encountered Them?"

"Yes," the two realize together.

"They are known as the Givers, Guides, Saviors—"

Zo sits up. "'Saviors'?"

Abigail Ortiz

"Yes, dear. They are known by Their character and by what They have done. As much as They created the path, They ARE the path."

The two sit motionless, holding their breath, eager to understand.

Zo finally speaks, "If the goal of the path IS the path, and the Trailblazers ARE the path, then They are also the goal?"

"Indeed, dear!" Aminah claps happily.

"Will we meet Them at the highest peak?" Augur asks.

"Why, you've already encountered Them, dears." Aminah's paws bounce on her belly. "They are throughout, They never stop moving."

"You are not traveling to Them," the third mole clarifies. "They are always traveling WITH you. As you continue along the path you are in pursuit of Them, even as They are in pursuit of you."

"Do you recall your appearance when you first looked into the river?" the first asks.

"Yes," Zo and Augur remain in sync.

"That was the reflection of the Trailblazers within you. The greater who that you are supposed to be, that you can only manifest through the path—through Them!"

"So our goal is to become a Trailblazer?" Augur asks.

"No," Aminah corrects. "One does not become the Three. Our goal is to know and reflect the path. And the pursuit of the path is our education through which we are made into its reflection."

The first adds, "And to each one, the path is as unique an encounter as every individual who chooses to travel it. My goal is not as Aminah's, nor is hers as your own. We each travel our own course, but it is the Three who have blazed our trails."

Just then, two more moles rush into the hut.

One points. "Aminah, your guests have been summoned to the Hill."

"The Hill?" Zo and Augur ask together.

"The finest soil mound in our grand community," Aminah answers. "Our founder resides there." She turns to the messengers. "Inform the Hill that our travelers are in need of rest and a good bathing. I shall deliver them first thing tomorrow."

The two moles look uncomfortably at each other, then curiously at Zo and Augur, before scurrying away.

"A bath sounds lovely." Zo smiles.

"Yes." Aminah's little, beady eyes squint into tiny slits as she too smiles. "I do think you shall enjoy it. Let's get you settled in for some rest then, yes? We can talk again tomorrow."

Aminah leads them to a different tunnel with a faint glimmer of light ahead.

Augur's sharp ears are first to pick it up, but he only grins.

Then Zo hears it, too. "It sounds like a waterfall." Turning the last corner, she gasps. "Oh! It's beautiful."

They enter a large chamber with a gently flowing pool. The entire far side is an open, grand cascade plummeting al fresco. This chamber is tucked behind a majestic waterfall, a cave bored by a mighty chute of the living waters of Maisha Maji.

"Here are some blankets and robes. I'll wash your garments while you bathe and they'll be dry by morning. I've had the robes fashioned in haste by our labor. I'm afraid they're not fancy, but they are clean." Aminah gives each a bundle.

"You may enter the waters on the other side of these dressing stones. You'll find pumice rocks to scrub with and root oils for your fur. Go on now, Zo, you take that side there." Aminah points, then grabs Augur's hand. "This way, I'll guide you."

Undressing, Zo remembers something she didn't get to ask, "Aminah?"

"Yes, dear?"

"When I first arrived to this world I was on the other side of the Marketplace, in a great forest."

"Yes, the Wanderlands, dear. Many, too, are lost there. Without direction they are stuck in their minds' endless reasoning. Such a sad, sad place. Have you found your root oil, dear? Just a few drops to comb through your fur while you bathe and it'll dry extra soft and shiny."

Zo enters the water. "It's so warm."

"Yes, dear. Scrub up. And don't go too far out. Wouldn't want you getting caught in the current. Woosh, over the edge and down the waterfall you'd go."

After a while, Aminah finishes cleaning their clothes and excuses herself to set them to dry. "I'll be back soon, dears."

Everything the moles shared is fascinating! But this water is too much perfection to not let myself relax... After scrubbing down, Zo soaks in the bath, but her thoughts don't settle. *Why am I here? HOW did I get here for that matter? I'm not from this world, so how do I fit into all—whatever this all is? More importantly, how am I ever going to find Quest?*

"Zo!"

She sighs. *His attempts at being quiet never are quiet.* "Yes?"

"Do you believe what they say about the Others?"

There goes trying to relax. "What's not to believe?" She takes the pumice stone to her feet.

"I know you think they're insignificant, but my experience has been different."

"Have you encountered them directly?"

"I haven't seen them, no."

She rolls her eyes. "Have you touched them? Held them? Felt their dirty little paws crawling on you? Have you caught one?"

"No, obviously."

"Then why do you insist on doubting what I and those who've had such experience tell you?"

"Shh! They're coming."

She soon hears the soft pit-pats of Aminah's return.

"Alright, dears, are you ready to turn in?"

Waking early after a full night's rest, and following a thorough stretching, Zo feels new.

She quickly and quietly prepares her daily meal. Then she closes her eyes and takes time to savor her bite. Sitting still and taking deep breaths, she centers herself. *I'm so grateful for this moment.*

Breathing deep, she reflects again on the lore of the moles and considers her journey in light of their wisdom, when—

"Good morning."

She sighs sharp. "Morning." She doesn't bother opening her eyes. *Why is his timing always the worst?*

"What are you doing?" Augur asks.

She takes another deep, irritated breath. "Spending time with myself."

"Oh. Did you eat?"

UGH. There's no reason to ask that. I just said I'm spending time with MYSELF. He's obviously testing me. A short, direct answer should clue him in. "Yes."

"Is everything okay?"

"Fine."

"What's wrong?"

"Nothing."

"Something."

"Augur! I was just enjoying some time alone and you don't seem to get the hint. THAT's what's wrong."

"So just say that." He sits down and takes out his breakfast.

She scoffs. "I did. Twice."

There is uncomfortable silence.

Then Aminah comes in. "Good morning, dears."

"Good morning, Aminah," Zo greets her.

Augur doesn't reply.

"Here you are, your garments are all dry. Your company is expected on the Hill today."

"Yes, ma'am." Zo takes her clothes. "What exactly is expected of us? We do hope to continue along the path as soon as possible."

"Yes, yes, so you say you want to continue on. Let's just see what you want once you've visited the Hill."

CHAPTER 25

*P*arading through the community and up the Hill, they are again accompanied by a procession.

At the top of the Hill are mud huts just like the ones below, but fewer and farther between. They approach the first hut and are instructed to go inside.

Zo turns back. "Aren't you coming, Aminah?"

"Me? Oh, no, dear. Never assume yourself at a place of honor until you have been called. The Hill called for you. Now go on, dears, they won't bite."

Crossing the threshold, Zo looks inside. *It's EXACTLY like Aminah's hut. What's the big deal about the Hill?*

"Welcome, welcome! We are thrilled you are here. Please come in, come in! Sit down, and be well."

"Uh," she looks around, but the room appears to be empty. "Where are you?"

"Please, do sit down and allow us to tend to you."

She whispers to Augur, "This is weird."

He shrugs. "Or intriguing." He passes her and finds another mole-sized couch.

Zo sits on the floor again.

There is prolonged, uncomfortable silence.

"Please, do sit ON the furniture. It is the finest in the Hermitage, fashioned from our richest soil—"

"Thanks," Zo looks around, trying to find the voice, "but I'm quite comfortable—"

"We MUST insist! Has Aminah failed to inform you…"

The voice carries on, but Zo ignores it and leans toward Augur. "It's all just dirt," she whispers.

He raises an eyebrow. "If it's all the same, just sit where they ask."

"But I'm fine here, comfortable even!"

He doesn't respond.

The mystery voice is still droning. "…and it goes without question that this soil is the most comfortable, it molds to your individual form, supporting every…"

Zo raspberries an exhale, and sits on the second couch.

"Oh, I'm thrilled you've decided to try it! Tell us, do tell, how do you like it?"

She speaks through her teeth, "It's just like sitting on the floor, but higher."

"Pardon?"

She clears her throat and speaks up, "It's a higher experience."

"Oh, yes! Very good! A 'higher experience,' excellent description! Quite right, indeed."

She leans toward Augur again. "Do they really believe their dirt is less dirty than other dirt?"

"Honored guests," the phantom continues, "we are proud to host you, and do welcome you to the Hermitage's most prestigious society, the Hill." The voice encircles them. "And now, without further ado, we introduce—" A drape is pulled, revealing a lantern housing several lightning bugs. "—our distinguished lineage."

One mole steps out of the shadows and stands tall with one paw firm against its chest. "My son, Zababa." He nods and steps back into the dark.

Another mole lightly steps forward, and the voice continues, "My daughter, Inanna." She also nods before stepping back.

"And I, I am the humble gardener to whom great love has been granted, and it is here, over the Hermitage that I exercise kingship. I. Am. Sargon!"

Leaping from the shadows, he lands with one knee and fist on the ground, his other hand is extended behind him, his head bowed. He is quite large compared to the rest of the labour. Plump rolls ornament his body like garland wrapped from his cheek-line spilling in tubular swells all the way down to his rear paws. Static, Sargon seems to be waiting for something.

Augur bursts into applause.

Zo is confused.

"Thank you. Thank you." Sargon lifts his stubby arms as he stands. "You are too kind." He leers in Zo's direction.

She offers a slow clap.

"Very good! Now, please do continue your appreciation for my beloved children." He claps twice and the two again emerge from the darkness, and bow beside him.

Augur's cheering rouses. Zo has lost interest.

"Thank you. Thank you. I do feel that went very well, yes." Sargon claps. "Very well, Zababa. Very well, Inanna. Yes, yes. Very well, indeed."

He picks up the lantern and, together with his children, sits nearer to Augur. "I'm so pleased that went wonderfully. We decided to make the most of your refusal to come forth last evening, and came up with our little routine rather spontaneously."

"We were very tired yesterday," Zo says.

Sargon's lips purse. "So we were informed."

"And quite filthy," Augur chimes in.

The mole bursts into laughter. "Of course! Oh, of course! Can't have you on the Hill if you are too dirty. You know, our soil here is rather special."

"Yes," Zo speaks flatly, "so we heard."

"So," Augur distracts from her impotence, "you just came up with that presentation last night? Circling around us while making introductions added quite a dynamic effect on such short notice."

"Yes, yes!" Sargon claps. "Oh! Only a fellow showman would appreciate such grandeur! Tell me, Augur, are you an entertainer?"

Augur smiles. "By trade."

Zo clears her throat. "I thought you said you are a gardener?"

"Was." He turns slowly toward Zo. "Yes, I WAS a humble gardener, deary. Now I preside here," he lifts his arms, "over this vast community." Then leaning back toward Augur, he continues with a lighter voice, "Do tell, give us some professional insight, a fellow craftsman's critique."

"How?" Zo cuts in. "How did a 'humble gardener' like yourself become king? And what exactly do moles farm? I'm incredibly intrigued."

Though he's not thrilled to be interrupted, Sargon does revel in the chance to gloat over himself. "Well, deary, that IS a tale...

"Before the Hermitage, we moles were nomadic in our ways, rather jealous of our territories, only coming together to mate. As a young boar searching for a territory of my own, I found myself beyond our natural land, lost in a world as bright and hot as fire itself.

"It was there, when I had finally resigned myself to a dire end, I met him." He pauses for effect before whispering, "Akki."

"Who?" Zo asks.

"Quite obviously the Trailblazers," Zababa speaks with the disdain of an entitled teenager.

"I have only known him as, 'Akki,'" Sargon continues. "He was a great shadow in that wretched land. He saved me, returned me to our borders and taught me the secret of farming the richest soil."

"So you harvest dirt?" Zo remains flat.

"It is from the SOIL, the richness of the soil which yields such exquisite harvest of worms and beetles and all wonders of magnificent and delectable bugs. It is with this enriched soil—that is the very extravagant home in which we abide, why the very furniture on which you now rest—that I was able to unite our labour, and I alone, Sargon, became known to all and founder of the Hermitage."

He smiles a toothy grin.

Ew, he reminds me of Yakov. The hair on the back of her neck stands as a shiver quakes down her spine.

"Now, Augur," the mole persists, "do tell me what elements a professional as yourself would suggest we add to our little production?"

The two performers discuss trivial matters.

Zo can't shake her discomfort. *What makes soil rich? Amma kept a compost in the backyard, so leftovers, fruit and vegetable peels, used tea leaves and coffee grinds, spoiled milk, anything stale, grass clippings and raked leaves, eggshells, even egg cartons, paper towels and newspaper went into that pile. Decomposition. But what is down here to decompose? And what's this 'secret' to this slimy mole's 'enriched' soil?*

A foul odor jolts her from her thoughts. Watching Augur and Sargon still discussing performance, Zo's eyes start to water and her face scrunches in disgust. "It smells like death."

The conversation stops.

"Excuse me?" Sargon fixes his beady eyes on her.

She turns in his direction, squinting away her tears. "Pardon?"

He lifts his nose. "You were saying?"

"You don't—" she sniffs the air "—you don't smell that? It smells like something died." She covers her nose with her arm. "It's overwhelming."

Sargon glances at Zababa, who disappears into the shadow. Then Inanna bows her head before stepping back. He turns his attention back to Zo. "Whatever do you mean? Augur, do you smell anything?"

"No. But to be fair, I'm quite certain I went nose-blind when we first entered the tunnels yesterday. There was a penetrating odor, and my sense shut down early."

Sargon leans forward, his toothy grin casts an unsettling shadow over his face. Narrowing his focus on Zo, his beady eyes seem to glow. "Would you like to know the secret of my soil?"

She flinches as a firm paw presses into her back.

Turning, she sees Inanna helping Augur up, and looks down to find Zababa extending his other paw to help her stand.

Zo takes a deep breath through the filter of her tunic, and gives him her hand.

CHAPTER 26

They're led to a large courtyard. Several massive composting piles stacked higher than the surrounding huts fill the center and are tended by teams of moles. Some water, a few use pitchforks to mix, and others bury themselves in the piles, boring holes. One mole is overseeing the entire operation.

"These are my other children," Sargon holds out his hands. "Though not my mated heirs, these few are entrusted with my secret, and so akin by privilege. After all, family first." His toothy smile is no less chilling.

He brings them to the foremole. "And this, this is my Tiberius." Sargon holds his arms out to embrace the mole. "Not my lineage, but my son by selection."

Zababa's small paw tenses against Zo's back.

"My father," Tiberius embraces Sargon. "I see you have come upon new travelers. Welcome."

Sargon turns back to his guests. "Oh, yes, quite new—"

The king mole can't contain his cheesy smile, and his hands are flailing like a kid meeting his superhero. Zo bites her lip to quiet her amusement.

"—just arrived last evening."

Tiberius crosses his thick arms. "And you're already to know the secrets of the soil? Impressive."

Inanna whispers, "Most travelers take more time to earn father's trust."

Zo sours. "What is this secret?"

"In time, deary. One must first appreciate the process to truly value the essential element." Sargon wafts his paws. "Now, son," (Zababa snorts) "if you will?"

Tiberius leads them through the compiles, offering in-depth explanations for each stage.

But Zababa is only interested in the visitors.

"Tell me of the path," he whispers. "What is it like? What have you seen? Have you come upon the Trailblazers?"

In a truly hushed voice, Augur shares his encounter at the canyon. Zo does her best to show interest to their guides, but her attention is split between the quiet conversation beside her and the awkward silence of Inanna, whose eyes dart uncomfortably between her brother and Tiberius.

"Inanna," Zo whispers, "have you traveled on the path?"

Inanna wiggles her nose and lowers her head. "I am not allowed."

"Not allowed? Why?"

"Father says it's too dangerous," she whispers, "but I know the truth."

"The 'truth'?" Zo asks out of the side of her mouth.

Inanna leans in close and, barely audible, adds, "You're not safe here."

"…and so as you can clearly see," Tiberius continues, "it is the decomposition of what has been that supplies every essential element for that which is to come. Isn't it wonderful how all that we are, all that we may ever hope or strive to become, at the end of everything—" he shoves his arm into a pile and pulls out a handful of dirt "—everything inevitably returns to soil. Soil is the end—" and he picks out a large earthworm "—and the very beginning of life."

Sargon bursts into applause. "Very good, very GOOD, Tiberius!" Turning to his guests, he urges, "Go on, now, feel it for yourselves, I must insist. Plunge your hands right in there and let it squish through your fingers. Feel how rich our soil is."

Without hesitation, Augur goes in double-fisted. "It's considerably warmer than I anticipated."

"Very good observation, yes." Tiberius nods, his paw cradling his chin. "A natural part of the process."

But Zo is lost in her thoughts. *Did I hear her right? I could barely hear her but, did she just warn me?*

Feeling all eyes turn to her, she clears her throat. "I'm quite familiar with composting—" She puts a hand into the pile and stops short, leaning closer. *Wow. This soil is really light. It's flakey almost, like snow. And holy cow! Look at all the bugs in just one handful!* She straightens and lets the soil slip through her fingers. "But what is this secret?"

Sargon leans forward, gushing his anticipation for this moment. "The secret, deary, is the right ingredients." He looks as though his prolonged withholding may cause him to burst. "Zababa, Inanna, lead our guests to the primary pile!"

They walk beyond the huts, to where the Hill recedes near the end of the cavern.

No moles work back here. There is only another, altogether larger compost heap. Their noses are once again resurrected by the palpable stench of decay.

Augur coughs and heaves.

Zo gags and covers her face.

Sargon holds out his hands. "This is where it begins!" He breathes deep and exhales with that exaggerated grin. "And THAT is the scent of power!"

"Zo is right," Augur chokes, "it smells like death."

"Come closer." He waves. "Come, see my secret."

Approaching, Zo recognizes the usual decaying ingredients, *Mulch, manure, peat. Nothing seems out of the ordinary— Wait. What is an entire tree trunk doing here?* "That's odd," she points. "Why don't you chop everything into bits?" *That's creepy. It looks like—* She leans in. "Wait. That bark looks—" *Oh, god. No!*

Horrified, she twirls back in time to catch Sargon's eager paws wringing just below his toothy smile.

His eyes narrow. "We aren't savages, deary."

Her knees hit the ground in time with her puke.

Assuming the stench has become too much, Augur reaches for her. "Are you okay?"

Everything is spinning.

"She'll be just fine." Sargon stands over her. "You both will."

Zo hits the ground, limp.

CHAPTER 27

*C*oming to, she can't move.

Her arms are restrained and her hands are covered. Try as she might, whatever holds her, holds her well.

"You know what I first noticed about you?" Sargon's voice seizes her. "Even before your snarky attitude and your irreverence in sitting on my floor?"

He's behind her, but she can't turn to face him. "Where am I? Where is Augur? What have you done to him?"

"It was your hair. I saw it the moment I laid eyes on you. Don't worry, you hide it well. I'm sure no one else caught it. But I have trained myself to notice such things. You see, it is this very thing that makes you a perfect candidate."

"'Candidate'? For what?"

His breath tickles her ear, "To be my secret."

She struggles to break free. "What have you done with Augur?"

"Do keep trying, deary," his voice is distant now, "you'll bury yourself much faster."

He's right. The more she moves, the more the weight of the compost pile tightens in around her. She's stuck.

I need help. Where is Augur? What did that dirty mole do to him? Ugh. I can't move! I can't just wait til I rot, but I can't move—OH! What touched my leg? A worm, probably a worm. Just a worm. There's got to be something I can do. I'm not deadweight yet. But if I move too much, it all gets heavier, tighter. Think, Zo! Stop moving and think.

Slowly, she begins to tunnel her fingers up, methodically pushing bits of dirt (and whatever else) beneath her palms. She does her best to pack down a good amount before bending her wrist to raise her hand. After repeating this process several times, her hands are now high enough that her next attempt will force her elbows to move. Now she folds her digits into her palms and uses her fingertips to gently sweep the sift under the backside of her hands until she feels a little avalanche loosen behind her arms. She presses back, carefully controlling the weight of her forearms, and pulls up just enough to begin tunneling her fingers upward again.

Finally freeing her hands, she looks around. She's buried on the far side of the primary pile. No one is around. She continues the painstaking method until at last her arms, too, are free.

She had already begun to sink during her initial struggles. But now that her arms are up, she feels confident. *I should be able to disperse my weight evenly across the top of the pile if I spread my arms in front of me, and slowly lean in and wiggle up. I think I can worm my way out of here.* Her fingers begin to tingle. *Now or never.*

Carefully, she leans into her arms, and begins moving her toes up and back, when—*What was that?*

Something big slithered beneath the heel of her right foot. And now her left.

No, no, "NO."

She drops a few inches. Her arms are now awkwardly bent above her shoulder line.

Breathe, Zo, breath. You've got this. You have all the time in the world. Just try again.

But it's impossible spread her arms wide enough, and compost starts sinking around them.

"No, no, no—"

Another slither beneath her feet.

"NO!"

She sinks deeper.

Her hands hang limp above her, numb. The weight of the pile is stifling her torso.

How the heck did we get here? Aminah was so kind. Why would she bring us here? She couldn't haven known about this, could she? No, there's no way. She shared too much. I felt like I was finally starting to understand, I was excited to get back to the path. And now, now I can't feel my arms and I'm probably going to die here. Buried by the filth of a dirty mole who only sees me for the remnants of my settlement...

There's nothing she can do.

CHAPTER 28

*S*he's sunk deeper.

I must have fallen asleep. She raises her heavy head, *OH,* and winces, *my arms.*

Although her muscles are numb, her bones ache where her elbows press into the compost wall. Her hands dangle just inside the hole, and she can't see beyond them.

Wake up! She commands herself over and over again. *It's only a dream, just WAKE UP!*

Sift falls in on her from the opening above and she coughs uncontrollably. She doesn't even realize she's being lifted until the sharp pains of recirculation surge back into her forearms.

As soon as her chest clears the pressure, she sucks in all the air she can. Gasping, she looks up through tearful and squinted eyes to find Zababa and Inanna are pulling her free.

Now lying facedown on top of the pile, her arms return to life with triumphant and devastating pain.

She moans and rolls over, bumping her head on something hard. Sitting up, she brushes away the rubbish and retrieves the object. It takes a moment for the heavy realization to sink in. She drops it and hastily retreats.

She looks at the siblings. They both stare blankly at the unearthed remnants of a mole's skull.

Inanna's eyes fill with tears and she turns to her brother. "Baba? Who was?" Her nose twitches and she scrubs her face.

"I—I have no idea." He's trembling. "I didn't know he went this far." He reaches to help Zo up. "You have to go now. Come with me. Inanna will retrieve your friend."

"Augur." Zo feels wobbly as she stands. "Where is he?"

"PLEASE. We must leave NOW." Zababa turns. "Nanna?"

Inanna nods and disappears toward the Hill. Zababa hurries Zo down and around it.

"Do you have more of the bright berries?"

"Yes, they're in my bag."

"Rub the juice in your hands again. It might help if you lose your way. But use it only if you need it," he orders. "If you can help it, you must keep your hands closed until you are beyond our borders."

"How will I know—"

"You will know. Inanna will send the blind one after you. Follow the tunnel to the right at three junctions. Left at the fourth. Middle-most at the last. You must remember!"

She recites the directions a few times.

"Good." He pulls her into a tunnel and stops, looking out with a careful eye. "The way will take you through twists and turns, but remember the junctions and it will return you to the path. You must remember the way and keep your hands closed throughout. Only open them if you're in peril at a junction, and only for a moment. Do you understand?"

"Yes. Please tell me, is Augur okay?"

"Move swift." He scurries out of the tunnel.

They remain in the shadows along the walls of the cavern.

Zababa whispers, "Your friend is well. He believes you are, too. My father has deceived him, told him you fainted from exhaustion and were returned to Aminah to rest—"

"Aminah. Did she know? She couldn't have known?"

"No. No one but the Hill knows what my father is doing. The rest of our labour go out on patrol, seeking the settled, but their intentions are pure. They believe the Hill provides aid. They are manipulated, they have no idea they are informants. The Hill uses their knowledge to dig out and bring the weak back to the pile. Their rotting flesh is the secret to my father's compost. He devours them."

"And what will happen to Augur?"

"My father is taken by his experience, but that will wear with time and he too will be in danger. Inanna will see that he follows you tonight."

Zo exhales relief. "Will you both join us?"

They arrive at the passageway's threshold.

"No. You must understand, we have only realized the depths of our father's madness. We cannot leave our kind subjected to his treachery." Zababa gazes back over the Hermitage. "This is our path." He turns back. "Now I leave you here. Do you remember the way?"

"Three rights, a left, then middle-most."

"Good. And whatever you do—"

"Keep my hands closed." Overwhelmed with gratitude and regret for misjudging him, Zo marvels at the cunning and bravery of this young mole, and smiles her crooked smile. "I'm sorry I'm so gross, or I'd give you a hug."

"No. No. Please don't. That stink could expose me." He hesitates, then adds, "I'm sorry my father forced you into his filth."

Though he cannot embrace her, his remorse fills Zo with warm vindication. "Thank you, Zababa. And good luck to you and Inanna."

"May the Three guide us all."

CHAPTER 29

*A*rms outstretched, hands tightly fisted, Zo makes her way through the dark tunnel as quickly as she can. When it's narrow enough that her outstretched fists can touch both sides, she is able to move quickly. But more often than not the wide passages stagger her pace, as she is forced to zig-zag forward, to ensure she doesn't miss a junction.

She reaches the first crossroad. *Come on, Augur. What's taking you so long? You should be able to run through this burrow like it's daylight.* She waits.

"What am I doing? Augur can do this with his eyes closed." She chuckles to herself. "Onward, to the right."

Two more rights and one left later, she comes the last junction, but it only offers two passageways.

"Three rights, a left, then middle-most. That's what he said. That's what I did. Where did I go—Oooh, CRAP." She hadn't checked for more than two tunnels at the third junction. *Sloppy. Just sloppy. You're better than that, Zo! Tired or not, you can't afford dumb mistakes. You have to be better than that!*

She drags her knuckles along the back of her neck and stretches. *Shake it off, kid. You're almost there, you've got this.* She heads back.

Sure enough there are three avenues at the third junction and she now takes the farthest right, pressing on.

I bet Augur came and went by now. I'm so tired. Don't slow down, Zo. Deep breaths, deep breaths. There. Keep going. Keep going. Remember Father, remember Ma and Bro, remember Quest. Keep going. Remember Mahdi, remember Pahana. Keep going. Remember Augur. Keep going. Remember the settled. Keep going. Remember Aminah and the siblings. Keep going. Remember the Three. Keep going. You got this! Keep going.

But despite her will, she's depleted.

Truly, that's all I've got. I'm spent. I need to rest. Just a quick power nap. Placing her rucksack beside her to mark the direction she needs to head, Zo eats.

Then she sleeps.

And she dreams…

The vine in her hair grows, and more vines sprout.

Her curls are now completely replaced with vines. She can't hide her settlement, and everyone gawks and shuns her.

She turns to run.

Gaining speed, the Three appear and beckon her. But the harder she pursues Them, the farther away They seem, until They disappear altogether into a cave.

She follows. But inside, the scene pulls back and she is swallowed by the toothy smile of Sargon.

His face is not natural. It's hewn in chunks and held together by a series of strings. He cackles, making it apparent that the strings that hold him together also command his movement.

Perspective continues to retreat, and the strings grow long through the dark until the crossarm of a controller can be seen. But although it's obviously Its doing, in the darkness the Puppeteer cannot be seen.

Zo's gaze is fixed, searching to find who wields the controls, but the crossbar suddenly sets toward her, and the vines on her head rush up, into the controller.

…She wakes.

Breathing heavy, pulse pounding, once again the stench on her becomes new. She gags and her hands open to cover her face. For a few moments, the green glow reflects intensely all around her.

She seals her hands tight.

But as the stink numbs, she lets one pinky out. The soft glow is magnified.

Without thinking, she holds out a hand entirely and stands in astonishment. The tunnel is lit up with the full brightness of a clear (green hued) day.

Floor to ceiling, the passage is comprised of a mirror-like rock. It's like a funhouse, some surfaces reflect taller, some shorter, some disconnected, still others zoomed in, focused on random areas (her knees, an eye, her fingers).

She approaches one seemingly normal reflection. She hasn't seen herself since she first drank from the waters of life. She gazes into her eyes.

I look kind. I never look kind! Gentle even, vulnerable? No one's ever said that about me. And I sure as heck don't want anyone to see me that way! Is that how people see me now, vulnerable? I mean, I guess there's a strength in that. Showing yourself openly instead of hiding, that can show strength. It's kind of beautiful, really. I mean, I'm not gorgeous, but there's something beautiful—I've never thought of kindness as strength before.

Her smile catches her attention and her hands touch her cheeks. *Oh geez, look how dirty I am!* The reflective stone responds to the focus of her eye, shifting convexly, putting the very grains of dirt burrowed into her pores on full display. *Ew, disgusting.*

"Disgusting," an echo resounds inside the tunnel.

Woah. Did I say that out loud?

She looks around. *I don't think anyone else's here. Just me looking back at me.* She returns to the reflection and brushing her hair away from her face, feels the vine. She pulls it forward and rests it between her eyes. *You've caused me quite a bit of trouble.*

"Trouble," the echo returns.

What the?

Again more thoroughly examining her surroundings, she still only finds her reflections. Looking at herself from multiple angles, she curls her lip. "I'm filthy."

"Filthy. Filthy. Disgusting. Trouble."

She catches it, *My reflections are parroting me.*

"Defiled," they continue, "Unworthy."

"Defiled?" she asks.

"Settled. Don't continue. Undeserving of the path."

Her eyes focus on an enlarged image of her self-loathing mouth, and she becomes entranced.

Sinking down to her knees, she begins to mimic the reflections, "I don't deserve it." She bows her head into her lap, but her eyes remain fixed, absorbing the degradation.

"Filthy... Defiled... Cowering... No escape... Much trouble... Settled... Not worthy... Disgusting."

The reflections stretch, crawling across the grimy floor and reaching toward her. But she doesn't move.

She watches as they cover her, not realizing a heavy layer of mud is growing over her feet and legs, up her torso, hardening to a thick crust almost as quickly as it moves. Hands open, the bondage continues its creep until it consumes the glow. As the crud finally hardens over her eyes, the echos persist in her mind.

I'm filthy. Not worthy. Too much trouble...

———

"Zo! Zo, where are you!" Augur's voice bounces through the tunnel. "ZO!"

Stopping nearby, he strains to hear something through the silence. "Zo?"

A faint heartbeat.

"Zo, is that you? Say something? Zo?"

Her pulse is steady, but she doesn't make a sound.

"Zo?" He inches closer. "Zo? I need you to talk to me. I know my voice is too loud for you to sleep. Come on, my lady, give me something."

He feels something large on the ground, and finding his way around it, her heart now beats behind him.

"Zo?" He kneels beside it. *But this feels like a boulder— and the pulse is stronger.*

He lays his ear against it. *What is this?* "Zo." He taps on the encrusted form and tries to pick at it. "Zo! ZO!" He hits it hard, and begins to pound against it.

Muted thuds call her awareness away from self-deprecation.

Narrowing her ears toward the rapping, the distant sound of a voice is muddled by her own endless chatter.

She is drifting.

"Zo!" Her name breaks clearly through the noise.

"Zo," the echos catch on, "Filthy Zo."

But Augur's voice bests the clamor, "Zo!"

"Unworthy Zo."

"You have to fight, Zo!" He has no idea what she's up against.

"Troublesome, Zo."

But he doesn't give up. "Fight, Zo! You're not a settler!"

"Settler Zo. Not worthy."

Consumed again, she floats through a dark void. With nothing to hold onto and no foundation to stand, she is lulled away.

Lost.

"Zo!" His voice fades into remote incoherence. "zo?"

Augur can't break the casing, but he heard Zo's heartbeat increase when he called to her.

His breath is heavy and he is tired. He presses his cheek against the crust. *Her pulse is strong.* "I know you're there, my lady. Don't give up. I'm not giving up." He sits back and rests his arm over the lump. "But I do need a break." He leans his head against the tunnel wall and sighs.

"Don't give up, Zo."

CHAPTER 30

*F*loating through the endless reflections of her mind, a light pierces between them.

What is that?

As Zo shoves mirrors aside, the light grows, then splits into Three, and dims into familiar images.

"Remember, Zo." They speak in unison, "Remember."

"Remember?" she questions, the restless echos still reverberate.

"Remember who you are."

"I'm... unworthy, filthy—"

"Zo," they insist, "remember WHOSE you are."

"Whose I am." She tilts her head. "Whose am I?"

The magnificent harmony of their voices rises above the swarm, "Salvador."

"I am," she closes her eyes to remember, but the reflections persist and manipulate the light like mirror balls of distraction, and she is swayed. "I'm unworthy."

But the Three magnify and the synchronicity of their voices resounds, "You are a Salvador. Zo, you are chosen."

"Chosen?"

They affirm, "Zo Salvador. Leader. Savior. Our chosen."

But again, the mirrors capture her eye.

"But I am filthy."

"You are chosen. We chose you, Daughter." Their voice resonates, stirring her.

Between the echos, she can finally recognize distinct voices. "Ma?" She casts aside the babbling reflections. "Ma! Father! Bro!"

"We chose you. Believe, Zo Salvador. Remember. Believe."

"Wait!" Frantic in her attempt to reach them, she can't find her footing and begins to thrash in her drifting. Her family is fading and the reflections swarm in full force.

But Zo is awake.

"NO! I am a daughter. I am a Salvador!"

Moans rouse Augur.

"Zo?" He moves his ear against her covered form. *I hear you.* "I hear you, Zo! Fight! Fight, Zo!" He begins beating at the crust again.

Zo is also now battling from the inside. Working together, the hard cast starts to crack.

Augur picks at the fissures. "Come on, Zo! Keep fighting!"

Then her elbow bursts through, and the casing shatters like a Prince Rupert's drop.

Augur falls backward.

She sucks in air and coughs as the dust settles, and brushes off the remnants of the shell. Then she stretches out beside her friend, who is still gasping for air.

She turns her head. "You came back for me?"

"And you," he's still catching his breath, "you elbowed me!"

She shakes her head and smiles. *He really is funny.*

He sits up. "What happened, Zo?"

"This tunnel is full of bad mirrors. Zababa warned me not to open my fists, but the way the green light magnified was beautiful, and then I saw myself, and I—my reflections entranced me and ridiculed me. I was helpless until…"

"Until I arrived." Augur beams.

"No, not you. I think I heard you, but you faded away. No. It was the Three!"

"The Three?" he forgets his pride. "You saw Them again!"

"Yes! No. Maybe? They were my family—my adopted family. Father, Ma and Bro, they told me to remember, to believe they chose me. I'm a Salvador."

"Okay, but how did you get out? I couldn't break through. I could hear your heartbeat, but I couldn't crack the shell, it wore me out! And then I heard you moan—"

"I remembered. And I fought because I believed them. I had to stop listening to what my reflections said. I had to choose to believe what they believed in me. And I'm sure you helped, too." She smirks. *Maybe he really does—no. Slow down, girl. Go with what you know.* "You came back for me."

"Of course I did. Zo, I—"

"Thank you, Augur."

He sighs. "It's my pleasure, my lady."

Augur leads.

Inanna gave him a new walking stick when she snuck him away. Sargon had summoned her to assist their guest in bedtime preparations, but rather than leading him to the bathing pool, she told Augur about Zo and sent him after her. When he made it to the border and Zo wasn't there, he knew something was wrong and determined to find her.

And now as they pass the final junction together, the tunnel begins a steep incline and Zo sees a speck of soft light ahead. She breathes a sigh of relief.

Augur takes notice. "Can you see it?"

"Can you?" she teases.

"I can feel the warmth of it. We still have a ways to go. It's all uphill from here. And it gets hotter."

"Do I still stink?" Zo asks.

He shrugs. "Not much. I think the funk got caught in the crust and kind of fell off with it as you broke through."

"Good."

He smirks. "Or I could still be nose-blind."

She playfully hip-checks him.

By the time they reach the tunnel's end, they're both out of breath and sweating.

The threshold is low and narrow and bends downward before leading up and out. Augur goes first.

Zo hesitates. *I've had more than my fill of tight spaces today.* Getting down to crawl through, her heart races and her breathing becomes shallow.

Augur reaches his hand back for hers. "I'm right here."

Her anxiety melts. *You're full of pleasant surprises today, and I'm incredibly grateful.*

She takes his hand and passes through.

CHAPTER 31

*I*t takes time for her eyes to adjust, but the pale blue hue of the moonlight is as welcoming as the memory of Amma's warm hugs. It's hot, but there's a constant, gentle breeze. The moon bounces like sliver over endless dunes and sand. This land is an extensive abandonment.

"Shall we rest?" Augur suggests.

"It's really hot. I think we should assume it'll be way hotter when the sun comes out. It's probably best to carry on now."

"Okay then," he holds out his hands, "which way?"

She sighs. "That's the problem. I can't see the path. We're in a desert and there's no way to know which way to go."

He grins. "So we rest."

"Yeah." She forces a short, defeated raspberry through her lips. "I guess."

They sit down to eat.

She bites her lip. "Can I ask you a weird question?"

Augur's eyebrows peak. "Sure."

"Did you have an encounter at the river?"

"'Encounter'?" He breathes deep. "Yeah, that fits."

"What did you— I mean, you didn't see anything. Did you?"

He grins. "Ah, but I did, my lady."

"What did you see?"

"I saw…" he shrugs. "I saw me. Happy. Not like laughing happy, but really content, you know? Satisfied. Fulfilled even. Confident and strong, but not haughty. And of course, flagrantly handsome."

She rolls her eyes. "Okay, but HOW did you see it? Did you actually SEE, with your eyes?"

"I saw it. I don't really know how else to explain it. When I got to the river, I was overwhelmed with everything. Everything. But I was determined. I pressed on, and at the river's edge I saw this—this ME. It was the image of who I really want to be, who I hope to be. I don't know why, but it made me thirsty, and when I drank, I saw me again, but…" He pauses, chewing on his thumbnail. "But that me isn't someone I want anyone to see. I don't even want to see him again."

He swallows. "I didn't want to cross the river then. I was afraid of being confronted like that again, of BEING that guy. I mean, I guess I AM that guy, but I was afraid the path would keep making me see him." He rubs his thumb and lifts his eyebrows again. "But I wanted to see you more." His grin illuminates his face. "Well, not SEE you of course, but you understand."

Good grief, maybe it's not just words. Maybe he really does like me. She shifts awkwardly. "So you're on this journey for me?"

"And you're on it for your brother."

"No— I mean, yeah, I was but," she nibbles her lower lip. "I'm changing. Pursuing this path—the Three, I clearly haven't found Quest, but I think I'm finding me instead. I don't know if it will lead me to Quest like I'd hoped." She stops, then exhales sharply. "But I'm here now in an actual desert and I need to carry on for my own sake, literally."

"You're not alone, Zo." Augur smirks.

She bites her lip again, *Should I be alone?*

Zo wakes up before dawn. *Dear god! The heat is already intense! Look at this wasteland. There's nothing here. Nothing. Sand and dunes. Dunes and sand. Nothing's even moving—no wait. What is that? A beetle? Hey little guy, where are you going?* "I'll bet you have a better take on this heat than we could imagine."

She watches it burrow itself beneath the sand, then looks up. *The sun is barely beginning to rise and it feels like the temperature has jumped 10 degrees in the last 30 seconds.* "Something tells me we're not going to like what we're about to find out. This day is not going to be pretty."

Augur moans, rolling over. "What is this? This heat is gross! I can't sleep."

"It's probably best we get started," Zo suggests.

He sits up. "You can see the peak?"

"No, just dunes. But I can see the sunrise, so I know the general way."

The midday is excruciating.

"Zo. Zo, I need to stop. Tracking through hot desert sand is not a blind man's idea of a good time."

"I don't think it's anyone's idea of a good time," she shrugs, "but here we are."

"Well," he plants his legs shin-deep, "I need to rest."

"Where Augur? Where do you suggest we rest? There's nothing but sand. Baking, scorched sand, everywhere."

He sits down. "I need to stop."

She huffs and crosses her arms, standing nearby.

He ignores her. "What if THIS is the peak?"

She scoffs. "There's no way."

"What if it is, Zo? All this time, all the work, what if THIS is it? It would very well explain why so few travel this path. And why those who do usually end up pissed by it."

"It can't be." She shakes her head, staring at the wasteland. "What mountaintop is a desert? Mountains are topped with snow and ice, not blazing infernos. It's impossible."

Augur challenges, "So where's the peak?"

"I don't know." She looks around. "But this can't be it. And even if it is, Aminah said the destination isn't the purpose. It's the path."

"So where's the path?"

"I—" her shoulders slump. "I can't see the path here, Augur. I see sand, endless, god-forsaken sand. Everywhere. And I see a cloudless, wide open sky. But no path." Tears swell in her eyes. She takes a deep breath and steadies herself. "But I KNOW it's this way."

"How?"

"Because it's always been this way. Just like in the dark forest, toward the sun til midday, then onward toward my shadow."

"But how do you know that's right? I mean, that led you to me so it was obviously right then, but why shouldn't it change? Why wouldn't it?"

She stands silent.

He doesn't wait. "We're wandering—aimless! And I can barely take two steps without feeling like I'm falling. And if we don't find our way, we're not going to make it." He grunts. "I need to eat."

She mumbles, "It's barely midday."

But he's already taking out his supplies. "Yes, and I'm drained. I need nourishment."

"Augur, we don't know how long we'll be here. We should ration our supplies."

He takes a swig from his canteen. "It's a good thing we each have our own rations then," and chomps into his bark. Then he leans back, as though he is enjoying bathing in this sun.

She rolls her eyes and sits down, back to the sun, pulls her poncho out and holds it over her head. "You're going to burn."

"Pardon?" He sucks his teeth. "I couldn't hear you over the sound of me savoring my meal."

Deep breaths, Zo. He's trying to get the best of you. Don't give it to him. Breathe. "Your skin is going to burn. You should use your cloak to cover up."

"Why thank you, my lady." He pulls his hood over his face. "It's lovely to know you care."

Inhale, two, three, four. Exhale, two, three, four Pay attention to your breathing. Pay attention to your present— Ugh!

She makes a clacking sound. *My tongue feels swollen and my saliva is thick—gross. Sand is sticking everywhere. Everywhere. It's jammed in the crevices of my eyelids, it's in my ears—trying to get my hair clean is going to be the worst—it's between my fingers, under my fingernails.*

Look at that. My sweat is evaporating in hazy plumes. Why does this poncho feel heavy all the sudden? My arms are aching. There, left arm, you can rest. Look at my fingers shake. Okay, your turn, right arm. And those fingers are shaky, too.

What is this empty feeling? Am I hungry? I haven't felt hunger in a long time. Geez, I'm tired. I'm hot, gross, exhausted, and Augur is just as snug as a bug in a rug. This heat is life-sucking! Eating again does seem necessary. Look at him! So cocky in his comfort. Ugh, but he sure is faring better than me. This isn't like any other part of the path, after all. It's rather unexpected. Eating again would be fine. We'll have enough to get by—

No. No. One bite of bark and one sip of water have always been enough for each day. I can hold out. I will hold out.

They wait for what feels like a miserable eternity under the thin veil of their makeshift canopies until the sun begins to descend and the temperature again feels tolerable.

With their shadows now before them, Augur holds out his arm to Zo, and they set off once more.

"No, wait. You're going to make me fall." She gives him her arm instead. "This way when you stumble, I can catch you."

"And when you stumble, my lady?"

"I won't." She smirks.

He laughs. "Of course."

"I see something."

"The peak?"

"No. A dead tree maybe? I'm not sure how far away it is."

"A dead tree, how inviting."

Making their way to it, Augur adds, "Why, exactly are we going to a dead tree?"

But Zo ignores him. "Hm, definitely not a tree. It's too small." She gets close to study it. "It looks like a stick, but it's not wood and it's hollow. There's sand stuck to it—fused, almost melted on—but it's smooth inside."

"Hollow and sandy but smooth. May I hold it?"

"No. Here." She grabs his hand. "You can touch it but it's buried pretty good. Maybe it's a marker for the path?"

"Is it pointing somewhere? It doesn't feel like it offers direction."

"Yeah, it's just kind of sticking out. I can't really tell, it's getting dark. Let's camp here and get a better look at it in the morning. I'm starving anyway."

He happily plops down on his rear. "I thought you preferred to travel in the cool of the night?"

"You gave yourself an extra portion today, Augur. This desert is draining my soul! It's not like any place we've ever been. Like, it's not enough to be hotter than Hades. No, in this extreme arid land, every step forward beneath the blazing sun is intensified by a trillion grains of sand sticking to every pour of my being. And apparently that's not enough either because there's humidity, too, which just makes moving feel heavier! And I did mention sand, but said nothing about trudging through it. I've been running on fumes, being your crutch, on fumes."

"Of course," he smiles, "an 'extra portion.' It couldn't be that in the desert you need to eat and drink more frequently to survive?"

"I'm surviving just fine—"

He scoffs.

"—AND I'm starving. So I'm going to ignore you and your smug face and this muggy heat, and take your advice and enjoy my meal."

He turns his attention back to the strange stick. "Well, it's definitely not wood."

"Thank you for that enlightening revelation, Inspector. Now please let me eat in peace." She bites into her bark and closes her eyes to savor it.

"Zo, uh, you wouldn't be done eating, would you?"

Mouth full, she turns to him and gasps. "You didn't!"

He is holding a piece of the stick in his hand.

"WHAT IS WRONG WITH YOU? That could have been our way out—AND YOU BROKE IT!"

"I didn't mean to, it just broke."

"In YOUR hand! You broke what might be the only direction we have in this endless expanse of nothingness!"

"We don't know that. Yes, yes, I broke it. But we don't KNOW that it would have helped."

"And now we'll NEVER know!"

"Zo. Look, I'm sorry, okay?"

"No! Not okay, Augur. Your 'sorry' doesn't fix anything."

"Well I can't fix it. It's a clean brea—OUCH! It cut me!"

"I have no sympathy for you."

Sucking his finger, he examines the hollow stick with his other hand. "Wait. This is glass."

"Why does it matter WHAT it's made of? We'll never know if—"

"It wouldn't have helped us anyway."

"You don't know that."

"Yes, I do. It's glass. And the only thing all the way out here that's hot enough to turn sand into glass is—oh. You mentioned it feels muggy, aye?"

"What?" She throws her hands in the air. "Why does that matter? You're changing the subject again."

"Would you say the sand is sticking to you because of your sweat, or because of static?"

"What? How does that even—"

"Sweat or static?"

"I don't know!"

"Is my hair lifted?"

"'Lifted'?"

Thunder crashes in the distance.

Augur holds his breath. "We need shelter."

CHAPTER 32

*T*he rain pours in torrents, causing the dunes to slip and flooding basins within minutes. Lightning has turned the night sky into an indiscriminate minefield.

With no hope for shelter, Zo and Augur lay flat on the windward side of a dune, about one-third of the way from the top. They hope to keep from getting swept away in the rising floodwaters while minimizing their chances of getting struck by staying below the ridge-line.

"WOOHOO!" Augur is belly-side-up.

"You're enjoying this?" Zo's breathing too quickly. "We could be struck by lightning or slip into an ever-increasing vat of quicksand—at any moment—AND YOU'RE HAVING FUN?"

"Describe it to me!"

A clap of thunder drowns his request.

"WHAT?"

"Tell me what it looks like!"

Belly-side-down, Zo's hands cover her neck. "It looks like we're going to die, Augur!"

"Then tell me what death looks like!"

"It's terrifying! There's more flashes of lightning than thunder! And it's all around! There's no way of telling where it's going to hit! It flashes often enough that I can see the rain changing direction in the wind! It's coming down in sheets! Sometimes it looks like it's not falling at all, like pages of water, like a flip-book in the sky—OH GOD!"

BOOM!

"That one was really close! It hit the dune right next to us!"

"WOO! My hair is standing!" Augur can't tame his excitement.

Now speechless, Zo laughs in terrified hysterics.

And Augur enthusiastically joins in.

CHAPTER 33

A simple tune rouses Zo.

Augur has turned the glass stick into a musical pipe. The storm passed sometime during the night, leaving mires in its wake. An eerie haze distorts the morning horizon. *I bet this is how Van Gogh first saw Starry Night.*

She breathes deep and slow, waiting for the melody to finish.

"That was a sweet song."

"Thank you." He smiles. "I've always loved music."

"You're good at it. A lot better than that nonsense you do in the Market."

"Ha! My lady, you wouldn't be trying to pay me a compliment?"

"You are, you're good. You should play more often."

Still grinning, he bows his head. "Your kindness is received. Thank you. Shall we be off?"

She looks around. "Are you familiar with mirages? I think I see something I don't remember seeing yesterday, but there's a lot of water in the air right now, so maybe it's not anything."

"With the storm we endured last night, I'm sure much of what you saw yesterday has changed."

"I suppose. I just wish I knew if I could believe what I see today."

"You know someone once told me—in the midst of utter uncertainty, mind you—it's probably a good idea to go with what you know. Or something like that, I can't remember exactly, I wasn't really listening at the time. I was hungry."

She smirks and takes in the hazy horizon again. "Okay. Let's go."

"Since you mostly keep yours closed, I'm guessing you're not dealing with this constant sand in your eye nuisance?" Zo's eyes are red and puffy.

"I am not."

"My eyes won't stop watering and twitching." She pulls her eyelashes to free whatever granules are embedded beneath the lid. "UGH. Hold on. I need to stop."

"How's your vision?"

She's rubbing her eyes so thoroughly that she doesn't pay him any attention. "ARGH. It hurts!"

"Can you see, Zo?"

"I'm trying to rub my eyes right now. I—"

"ZO. I need you to stop rubbing and try to see. Can you see anything?"

"Give me a second, my eyes are really watery and—ARGH. It hurts to open them!"

"Try, Zo. You've got to try. Can you see anything?"

"It really hurts!" Forcing her swollen eyes open, she pauses. "I—I can't. I can't see anything. Augur, I CAN'T SEE!"

He sucks his teeth. "Sandman's eye. I should have known."

"What? Wh—what is that?"

"We're in a desert. Your eyes haven't had any break from the sun."

"And?"

"And the sun has blinded you."

"WHAT? Just like that?"

"Can you see?"

"No."

"Sandman's eye."

"Okay. Okay." *Just use the*— "ARGH! No! I gave my sap to Pahana."

"I have some, but it's a temporary fix."

"What do you mean?"

"It will heal you, but it won't prevent it from happening again. We have to get out of this desert, Zo."

"That's what I've been trying to do, Augur!"

"I know, I know." He bites his thumbnail. "Listen, let's get that sap in your eyes. But hear me out, you're going to have to cover your eyes."

"What? Cover my eyes? That makes no sense."

"Zo, it will just keep happening, and who knows how long we'll be here, and we—I only have so much sap. You have to keep your eyes covered, it's the only way."

"And, what? We just sit here and wait? Become settled? Or better yet, you take the lead. The blind quite literally leading the blind—"

"Yeah. I lead. You can lean on me this time."

"Augur—"

"It's the only way. Believe it or not, I have a pretty good handle on this whole being blind thing."

"That's not—"

"I've got this, Zo. Trust me."

She sighs sharp and covers her face with her hands. *My eyeballs feel like fire. I definitely don't ever want to experience this again.* "Okay."

He tears his cloak to fashion a blindfold, while she manages to get a drop of sap in each eye. After it bubbles and soothes, she takes one last look around, then shakes her head before covering her eyes.

This time she takes his arm, and once more, they set out.

CHAPTER 34

*D*uring the day she keeps her eyes wrapped as they trudge through the heat and sand, but at night she searches the horizon for anything that might direct their way.

By the time she realizes she's lost count of the days, she's already begun to lose hope. "I'm starting to think this is it."

"What? No. I've got this, Zo."

"I feel like we're going in circles. We HAVE to be going in circles! There's no way this desert is this big! It's on a mountain, for Pete's sake—it HAS to end! Even just to drop off."

"Maybe the moles brought us elsewhere?"

"No. No, Zababa and Inanna were true. They could have given us each different directions or let us be turned to soil for that matter. No. Something's off."

"What do you mean?"

I don't like the way he said that. He was just trying to cheer me up. Why is he sensitive all the sudden? Why does saying something's off strike a nerve? "I don't know, I can just tell something's not right. Ever since I started covering my eyes."

He is silent.

That's not like him. "Why are you so quiet? What's on your mind?"

He shifts uncomfortably. "I just—" he sighs. "Perhaps I'm not very good at leading here."

"What do you mean? You said that you had it, to trust you. Like you literally just said it again a minute ago. What do you mean, maybe you're not very good?"

"I—I don't know what I'm doing, Zo! For all I know we HAVE been going in circles." He shrugs. "I don't know."

"Wait. You made me believe you."

Silence.

"Augur, you made me believe you! You've reassured me again and again. And now—what? Nothing? It was for nothing! Because now that I'm exhausted enough to say something, now you admit that you don't even know if we've been going in circles! Have you had any direction at all?"

"No."

"NO?" She scoffs. "Since when? How long, Augur?"

"The whole time."

"The whole time?" Shaking her head, she scoffs again. "The whole time."

Silence amplifies their tension.

Finally, he pleads, "Do you think it's easy to follow you?"

"What?"

"You think it's easy it have to lean on you for everything here?"

"You cannot—no." She bites her lip. "You're not seriously trying to pin this foolishness on me. You followed the wrong girl for that! Do you think it's easy for ME having to carry YOU everywhere? And you stop and eat whenever you feel like it, and I'm starving—barely surviving! DOING EVERYTHING IN MY POWER TO KEEP YOU ALIVE!"

He throws his arms to the sky. "I'M SORRY!"

"You're what? No, you're not! Who yells an apology? You don't want to deal with the ramifications of what you've—"

"I'll accept whatever consequences." He rubs his temples, shaking his head.

She scoffs. "You don't get it, and that's how I know you're not sorry. What consequences, Augur? The fact that I'm angry? I HAVE TO DEAL WITH THE CONSEQUENCES OF YOUR CHOICES. ME! I trusted you! I—" she softly gasps. "I trusted you. And you?" *Even his silence stings. He has no remorse for what he's done.* She takes a deep breath. "You—no. I need space. I need time and I need space."

She gathers her belongings. "I'll be on another dune. I can't. Maybe we can talk tomorrow—or never, I don't know right now, but I need space." She grabs her bag and stumbles over to the ridge.

Augur makes no attempt to stop her.

He obviously knows he's wrong!

He knew he was wrong all along, and yet he continued. And what, if I never mentioned anything—we would have just kept going in circles! AND HE KNEW IT. He's a liar. A liar! And he justifies himself because he was jealous. Jealous? Of ME? But HE followed me! I never asked him to and I sure as heck didn't force him. And, dammit, I've been doing EVERYTHING to keep him going. Me! He's betrayed MY trust. HE's screwed us both over! But it's all good because he'll 'accept whatever consequences'— bullshit! What consequences? WHAT ABOUT ME? I didn't get a choice in those consequences! I didn't opt into his foolishness! But 'whatever consequences' are MINE now because HE chose them. IDIOT!

Breathe, Zo, breathe. Inhale, two, three, four. Exhale, two, three four. Just breathe. Nope. I can't even give him all that credit. Of course it's my fault because I'm a fool. I'm always too quick to trust people.

Quest, I miss you! You would have set me straight. You would have known not to trust him. You would have seen me getting myself caught up in the flattery, the fake chivalry. You would have known. Brother, where are you?

I was right once, though. Father, Ma, Bro, I miss you, too. Your acceptance was true, unwavering, unconditional. God, I miss you.

Snuggling into her satchel, Zo wipes her face against it and whispers through tears, "I miss you, Daddy." She buries her face again and covers her head, trying her best to smother the sobs.

Losing any awareness of time to her misery, a bright light cuts through her barriers, overpowering her sorrow and commanding her attention.

What in the— She lifts her head. "It's about time!"

CHAPTER 35

The white light is cooler than the desert. Zo's less anxious this time and sits calmly, waiting. *I'm finally waking up—*

"Daughter, oh my darling, how beautiful you are."

The sound of her tender voice moves Zo to tears. "Ma?"

"My beloved child, how I've missed you!"

Zo covers a sob with her hands and squints to see beyond the light. "Ma?"

"Come here, sweet girl."

Crying and with arms extended through the bright, she runs into Ma's embrace, practically knocking her over.

"Let's have a sit, dear. Let me get a good look at you." Ma gasps. "You are gorgeous. Come here."

Oh, I've missed this! Ma's hugs are better than I remembered.

Burying her face, Zo weeps in the arms of her mother.

After some time, Ma speaks, "My darling, do you remember when you first came to us? You were so desperate to stay, you said everything you thought we wanted to hear, did anything we asked, agreed with everything we said."

Zo releases a gentle laugh. *I did!* "I didn't want you to send me away. I thought if I was perfect, you would keep me."

"Yes dear, you were a child eager to please because you were afraid. But that wasn't what we wanted at all."

"I remember we talked, you, me and Father, while Bro and Quest played video games. You said you loved me," she wipes her face on her tunic, "and you wanted to know me, the real me. You said I am so important that even if we don't like the same things, you'd still love me. And that I could teach you about things you'd never tried before."

"That's right. And that is when you looked up at Father with your big, sad puppy eyes and your pouty lower lip, and told him you didn't like to watch golf." Ma smiles. "And then you told me you didn't agree with my roasted carrots, remember?"

They laugh.

"And then I broke down crying because I knew I had to tell you about the spelling tests I hid from you." She shakes her head. "I hated spelling!"

"Yes!" Ma laughs and squeezes Zo. "But, do you know what, my love? Your Father and I adored you just as much! You were honest with us, and we could finally begin to get to know you —really you! Why, you filled us with so much pride because you trusted us enough to be true to yourself, even though you were scared."

"Yeah, I was terrified to do it. But I was so relieved."

"Of course, Darling, that makes complete sense. Because of your courage, then we could work with you together, and your spelling improved! And believe me, dear, I know how boring golf is to watch! And you know what else?" Ma drops her chin to whisper in Zo's ear, "I never much cared for cooked carrots either."

Zo smirks and rests against her mother. She sighs, *This isn't just about nostalgia.* "But Augur didn't lie about carrots, Ma. He's caused us to wander aimlessly for—I don't even know how long. He's led us off the path. It's a big deal. And, I trusted him."

She pauses. "I feel betrayed and foolish for trusting him in the first place."

Amma holds her tighter still. "Remember who you are, daughter. Remember us and remember who you are."

Zo closes her eyes, snuggles tighter and breathes deeply. "You still smell like the garden, Ma."

...She smiles and looks up, but she is holding her lumpy rucksack.

The dawn is breaking and a soft light stretches over the dune where Augur sleeps.

Remember, her mind echoes, *Remember*.

She sighs.

"Wh—wh—WHA?"

Augur jumps up out of his sleep, startled by something landing on his legs. Frantically examining his surroundings, he realizes Zo's bag is lying beside him.

"You're a liar." She sits nearby. "And I don't know how I can trust you."

"Zo, I've wanted to tell yo—"

"No. Stop. You SHOULD have told me all along. Before you ever even spoke to lead, you should have said what a dumb idea it was to even consider it—when I asked you in the very first place! Or you should have said something when you were leading us nowhere. Or when that initial doubt turned into the certain realization that you couldn't do it. Or at any point on any given day thereafter that you knew you were not truly leading. You SHOULD have said something. And now—"

"Zo—"

"Shh, shh, shht!" she points. "NOW you don't get to speak. Just listen."

He drops his head.

"You're a liar and you're deceitful, and I don't know how or if I can trust you. You led me to believe I could, and I was dumb enough to do it. You've had us wandering—I don't even know how long—and chances are we've been going in circles. I gave you my trust and you intentionally betrayed me day after day and on and on. Who knows where we could have been by now? But here we are still stuck in this soul-sucking desert because you refused to buck up and be honest."

She breathes.

As the sun steadily rises, she remembers her eyes and pulls out her blindfold. She measures how far apart her eyes are, and uses her teeth to thin the fabric in two small areas before putting it on.

"You took advantage of me in my weakness." She shakes her head. "In my weakness."

He's kept silent and now sitting with his head low, gives no indication that he has anything to offer.

Scanning the horizon through her makeshift sun filters, she thinks back to her vision with Ma, *I was so scared.*

She shakes her head. "But it's all good because you're 'ready to accept the consequences,' right?" She scoffs. "You haven't even considered that I have to carry the burden of your consequences. Your actions aren't your own, we're traveling together—what you do affects me, too."

Dragging her hands through her hair, she pauses at the vine and sighs. *And now what?*

Her head low, she taps her chest loud enough for him to hear. "And now it's on me to either leave you here to burn—which I can absolutely justify. Or forgive you. Just give up my reasoning, let go of the days and weeks and who knows how long we've wasted here—not to mention the fact that you chose to harm me—and rather than retaliate with complete justification, choose to let go of my righteous vindication.

"I don't want to forgive you, Augur, because you don't deserve it because, dammit, this wrecks me. You've WRECKED me!" Holding back a sob, she lifts her head and swallows hard. "And you know what? It's my fault because I gave you my trust. So it all comes back to me anyway." She sighs heavier.

A restlessness sits uncomfortably between them.

Ugh, this sucks. I hate this so much. Blech. I can taste it, it's sour and bitter. How is that even possible? Too early and too late. Come on, Zo, just say it. You've already decided, now come through.

Throughout her scolding, Zo steadily avoided looking at Augur. But now, she looks. His head is low, his skin is flush and wet with tears.

Her heart leaps for him, and she hates herself for it. *Loyalty is going to be the death of me.* Stomach acid burns her throat. She swallows hard, shaking her head. *I hate the taste of vomit. Giddy-up girl, stop stalling. You've made up your mind, remember.*

She pulls her shoulders back and stretches her neck high, pursing her lips. Her vocal cords tremble, pleading with her to reconsider before she makes a sound. She swallows again and takes a deep breath. *I remember.* Looking directly at Augur, the stale taste of acid still thick on her tongue, she breaks the spell.

"But I forgive you."

Though the words pass through a clenched jaw, relief lifts her, like a heavy weight cast off of her soul.

Augur can't contain his composure and crumbles into himself, weeping.

She wants to reach out and comfort him, but still feeling the sting of betrayal, she silently doubts his resolve.

Watching him, she remembers the relief she felt when she confessed her truths to her parents. Her thoughts shift to how painful it was to determine not to settle, to break free from Pahana and leave the Gathering Place, and how scary it was to cross through that field. But the liberation she knew once she was again traveling the path, *it was more than anything I could have ever hoped for. You'll understand that freedom soon enough, Augur, I know you will.*

For that, and the pervading peace despite the doubt and pain, she moves in to sit close and reaches out to comfort him.

I made the right choice.

The two set off again together. Zo directs their path toward the rising sun.

For the first time, Augur talks about himself in a manner that isn't silly or intentional, he simply shares as his thoughts give rise. And Zo's fondness toward him increases.

The sun hasn't yet reached midday when the temperature abruptly drops.

"The sky is getting dark. It looks like another storm."

"Really? The air feels dry."

Lifting her eye band, she steadies her focus and a faint gasp escapes her like the shallow remnants of a breath she'd already exhaled.

"What is it?" Augur asks.

"We," she swallows. "We—we need shelter. NOW."

"What do you mean? What do you see?"

She turns in circles, but there's no safety anywhere.

"Zo, what is it?"

"I, I think—it's like, uh, uh, a rolling cloud of dust—a sand storm! It's a sand storm! And it's coming really fast!"

"Do you see anything? Anything at all we can use for shelter?"

"No. There's nothing!"

The sounds of heavy winds catch up to them, and grains of sand begin to lift, swirling around them.

Augur holds his hood low over his face. "Then we should run."

"What?"

"RUUUUUUUUN!" He grabs her hand and takes off.

But Zo doesn't budge. For an extended moment, she stands staring. *Look at him go. He moves when it counts, I'll give him that. Ha! Those long legs trying to speed through the sand.*

Remembering the approaching gale, she turns back toward it—again motionless for too long, overwhelmed by the enormity of the dust cloud (which somehow has yet to reach them). Her mind flashes, recalling her to the only other living thing she's seen in this wasteland.

She spins back around. "AUGUR!" But her voice is lost to the roar of gusting winds.

She pulls the guard back over her eyes and takes off after him, covering her mouth with her hands to breathe free of debris.

He has a good lead on her, but his stumbling slows his pace enough for her to catch up. Tackling him, she cries, "DIG!"

"WHAT?"

She's already on her knees, scooping up sand. "Dig! Like the beetle!"

"BEETLE?"

"We have to get under the sand! DIG!"

The hole is soon large enough for them both to lie down in, and the two heap sand over themselves. Augur puts his cape over his face, and Zo buries his head.

The swirling grit whipping through the air stings her exposed skin. She covers her face with her poncho, then drags a heavy layer of sand over herself. She pulls her hands under just as the front hits.

Beneath the stratum of safety, Zo exhales and listens to the surging winds above. Granular loosens beside her hand, and she pulls back, fearing the torrents are picking up. But the touch of Augur's burrowing fingers is a welcomed relief.

Holding hands, they wait for the storm to pass.

CHAPTER 36

*E*verything is calm.

Augur digs himself out from the weighted blanket. "That's a good workout." He shakes his head, sending sand flying, bats his neck and picks at his ears. Then he turns toward Zo. "Allow me to assist you?"

But she's already up.

She clacks her tongue. The stale taste of dust coats her mouth with a thick, dry film. "We should keep our faces covered for now." She looks around and spits. "The sand is down but the dust hasn't settled, it's blocking a lot of sunlight like a yellowish-brown fog."

Augur is still patting sand off himself. "I feel so dirty."

She glances at him. "Yeah, you're gross."

"Of course, you must have it altogether." He grins.

"Haha. I'm sure we're both a mess."

"Sit tight until the air clears?" he suggests.

"Agreed."

"Good," he rubs his hands together, "then I can eat."

"You're constantly eating."

"Spitefully spoken by the one who is depleted every night." He pulls out his feast.

Zo looks at him sideways. "Touché."

"Augur. Augur, I think I see something. Remember after the monsoon, I thought I saw—"

"The mirage? Yes, I remember."

"Maybe not," she tilts her head. "The dust is still thinning, but I think I see something."

"So you said. What do you see?"

"It's not entirely clear, but it's SOMEthing in this desert of nothing. I say we have our heading."

He lifts a heavy eyebrow. "You're certain it's not just a mirage?"

"I'm not. But it can't be any worse than our wanderings thus far." She takes his hand. "Let's go."

The dust thins as they travel, until Zo pauses, awestruck. "That's it."

"What?"

"The peak." A gentle gasp escapes her crooked smile. "I think I see the peak."

It rises out of the desert higher and steeper the nearer they approach. The "peak" is quite an impressive mountain itself, enveloped with clouds so thick that its pinnacle remains buried. It's clear, though, this is the final stretch.

It's a full day's walk before the arduous sands begin to shore and they stand on solid ground again. The moon is shining bright in the star-lit sky when they finally reach the base.

Zo looks up at the mountain and whistles through her teeth. "It doesn't look like it's going to be easy."

"Ha!" Augur scoffs. "What about any of this path has been easy?"

She sighs. "I don't know how we're going to do it. It's basically straight up from here. Have you ever climbed a wall?"

"Have you?"

"Yeah. In a gym, with brightly colored holds to grab and stand on, wearing a harness and rope, attached to the top and anchored at the bottom. Also spotted by a trainer. So nothing like this."

"Aye, you have experience then?" He nods. "Good!"

She scoffs, rolling her eyes.

"I'm not kidding. I believe in you, Zo. You just brought us through a desert in no time. I couldn't do that with all the time. You'll figure this out." He laughs. "We're going to climb a cliff."

Looking up at the moonlit mass, she feels exceedingly small. *It would be hard enough trying to do this on my own. How are "we" supposed to do it?*

Searching for the best route, Zo walks alone around the base. *Everything looks the same. There's no easy way up.* "And here I thought the desert was rough," she mumbles.

"Zo!"

A long-forgotten voice echoes down the cliffs, "Zo!"

Searching, she spots a climber high in the distance.

"Hey Sis!" he waves.

"Bro?" her voice is slow, as though her eyes haven't yet convinced her of his presence. *No. No, that's definitely him!* "Bro! Broden!"

"Follow me, Sis!"

"Follow you? WHAT?"

"Follow me! You can do it! See that cranny to the right of you, I've marked it, start there!"

"HOW?"

"Climb!"

She throws her hands in the air, rolling her eyes. "'Climb,' he says. What do you think I've been trying to figure out?"

She looks in the narrow opening he pointed to and gasps. *What? Ha! It's right here, just like at the boulder!* She runs her fingertips over the grooves of a new etching of her family's crest.

"I found it!" she calls up to Broden.

"Follow me!" he urges again.

She looks up, but he's gone. Stepping away from the wall to get a better look, she trips backward and begins to fall—

...She wakes up.

She rolls over and whispers, "Augur?" But he doesn't stir, snoring strong as ever.

She grabs her bag and slips away.

Letting her fingers glide along the rock face, she walks around it, studying its features. *Come on dream, manifest your glory here. This is your chance to be more than just my sad and desperate imagination. OH! I forgot—*

She stops to pull out a glow pod, then re-sweeps the area she's already passed before continuing on.

"I'll find it, Bro. I'm coming."

As the moon begins sinks low and the lustrous coat of the night sky folds through iridescent shades of dark to subtlety softening purples, she picks up her pace, dragging her fingers as she goes, until—

This is it!

She's found a crevice with a texture smoother than the wall. But looking nearer, the markings are not her family's crest.

"Where's the angry kid who scratched out their drawing?" She smirks as she circles the scraping with the juice from her pod. Then she runs back to camp.

"Oh!" she startles. "You're awake?"

"And a good morning to you, my lady."

"No. Sorry. I just didn't expect to find you—"

"Awake?"

She shrugs. "Yeah."

Augur smiles.

She melts a little, then straightens. "I had this dream—"

"Did you see the Three?"

"No, but Broden, my adopted brother, was climbing the peak and he told me to follow him, and our family crest was carved into the wall below him. So when I woke up, I went looking for it and—"

"You found the way?"

She hesitates. "I think so. I definitely found something. Come with?"

The morning's light is magnified by the surrounding sands, making for a very bright, very hot start. As they walk, the shadow of the peak is a crisp respite.

Augur takes a deep breath. "Assuming you didn't find the crest, what did you find?"

"I'm not sure. I'm guessing the daylight will make it easier to see. I marked it with the glow juice. It should be," she falls silent.

"Well?"

"It should be here. Like, right here." She's holding her breath. "I marked it with the glow and everything!"

Augur stands solemn for a few moments. "We were attacked."

"Excuse me?"

"They attacked us. It's the Others. Don't you see?"

She sighs. "No, Augur, there's nothing out here, no one out here, just us."

"No. No, you're wrong—unless you dreamed the entire thing up, unless you were sleepwalking and ran back to me in your sleep—you're wrong. They're trying to keep us from the path. Can't you see?"

"I'm not the one who's visually impaired."

He laughs. "That, that was good."

She blushes. *His smile really is beautiful.*

"Zo, I need you to hear me. I know the Others."

"Wait," she tilts her head. "What exactly do you mean, you 'know' the Others?"

"I mean—" he hesitates. "I've been in this world longer than you, right? I grew up in the Market. I'm very aware of the Others, and of the Puppeteer. And I'm telling you, this is them. They're trying to prevent us from moving on. They're desperate, so they're not being subtle anymore. It's the Others, Zo. I know it."

That could explain why it was all scratched up where the crest should have been. "So what? If it is them, they've already hidden the crest and my marking."

"The glow?" he asks.

"It's gone."

"There has to be something. Something else you remember? Anything?"

She takes a minute.

"In my dream, I found the crest inside a narrow opening. The scratching I marked was also in one."

"Okay. That's good. And you're sure it was around here."

"Yes. It was somewhere..." her voice trails as her eyes search the stone.

Augur searches, too, patting around the wall, until—

"Zo. Come here, feel this. It's smoother here."

"You blind seer, you found it! Yes! And look, there's bits of glow residue on the ground. Augur, you're brilliant!"

"I am. It's true." He pauses. "Now what?"

"Now," she lifts her head, "we follow Bro." She takes a deep breath, studying the accession. "Up."

He points. "Up?"

She clacks her tongue. "Up."

"How?"

"I don't know." Closing her eyes, she can still see Broden climbing. "But Bro did it, and he said to follow him, and I know we can trust him."

"You also do know it was a dream. You're suggesting we commit our lives to a figment of your unconsciousness." He sucks his teeth. "It sounds more than a bit absurd when you consider it objectively."

"It does. And it is." She sighs. "But here we are. I'm going to follow him." She faces her friend. "Are you coming?"

"A blind man scaling a vertical cliff to follow a lady chasing a dream?" He smiles. "Of course I'm in."

Zo ties the rope to her waist.

Stretching her arms and legs from one side of the crevice to the other, she lifts with her legs, using the narrow gap as her brace. She steadies herself with her arms and again pushes higher. Augur lets his end of the rope trail after her.

After 12 repetitions (about 25 feet up), she looks down. "Oh geez!" She shuts her eyes. "I don't know if I can do this!" Her body quivers, and she barely stops herself from falling. "I feel dizzy all the sudden. And sweaty, and my arms are shaky."

"You can do it." Augur calls from below. "We were much higher descending the ridge."

"Yes, but I couldn't see that then! I hate heights! I don't think I can do it."

"Don't look down," his voice is steady.

"Easy for you to say."

He chuckles. "Look up, Zo."

"My arms are shaking."

"ZO. Focus. Look up. What do you see?"

She looks up. "I see more rock and the sky—and I'm shaking!"

"Focus, Zo! Deep breaths. Find the next place for your hands, breathe, and move on. Keep your head up."

She takes a few deep breaths and finds a good spot to place her hands.

Up, Zo. Focus. Up.

She sets her hands and pushes with her legs.

Exhale...

She moves higher.

Focus. Breathe...

Higher.

Up. Breathe... "Augur!" She doesn't look down. "There's something hanging out of the rock!"

"What is it?"

"I'm not sure. Some kind of string, maybe? I'm almost there." She climbs higher. "It's a D-ring hanging on a cable. A looped cable. It's attached to a metal thing—like a nut or something—that's wedged into a crack." She tugs at it. "It's in there good. I think it's an anchor. I'm going to thread my rope through it."

"Be careful!" Augur warns.

"This could be exactly what we need to climb!"

The line slacks in Augur's hands. "Zo! Is the rope secured back on you?"

"I'm tying it now! Okay. I need you to pull the rope taut and anchor me. I'm going to test my weight on this thing."

"Zo—"

"I don't want to fall, Augur! I'll be careful. Are you ready?"

He wraps the rope around his hips twice, and sits on the ground, with his feet up against the crevice. "Yeah, I think so." He leans back.

Setting her arms, she tucks her legs in and slowly lets her weight down on the cable. *Now or never.* She exhales and pulls her arms.

The rope groans as she sways against the stone face.

"You did it!" Augur raises a victorious fist.

"HAHA!" She puts her feet back on the rock, leans out and looks up. *There! There's another clip up there. And another beyond it!*

She closes her eyes and smiles. "Thank you, Bro."

CHAPTER 37

"Alright, this is how we're going to do this." She turns over her rucksack, and after rummaging through its contents, grabs the knife. "I'm going to make a harness for each of us. Yours will be one piece with the rope. Mine will be detached."

"Detached?" Augur raises a thick eyebrow in objection.

"Yes. I'm going to tie my end of the rope to this D-ring, then the D-ring will clip into my harness. This way I can easily unhook to thread the rope through the secured cables as we climb. Once the line is looped through the cable, I'll reattach myself.

"You'll have to pull up the cables as you pass them since your harness won't disconnect. They're wedged, so it'll take some strength, but as long as we're both locked into the other cables, we should be fine. And this is just a test run, so—"

"Zo," he grates his forehead against his open palms. "This is not going to be easy for me. I'm going to be depending on you to guide me. It'll take longer, and it's going to be extra hard for you."

"I know, but I can't leave you. You haven't left me. I won't leave you."

His shoulders slouch.

She looks at him sideways. *That was a strange reaction. But we're waisting time.* "Come on." She tugs on the final knot of her harness. "I'll spot you for a practice climb now, and we can set out first thing tomorrow."

"Zo," his head is low and he tugs at his cape's collar.

Geez, he's really scared. "It's alright, Augur. I won't let you fall." She snickers and squeezes his shoulder. "At least not too far."

He grins halfway through a sigh, and takes his end of the rope. "Yeah, alright, let's go."

It takes some time to coordinate Augur's movement with Zo's directions from below.

He shows remarkable trust in her, even though she fumbles over her left's and right's, and isn't able to offer as precise instructions as she intends. Still he climbs, and after a few near slips early on, he's developed quite a knack for it.

He's a natural! How is that even possible? His progress is really impressive. He's totally shaming any limitation I would of assumed for a blind person. It's really cool.

When he finally reaches the cable, he hollers out enthusiastically, and she happily joins in celebrating his victory. "Amazing! Truly incredible, Augur! I bet no one at the Marketplace would recognize you now! Well done!"

"HA! WOO!"

"When you're ready, plant your feet, get a firm grip on the rope and lean back. Then you'll push out like you're jumping, while I release some slack. Not too strong. Nice and easy. That's it. Perfect."

"This is exhilarating!"

"And... gently... down. You did it!" She embraces him.

His proud grin is infectious. "Not too shabby, if I do say so."

She pats him on the back. "You did really well." Her hand rests on his shoulder. "Tomorrow will be different. I'll be calling directions down to you from where I pass, but the way you just handled it, I really think we can do this."

Still smiling, he bends down and in one swift swoop, clips her knees, picks her up, and leans in to kiss.

"Woah there," she pulls away. "I get that you're excited, but no."

"I'm sorry." He awkwardly puts her down.

"No, it's fine. Forget about it. Let's eat and rest up. Tomorrow we climb."

She leaves him standing alone, still wearing his harness.

I should have kissed him. No! No, I'm glad I didn't. I need to focus on the quest—on MY quest. But I could have kissed him! I want to kiss him. UGH. I need to find Quest. And we need to get home. I do like him, though. He's fearless, when he's not scared of the Others. And loyal, when he's not trying to show off. And despite his insecure boasting, I've seen a genuine humility in him. UGH, stop thinking about him! Focus on the path, the Three—

"You okay up there?" Augur calls.

"Yep, almost to the next cable. Just... a little... closer... There. I'm running the rope through now. Okay, clipped in. Your turn. Before you come up, you need to—"

"Pull out my cable. I'm on it."

"Be careful." She braces each time he has to raise an anchor. The force is more than enough to throw him off balance and out of the crevice.

"ARGH. Woah! Woah. Okay, got it. And up." He clears his throat. "So, about yesterday, I want to apologize—"

"Augur—"

"No, Zo. I shouldn't have—"

"It's fine. Really. Just pay attention to what you're doing. Focus on the climb. 'Up, focus, up,' remember?"

He smiles. "But you're my 'up,' Zo."

She shakes her head. "The climb, Augur, focus on the climb. I can see the next cable, but beyond that is a bulge. I can't see over it. It might be the peak, but I doubt it. It doesn't look too hard, I don't think we'll hang upside-down or anything, but I'm going to have to climb out of the crack to get above it."

"You should probably get started, then." He continues steadily up. "Conserve time by moving forward. I can handle this crevice, but we need to know what's next."

"Yeah, point taken."

She passes the next cable with ease before Augur makes it to the second. *The narrowing tapers from here. It seals entirely just below the bulge. Looks like it's about six feet up. I've got about that in slack. I'll have to climb outside the rock from here, but that's where we are now. Come on, Zo, up, focus.* She pauses to look at her partner. *He's already pulling up at the cable.*

Looking up, she reaches out of the crevice. There's a notch within reach, perfectly fitting to her hand. Grasping it, she pushes up with her legs one final time and sticks her head outside the crack.

Woah. She gasps. *That's a chilly breeze! My heart just skipped a beat. I hadn't even noticed how hot I was. My face is so sweaty!* She smiles into the wind and breathes deeply.

"You giving up?" The nearness of Augur's voice startles her. He's just a few feet below.

"You caught up fast."

"I'm a quick study."

"Yeah, well," she looks up, "that's good, because everything is about to change. We should probably stay close from here out. Can you slide those extra cables up the rope to me?"

He begins to, then stops. "You should tighten the slack first. If one of us slips, it would be better if it's just a slip rather than a long fall. The force of a big drop might be enough to pull us both down."

"Point well-taken." She creeps back into the crack, uncomfortably close to him. "Sorry."

"No need to apologize, my lady."

She adjusts the rope, securing the D-ring, and he slides up the spare anchor cables. Zo ties one to the far end of the rope. "A failsafe I hope we don't have to use." She takes a deep breath. "Ready?"

"Yes, my lady."

"Okay. Pay close attention. You're going to need to follow my directions exactly. This crack closes just above me. We're scaling up, from here out..." She details instructions for his progression outside, then goes on to explain everything she is doing as she climbs.

Augur follows with complete trust and obedience.

Come on, Bro. How is it that the cables set in the cliff's open face are spread farther apart than the ones inside the crevice? No use in complaining now, but really? Phew. Come on, Zo, you got this.

By the time they reach the third anchor, she takes a moment to appreciate Augur's tenacity and ability. *He is quite surprising.*

Searching for the next cable, she realizes the stretch that lies before them is hidden by a heavy cloud. She looks over her shoulder, *Clouds are just fog in the sky. Fog means reduced visibility and increased moisture. But the sun is still pretty high, I'd say it's early afternoon. We can do this. We don't have another choice. We have to do this.*

"Okay. We have a thick cloud ahead. That's going to mean moisture, which will make for slippery rock. We HAVE to be careful. How are you feeling?"

"I'll be happy when we summit."

"You and me both. It can't be too much farther now. Shall we?"

She was right. The rock is slick.

And the clouds only allow a couple feet of visibility. Zo has to feel her way upward, and their pace slows to a stunted intentionality.

"How's it coming?" Augur asks.

Absorbed in determining the next move, she doesn't hear him.

"Zo?"

"Huh?"

"Are you okay?"

"I just need to figure this out."

"Should we belay? Try again when the clouds clear?"

"No. No way. We've come too far. It can't be much farther. And there's no way of knowing when or if these clouds will clear. No. We can muscle through." She returns her full attention to the task.

"Can we?" he asks.

Her jaw is locked. "We must."

"AAAARGH!"

Altogether caught off guard by his slip, she couldn't have prepared herself for the pain of being slammed into the rock and the constriction around her hips.

Augur dangles, flailing for a few too many moments before hysterically laughing.

"This—" She tries to brace herself, but his weight thrashing about the line pins her to the rock. "This isn't funny."

"HaHA! HAha!"

"Seriously, Augur, you're hurting me."

"I'm sorry, I'm sorry. I'm sorry! It's just the RUSH! Just a fraction of a moment free-falling, and that fraction feels like eternity of certain death. Then suddenly—ZOOP! Not today, Augur! YOU'RE NOT DYING TODAY! HA!"

"Yeah well, your weight on the line has me pinned. I feel like I'm being crushed to death. I need you to get back on the rock."

"Can you see me? Can you help me get back on?"

She looks down searching for his figure. "I can't— UGH! The clouds are too thick."

"I'll figure it out, my lady."

"I'm going to throw the extra rope up. Maybe we'll get lucky and it'll catch something."

But it doesn't catch. After several failed attempts, she pauses. *This hurts. And it's all too familiar. Like, maybe it's my destiny to be stuck, pressed into a cold, jagged stone, almost there but not quite.*

Her hips feel every ounce of Augur's weight double in force with each unsuccessful attempt to mount the rock. *Don't think about all the bruises he's forcing on you—UGH—with every slip my bones are crushing into this jagged stone! It's like the life is being kicked out of my lungs. Every pulse throbbing through my legs adds more pressure against these damn ropes—* "I NEED YOU TO GET A GRIP!"

"WHAT DO YOU THINK I'M TRYING TO DO?"

Biting her lip, the pain is unbearable, and she begins to cry.

"I'm trying, Zo!"

Through muffled sobs, she whispers, "You're killing me."

"WHAT?"

"YOU'RE FUCKING KILLING ME!"

"IT'S NOT EASY, ZO!"

He's met with hard, heavy silence.

It's pointless. He can't see what he's doing to me. Even if he could see, he wouldn't be able to see beyond this cloud. I have to bear it. God, I hate him for it! And I hate me for bringing him along. Mahdi tried to warn me. But that smile charmed me, and I let it—I let him in. And here I am. I deserve this. Dammit, I deserve this.

"Zo!"

Startled out of her thoughts, the pain returns and she moans. She can't tell if it's tears or sweat or the mist of the cloud, but her face is dripping wet.

"ZO, I'm sorry. I'm sorry, Zo, really. I know I'm hurting you. I know you're carrying me. And I don't know how to fix this. Zo? Zo, listen. You have to cut the rope. Cut the rope, Zo, let me go. You need to go on. It's okay. It's okay, Zo. Just cut the rope."

What did he say? I know he's talking, but I don't know what he's saying. I can't see him, and now I can't hear? This is so weird. At least my legs don't hurt anymore—wait, why can't I feel anything below my waist? It's all just dull and uncomfortable. I feel dizz…

Her head drops back.

Looking up through the haze, curiosity stirs as two sets of hands reach down to her.

She passes out.

CHAPTER 38

*L*aughter calls through the dark.

Zo takes a deep breath and opens her eyes. The sunlight is bright and unexpected. Squeezing her eyelids, she stretches, yawning languorously before snuggling back into the comfort of her dreams.

Until she hears the laughter again.

Quest must have—wait. WHO is that?

She pries an eye open and turns toward the conversation. *That's obviously Augur, and he's obviously entertaining those people, but who are they? They sound so familiar.* Blinking, she clears her throat. "Augur?"

The voices cease and all eyes turn to her.

"My lady!"

She leans on an elbow and stares.

Augur stands up and smiles. "You're awake."

It can't be. She begins to shake and tears blur her vision. "Father? Ma? Bro?"

"Yes, Daughter."

"My beautiful child."

"Sis!"

They rush to embrace her.

Augur stands alone. "Aye," he calls over his shoulder, "have you any idea what's—"

"SHUSH." (Another unmistakable voice.) "Can't you see they're having a moment? Well, I do suppose you can't very well SEE that, now can you? Humph," he chitters.

"Mahdi?" Zo's head pops up. "Mahdi! You're here! You're here, too!"

Smirking, he tilts his head toward Augur with more than a hint of bullied satisfaction, then joins the welcoming. His wings cover the group in a feathery cradle.

Augur folds his arms and sits down.

"Oh, Augur," Zo calls. "Come here, please, come meet my parents."

"Your parents, my lady?" He grins. "Surely you are in shock. These are the Three. Plus the bird."

She straightens. "What?" And smiles. "No, Augur, this is my family. And of course you remember Mahdi."

"My lady, I must insist, do ask the bird. We are in the company of the Three."

She looks deeply into the gentle eyes of her family. "Am I in shock?"

Ma smiles warmly. "It's really us, dear one. We're really here."

"Not another dream?"

Father reaches out and lifts her chin, beaming with pride. "Not another dream."

She grabs his arm and embraces him again, and reaching out, pulls Ma and Broden in, too. Then lifting her head, she tugs Mahdi by the feather. He whistles a short, happy note and again wraps them beneath his wings.

Augur still sits. "But Mahdi, they're the Three. YOU told me they were the Three." He whispers, "They know things about me—" he clenches his jaw "—PERSONAL things." *Surly they're jesting me.* He lifts an unbelieving hand. "Come now, bird, her family is passed!"

Mahdi only rolls his eyes and shakes his head, still absorbing the group.

Shifting uncomfortably, Augur exhales dramatically. "I'll just be here, then."

"Wait," Zo pulls away and searches her family. "Does this mean— Have we all died?"

"In many ways, yes," Father answers.

"So I'm, dead? This whole time? My searching for—OH, Quest! He must be a wreck!"

"No, Love." Ma gives Father a riled stare.

"Well, it's true," he holds. "We have all had to die many kinds of deaths to ourselves—"

Ma cocks her head. "Now is not the appropriate time for metaphors, Papa. She's just come to. No reason to thrust her into shock with your wormhole analogies."

Father smiles, pleased with his pestering. "You just used an analogy to describe my analogies."

Broden smirks and shakes his head.

Ma turns back to Zo. "Don't mind your Father. You know how highbrow he can be. You're not dead, Zo. None of us are. In fact I'd say we're more alive right here than we've ever been."

"But we buried you and Bro— I mean, you were cremated. We had a funeral, the whole town showed up!"

"Yet here we are." Ma's smile is kind.

"So if I'm alive here, am I dead back home, too?"

The three exchange knowing glances.

Zo lifts an eyebrow. "I feel like you're all in on a secret, and even though I'm aware of it, you're not going to let me in on it."

"My sentiments precisely," Augur cuts in, "but don't mind me."

She rolls her eyes, grinning. *Leave it to Augur to pick the worst moment to cut in— Why is everyone giggling?* Her face flushes as she looks around.

"Sorry, Sis." Bro stifles his amusement, then leans in to whisper, "I still see you as that little kid."

Her eyes widen catching the end of a glance Ma gives Father, and Zo bites her lip. "So you've all met Augur then?"

They smile.

This is awkward. Geez, my whole face feels red! "Alright, um." She clears her throat. "How long was I out? And what actually happened?"

"You followed me, Sis." Bro puts his arm around her shoulder. "And you brought Augur along. I'm seriously impressed."

"Thanks, Bro. But we didn't make it all the way."

"So we carried you. Father and I pulled you up while Mom managed us."

"Ha! Listen to him, 'managed'?" Ma muses. "More like encouraged whilst sitting on your legs."

"That's right, Ma, you were our anchor!"

"It's all quite astounding, actually," Augur cuts in, "their strength is rather unnatural."

"Mahdi was a tremendous help," Father says. "He pulled by the rope while we had your arms."

She sits quiet, letting it sink in. "So we, we've all made it to the peak?"

"Yeah, Sis." Broden smiles, stepping back so she can have a look around. "You did it."

The sun hangs past noon, but shines as bright as the midday. Zo closes her eyes, soaking in the warmth of it. For all the time she's spent being scorched beneath its oppression, she's missed reveling in it.

Eyes sealed, she listens. *What is that?*

Turning to look, she's slightly let down to find another peak still stands before them. But her disappointment doesn't last. Eyes wide, mouth dropped, she takes in the wonder, and whispers, "Is that the source of Maisha Maji?"

"Indeed," Mahdi is also taken by the beauty.

Absorbing the sound of it, Augur asks, "Describe it to me?"

Zo's words barely rise above her breath, "The peak, it's a small mountain, but it's shaped like, almost like an overstuffed armchair—like a throne! It's probably the size of a downtown city building, um, I don't know what to compare that to here— 40 or 50 meters high, give or take? But the seat is maybe a quarter of that. The rock is like a kaleidoscope, maybe that's from the bright waters? It looks like a marbled mash-up of deep black opal and pure white pearl, but also iridescent, so I can't exactly tell. There's a raging, bright waterfall bursting out from the highest point that spills onto the seat, then down the throne and pours into a swirling pond that's covered in a misted halo of dancing rainbows." She sighs. "I know I'm not doing it justice, though. It's amazing."

Augur breathes it in.

Drawn to it, Zo tries to get up. "OUCH!" For the first time since coming to, pain surges through her hips.

"You're still hurt." Mahdi digs through his satchel. "Here, I was waiting for you to wake up to give you some." He pulls out his sap.

Remembering the bitter taste and pain of it, she cringes. But recalling how she healed, she relents. "Thank you, Mahdi." *I don't want to, I don't want to, I don't want to.* She closes her eyes and tilts her head, her tongue just barely poking out between her teeth.

It's different this time. It tastes sweet. Soothing. Eyes still closed, a smile fills her face, as tingly warmth moves down her body. It settles in and radiates on her pelvic bone first, then lifts to her muscles and finally out through her skin.

"AAH!"

Everyone looks.

Augur is retreating from the edge of the waters and stumbles back against Broden. As he tries to get back on his feet, Broden embraces him, and Augur begins to weep.

Zo stands to go to him, but Father stops her. "Give them time, Beloved."

She bites her lip, watching them. *I'll check in with him later.* She turns to Father. "What is this place? How are we here? And why does Augur insist you're the Three?"

"My beautiful daughter, I love you and am so proud of you. And, oh, how I've missed you!"

His kind smile gives her a peace she hasn't known in a very long time. *I've missed you, too!*

Long before waking in this strange world, even before he passed away back home, she hasn't felt this way since the last time summer before she left for college. She hugs him, pressing her head against his shoulder.

Holding him close, she relaxes in the company of her daddy. And as she exhales, Ma's warm embrace snuggles in, too.

"I've missed you both so much!"

"We're together now, Beloved. We aren't going anywhere."

I've missed my family— She jumps up. "Are other travelers here?"

"There are."

"And Quest?"

They're silent. Look, Father's eyes have shifted. Quest's not here.

She buries her face in his chest and cries.

CHAPTER 39

*T*ime is different here.

Though the sun appears to move, it doesn't set. Instead, it circles the peak as if the true state of its being, the very source of this world's light, of warmth and life itself, is to enshrine the source of Maisha Maji. It's a marvel to behold.

Rest is different, too. It's abundant and familiar, but rather than sleep, it comes in warm embraces with family and laughter, reflective moments and awe-filled, delightful pauses. Being present on the peak provides a constant state of rejuvenation.

Even the travelers here are different. There are far fewer than those at the Market, and even the Gathering Place. But similar to the Market, they are of all kinds, and each bears some sign of previous settlement. They welcome the new arrivals with celebration and all the warmth and generosity of family.

At the peak, there is a communal sense of camaraderie. Notwithstanding difficulty and desire, all have subdued their temptations, defied their settlement and pursued the path. In addition to the sense of belonging, usefulness and confidence abound in this fraternity, every being has a unique purpose to enrich the community as a whole. None are left out, nor frowned upon. Beauty and importance are given to every function without hierarchy. And celebrations seem constant, as frequently as new ones are welcomed, others are honored before setting off again along the path.

"Utopia," Zo mutters.

"Hm?" Mahdi's yellow eyes dart at her.

Oo, I said that out loud? Awkward. She clears her voice. "Have you gone to the waters since you arrived?"

"Indeed, dear one."

"Was it like before?"

"It was," his head twists. "And it wasn't."

Giving her old friend all her attention, she notices something truly different about him. *The coloring of his feathers is changed. He's still black, but it's not just blue in his edges. There's so many colors! Every feather has a different tint—blue still, yes, and purples and reds and pinks, oranges and yellows, greens and teals. It's like the leaves on Maisha Mti.*

And look at his eyes! He's intense still, but I see a tenderness peeking through. He had tender moments before, but he rarely showed it. This new look is solid and sincere.

"Mahdi?" she smiles, still staring.

"Hm?"

"You're beautiful."

"HM?" He looks at her sideways.

She swallows and looks down. "I'm sorry we lost you in the dark wood. I'm sorry we didn't go back."

His eyes glaze over as he remembers the damnable forest. "Yes, well, I always told you our paths would part."

"But—"

"Think not of it. All is long forgiven. We've each undergone our own journeys." He smiles warmly at his old traveling buddy, whose stare reveals she is again captivated by his beauty.

"You've changed," she returns his smile.

"Humph. Yes, I suppose I, too, have changed."

"'Too'?" Her eyebrows lift, then pinch.

"You've not yet seen yourself, young one?"

Her heart leaps. *Why does that terrify me?* "No."

"Well, HUMPH, what are you waiting for! Come now, go, go, go! Go on, child, see! See what you are becoming. See who the path is making you. I can see you. I've seen me. Now you must see!"

"But," she turns away.

"'But'?" He follows her gaze to Augur, then throws his frazzled wings in the air. "See for yourself, child! Go! Trust my words, now. GO."

Standing slowly, she takes a deep breath. *Come on, Zo, buck up. Let's go.*

She stands at the water's edge.

It's so beautiful! It's even more spectacular here than back at the crossroad. And powerful! I wonder if this is what Niagara Falls is like?

Gazing at the cascade, the movement is so swift that her vision blurs. She rubs her eyes and focuses in on just a single drop —defying everything around— it appears to plummet in slow motion, splitting the light within into a spiraling prism.

She closes her eyes, then refocuses to take in the entire waterfall. *It's like a molten force of mirror-balls. And all the rainbows dance around the base like a multi-layer, ruffled skirt.* She lifts her head and just listens, *There must be a song in the booming thunder of those falls.*

The pond is a singular, massive whirlpool. Though tame at the water's edge, its center pulls into a mighty vortex, spinning the bright water with such force the light bends in a spectacular laser show as it's sucked down the hole. *It's beautiful and frightening*. The hair on Zo's neck prickles, and she takes a half-step back.

Alright, girl. This is great and all, but you're here to look at you. Stop getting distracted. It's time to see me. A shiver creeps down her spine. She closes her eyes, steps forward and takes another deep breath.

Then looks down, and smiles.

Hi there. The matured beauty of kindness, humility and strength she remembers from her first encounter joyfully returns her gaze.

Her thirst rises with a force as powerful as the waterfall itself, and she plunges her hands into the water and drinks deeply.

Looking again, Zo's taken by her hair. *Look at this gorgeous, wild mop! Holy cow, it's grown so much! It's a vibe, though. I clearly forgot that I braid it when I'm thinking deep, and I've obviously been overthinking a lot. But it looks like I left them with perfect intention. And what is this?* Two small patches of white hair now spring from each temple. She smiles. "Hello wisdom."

Then she sees her vine.

Its bright green sticks out like, well, like a vine against dark, curls. It's already two-thirds the length of her longest lock. Holding it in front of her face, her enthusiasm fades.

They've all seen it, Ma, Father, even Bro. I don't want to imagine what they must think of me.

A tear rolls down her cheek and into the waters, drawing her attention back to her reflection. *You know what?* She smiles, *They already saw it while I wasn't even awake yet, and they responded to me just as warm as ever, honest embraces. They're not ashamed of me.*

An unknown burden lifts, and she considers the vine differently. *There is a beauty to it, standing out among the curls.*

And it kind of fits the vibe with my random braids and white streaks. It's hip and mature. I'm digging it.

Then she sees her eyes.

Geez, I'm piercing my own soul here. My eyes are deeper than I remember, more intent. They've seen things and shed tears, but they're not cold, they're not still hurting. I see astute awareness, and fierce, unapologetic love. And there is a bit of sadness, too.

She changes her focus before sorrow overwhelms her, and she sucks her teeth.

Look at those chapped lips, girl! HA! They have a pretty color, though. She smiles and beholds the beauty of the crooked grin she realized she could love at her first encounter.

Her skin has tanned and is rather dirty. But her rosy cheeks still show through. The very beginnings of the wrinkles she knew were coming are taking form. She admires them for the many laughs and cries they represent.

Wait. This reflection's not shocking or hideous. I can't believe how much I've grown from who I saw before. I mean, I'm not too far from the first image at the crossroad, "the 'you' you are meant to be."

She looks away, then checks again—*Just to be sure*—and is comforted by the same reflection.

She turns back to find her family, with Mahdi and Augur, all patiently waiting for her.

"I've changed," she says, nodding slowly. She stands and walks to them. "I have a ways to go, but I've really changed."

CHAPTER 40

"So what did you see?" Augur and Zo finally have a chance to speak alone.

"I saw me." Her eyes recall her reflection. "A much better me than the reflection I saw before crossing the river."

He is biting his thumbnail. "Better, how?"

"Well, I didn't scare myself," she grins.

He presses his palms into his forehead.

"Augur, I was joking, I didn't mean—" She sighs. "I'm sorry. That wasn't funny. Please, what did you see?"

He shrugs and returns his thumb to his teeth. "I saw me."

"Changed?"

"Yes." His nod is slow and methodical.

"So you were surprised by your growth? I was, too."

"I was… surprised." He purses his lips.

She studies him. "But?"

"Shocked is more fitting."

"Wow, that's a lot of change."

"No, that's just it. There wasn't much change at all. None for the better."

"What do you mean? We've traveled long and hard together. And all the traveling you did alone?"

"Yeah," he shakes his head, "I know."

"Are you sure? You never settled. Maybe you just—"

"I'm sure."

Take a beat, Zo. He's being sincere, and it's bleak. Change the subject. "How long do you think we've been here?"

He takes a deep breath, and his brows pinch together in thought. "It's hard to say." After some reflection, he adds, "Time feels different here. Faster. And slower."

"Yeah, you get that, too?" She sucks her teeth.

"The Three will know."

She smirks, mocking him, "'The Three.'"

"Mmhm." He smiles big. "The Three."

———

"Bro?"

"Yeah, sis?"

"Can we talk about this, 'the Three' business?"

"Sure."

"Well," Zo shifts awkwardly. "Are you? And Ma and Father, are you guys 'the Three'?"

Broden smiles. "Why do you ask?"

"Because Mahdi and Augur seem to think you are."

"And what do you think?"

She pauses. *Why doesn't he just answer the question?* "I don't know what to think, that's why I'm asking." *I know that look. He's expecting me to think more about what I think.* She bites her lip. "You're my family."

"Absolutely," he affirms.

"Well, I've heard the Three created this world and that They maintain it. That They always have and They always will. But you've been my family. You guys were a family before me, like back home. You couldn't have been here while we were there?" *Although, time does seem different here.* She sighs.

"What do you believe, Sis?"

"I BELIEVE that I don't have it all figured out. But I KNOW that we are family."

"Is that enough?"

She scoffs, shaking her head. *He's definitely turned this conversation away from my question. 'Is that enough?' Is it enough to know that we are family, yeah. Of course! I want to know more, but that's always been enough.* She takes in a deep breath. "Yeah, Bro, that's always been enough."

He playfully tousles her hair. "THIS is enough," he laughs.

"THIS is my crown of wisdom, thank you."

"You must be very wise, Sis."

She laughs. "Oh, wow! Look who's gotten funny all the sudden."

"Aww, come on! I've always been hilarious."

"HA! Now THAT is funny."

"Zo!" Father calls from a distance. "Come, walk with me, daughter."

He leads her along the shore.

Zo's eyes brim. "It's so beautiful here."

Father smiles. "Do you like it?"

"Very much…" her voice wanders with her thoughts.

"Are you disappointed?"

"No. I mean, not at all by you or this place…"

His face softens and he nods. "You hoped to find Quest here."

"Why isn't he here? Where is he?" Her eyes plead for answers.

His smile is kind. "Beloved, here is simply here. This is not the end of the journey."

"But this is the peak. And," she scans their surroundings, "just look at this place. It's like a dream." She exhales. "Only a fool wouldn't settle down here."

"My dear daughter, listen to your words. What has the path taught you about settlement?"

"Yes, but this is THE peak. This where the path leads." She raises both hands in emphasis. "We made it."

"Did we?"

Her hands drop with a slap against her thighs. "What more can there be?"

"Hm?" He taps his raised chin, peering down at her.

She sighs. "Quest."

He nods.

"And Augur is edgy," she continues, "and Mahdi is busying himself about, like a caged bird set beside an open window. But YOU'RE here, and Ma and Bro. I just got you back. I don't know if I can leave you—"

"Have we not been with you?"

"Not like this."

Father agrees, "Not like this."

"But we're not complete," she resigns.

Helping each other, they climb up to the lap of the waterfall's throne. The stone here is smooth and sheer and steadily misted. The rock is too slick to go any higher.

Zo looks out. *Woah. This has to be some kind of optical illusion. I can see everything from here! Over the clouds and beyond the desert, all the way down to the wide road. It looks like someone dragged a stick to draw a trail in sand. There's the Marketplace—wow. It really does look like a labyrinth. And the Wanderlands beyond. Hm, I can't see the path, but even at this distance the tree still looks magnificent and the river flows just as mighty.*

She smiles her crooked grin turning her attention to the billowing dance of rainbows all around. *Look at that hypnotic whirlpool. There's a magic here. And being here with my family! But Quest... I left him all alone. He needs this. He needs us.*

"Father," her lips pull taut. "We need to find Quest. He needs us—all of us. We have to find him."

Moved by her resolve, his eyes gleam. "We will, Beloved."

CHAPTER 41

*T*heir company is seated around a large, disk-shaped stone. A feast has been prepared.

Zo raises an eyebrow. "We've only eaten the bark and drank the waters for so long. We haven't needed anything else."

Father smiles. "You're wondering why this meal? Why now?"

"Yeah," she nods, as they approach the table. "Why?"

"So few travel the path, and of those few, far fewer persevere this far. As you are well aware, the path is not easy."

She tilts her head.

"It's our desire that all should travel it, that all should see their unveiled selves, journey with us as family, and become their truest intention.

"Many wonderful things await those who bear the path, greater things. But so few suffer it." He lip quivers and he sighs. But then he turns to her, beaming. "But you've made it, my child! So we celebrate. This meal is but a representation of the good you have become, the who you are becoming. ¡Salud!"

Everyone raises their cups in cheers, "¡Salud!"

Father sits between Mahdi and Augur. Beside Mahdi is Ma, beside Augur is Bro, and Zo sits between Ma and Bro.

Ma smirks as she leans close and gently nudges Zo. "Roasted carrots?" They laugh.

And they eat together, sharing and delighting in each other's company.

I haven't felt bliss like this since that night at the Diner... Zo shivers, takes a calming breath, then swallows. *It was worth it. If that's what was needed to bring us all back together—*

Her eyes blaze with wild urgency.

"Family," she stands. "This place is beautiful, beyond description. And to be here with all of you, I couldn't have imagined myself this happy in my wildest dreams. But I've realized this is not the end of my path. I must continue on to find Quest. He needs to be here with all of us. We're Salvadors after all.

"Since I haven't found him on the path, I'm going to return to the Marketplace. And if I can't find him there, I'll search the Wanderlands."

A hush falls over their meal.

Father nods toward Zo with an approving smile.

Ma's eyes are brimming.

Bro grins from ear to ear.

Mahdi whistles a pleasant note as he glances from face to face. "HUMPH. Well, it's settled then. Let's away!"

Everyone discusses with enthusiasm their expectations and hopes for what lies ahead.

Except Augur.

He sits motionless for a few suspended moments before returning to his meal.

Taking notice, Zo reaches out and squeezes his hand. "You will come with us?"

His hand barely responds to her touch before he pulls it back. "Why? Why would I leave this place? It's perfect here. There's nothing to want for here. Why should I possibly go back there?"

He shakes his head. "And why should you? There's no guarantee your brother is even in this world. And what if he is? Has he searched for you? What effort has he put into finding you? All this time you've been searching—risking everything—and he's not been anywhere along this path! If he's here, he's obviously moved on. Don't you think it's time you did as well?"

Her eyes blur and she snatches her hand back.

Augur continues, "Use your blessed eyes and look around, Zo. You said yourself, this place is a dream! And your family is here." His nostrils exhale with exasperated force, "Consider what we can have!"

The table is again choked in silence.

Zo's jaw flexes as she stands up. Finally, shaking her head, she looks once more at her desperate companion before leaving the table.

"Zo?" Augur calls after her, "Zo!"

She looks at her feet. The shoreline is granules of the same opal-pearlescent rock that makes up the fountain's throne.

Sitting down, she removes her boots and lets her toes and fingers dig into the cool of the pebbled beach. She leans back and closes her eyes, absorbing the sun and inhaling the sweet scent of crisp, waterfront air.

I love this moment.

But her brief attempt at mindfulness is overrun by the very fresh memory of Augur's dispute. She tenses. *He's wrong. He's so wrong. He doesn't even know Quest. Who is he to make such nasty assumptions? He has no idea. I know my brother. He's looking for me, if he can. He has to be caught up or held by something—or someone. He'd find me if he could. Augur's a jerk. A selfish jerk! He doesn't understand. His family isn't like ours. He doesn't understand. He can't possibly understand.*

She wipes her face.

Why am I so upset? Who cares if Augur doesn't get it? Why should I care so much?

Staring mindlessly at the sky, she sighs.

I do care. WHY do I care? He's been a loyal friend, even though he is selfish. He doesn't know Quest. Maybe Augur is thinking of me? Maybe he's worried that I'll be let down? But he doesn't know Quest. If he knew him he'd never—

"Daughter?" Ma approaches.

Zo quickly wipes her face again.

"May I sit with you?"

"Of course." She manages a wired smile.

Ma wraps her arms around her.

I haven't snuggled with Ma since I was a kid.

They sit quietly together. And after some time, Zo begins to whimper.

"My brave girl," Ma holds her tighter. "Sometimes the overflow of tears helps relieve our brimming minds. You go on and cry, my Love. I'm right here."

In the safety of Ma's embrace, Zo weeps.

She cries for missing Quest. She cries for Augur's inability to understand. She cries for the joy of being reunited with her family. She cries for the many relationships she's made and lost along the way. She cries for the beauty of the path. She cries for the pain of it. She cries for the sheer exhaustion of everything. She cries for nothing at all.

Until she is done.

She was right, Zo rubs her cheeks and neck dry on the loose sleeves of her tunic, *my head feels clearer now.*

She exhales. "I have to go, Ma. I need to know."

"Of course, Beloved." Ma smiles. "And we will travel with you."

"Zo? Zo, I'm sorry." Augur has finally found her alone.

She exhales deep irritation. "Please don't do that."

He tilts his head. "Do what?"

She sighs. "Why are you apologizing?"

His thick eyebrows lift. "Because you're upset."

"Don't do that," she quips.

He frowns. "Why?"

"Don't apologize just to appease me." She shrugs. "It's not a real apology."

"Zo, I'm just trying—"

"To make me feel better? An insincere apology won't do that."

He sighs. "I'm just trying to apologize."

"Why, Augur?"

"Because you're upset!"

"Exactly." She shrugs. "No thanks."

He shakes his head. "You don't make any sense."

"Because I believe an apology should be honest?" she snaps. "Obviously you're right, how perfectly bonkers of me."

He scoffs. "What gives you the right to say whether I'm sincere or not?"

"You're the one trying to apologize to me, I'd say that gives me every right. I don't want an apology because I'm mad or sad or whatever. I have feelings. Feelings happen. Don't apologize because of them. If you genuinely want to apologize, maybe consider apologizing for your behavior, not my reaction to it."

He spreads his arms. "I don't think you should go. I don't. I make no apology for that. I think it's in yours—and all of our best interests to stay. I won't apologize for looking out for you."

Her arms are crossed. "Then don't."

"What?"

"Apologize."

Exasperated, he nibbles his thumbnail. "You're incorrigible."

She shrugs. And after a few tense moments, she sighs. "I'm going."

He shakes his head. "Yeah. Yeah, I know. I figured."

"Well," she waits.

"'Well'?" He waits.

"Well, are you coming with?"

He smiles. "Is that your best attempt at an invitation?"

Both annoyed and yet pleased with their repartee, she exhales (intentionally overdrawn), then drops to a knee and grabs his hand. "Dearest Sir. Augur, it would bring me the greatest honor if you would accompany me and—"

"Stop, stop," he's gushing, "you had me at 'dearest.'"

She gawks. "And I'm the incorrigible one?"

CHAPTER 42

*A*ll of their company stand on the waterfall's throne, staring into the whirlpool below.

Except Augur.

His hands are covering his ears. "This is the best way down?" he yells. "I don't mind the water, but I can't stand being soaked in my clothes. It's uncomfortable, a bit overstimulating, you know? Aye, bird, can't you simply glide us all down?"

"My wings aren't quite up to par. Humph, but I'll happily take YOU over the edge."

"Mahdi?" Father laughs.

"Humph. Were you not thinking it?"

"This is the best way, indeed," Father reassures. "Fastest and safest. Frightening perhaps, but more so exhilarating. Think of it like a waterside."

"I'd relish it, if not for being fully dressed. I hate wet clothes."

"It'll be fun." Broden's grin is spread from ear to ear, and his eyes are saucers of anticipation.

Zo's heart is in her throat. "I hate heights."

"Alright, let's join arms." Father steps forward and motions. "Double check to be sure your bags are secure." He steps

Abigail Ortiz

back in line. "Okay, on the count of three!" He grabs hands with the group. "ONE. TWO. THREEEEEEEEEEE!"

They run the few steps together and leap over the cascade and through the dancing rainbows, falling feet first into the rushing lake.

Their splash is enough to break their link, and the rip of the current drags them apart. One by one, they encircle the vortex, Broden first, then Augur and Mahdi, followed by Ma and Zo, and finally Father.

"Everyone good?" Father yells.

"Breathe!" Ma warns, "Don't forget to breathe!"

"I'm going in!" Bro's excitement would be contagious, if not for the terror of it. "See you on the other siiiiiiiii—" he's sucked into the swirl.

"Steady breaths!" Ma calls after. "Steady! Steady brea—"

They're gone.

Down, down, down the great cyclone they ride.

I can't even hear my own scream.

They all attempt to call to each other, only to realize the deafening sound of the rapid saturates the empty space leaving no room for trivial cries.

Beneath them is a massive hole, and beyond that Zo can only imagine before—

They pass through.

They're falling through an immense chute.

Large openings are cut down the sides, like a giant's finger holes along a monstrous flute.

This must be the same waterfall that feeds the bath at the Hermitage. I hope Zababa and Inanna were successful. I know Aminah would help them. I bet one of these openings leads runoffs to the Gathering Place. Bleh, that awful beer. I wonder how Pahana is? I miss her.

Zo looks around at her present, free-falling company.

These people, right here—all that we've been through, endured, overcome... I had no idea what I would have missed when I considered settling. And now that I've lived it, I wouldn't want a life settled on or apart from the path. I am glad for the time I shared with Pahana— I learned so much! But these people right here, falling endlessly through fierce waters with me, with no idea what lies ahead, these are my people.

She looks down. *Is that? Another plume of dancing rainbows—we're going to die. Oh god, we're going to die!*

"Feet first!" Father yells, "Feet down!"

"Hold your breath!" Ma manages just before the echoed booming below cuts in. Then—

SWOOSH

Rather than breaking the water's surface, the group drops onto a natural, almost vertical waterside, grading subtlety down, gently slowing the flow before banking wide to the left, then to the right and finally spilling out into a pool-filled cavern.

Submersion in the waters is sudden and sublime.

For a moment, buoyant amidst the bright, Zo flashes back to the light that ushered her into this world, then the light of Ma's warm embrace in the desert. *There's an odd security drowning in this shine.*

Overcome with a sudden desperation to breathe, she comes to her senses and swims up for air.

The water continues to flow out of the cavern, but the company swims sideways for the cave's shore.

The ceiling vaults high, and the dancing rainbows paint the walls like an extravagant party. Closing her eyes, Zo quiets herself, lying on the ground, again listening for the music amidst the magic.

"HUMPH. I am a very soggy bird."

Zo rolls over. Her traveling buddy is matted and appears weighed down by the moisture. "Is there anything I can do to help, Mahdi?"

"Not at all." He gives himself a shake and begins preening.

"Have you managed to save a dry garment?" Augur is crawling out of the water.

Zo heaves her saturated rucksack, and pulls out her thoroughly soaked poncho. "Afraid not." She begins wringing it out.

"Humph. Is anyone else exhaustively chilled?"

"I am exhausted," Augur chimes.

"Broden, Augur and I will find preparations for a fire," Father speaks, "We should all dry off before we head out."

Ma asks Zo for rope, and together they fasten a line to hang their gear. Then they get to work wringing and shaking off all their items. Mahdi continues to preen.

"Ma?" Zo asks.

"Yes, Darling?"

She waits until she knows she has Ma's attention. "What do you think of Augur?"

Ma smiles. "A more important question might be, what do YOU think of him?"

Zo sighs and thinks. "I like him. I worry that I like him too much."

Ma's forehead wrinkles. "Why is that a worry?"

"Well, in the desert for instance. Sometimes it's like he's only looking out for himself. Like he's afraid of complete honesty."

She nods. "Honesty can be scary."

"Sure." Zo sighs. "But how can any relationship exist without honesty?"

"Hm." Ma's head is downcast. "Many relationships exist with very little, if any at all, Beloved." Then straightening, she adds, "What kind of relationship are you pursuing?"

"'Pursuing'? I'm not—" The kindness in Ma's eyes reminds Zo that she also needs to be honest. "—I mean, I do like him. He's proven himself loyal, for the most part. And he's made it clear he likes me. I just wish he'd be more himself, you know? I feel like he's trying to hide something or be someone he's not. Someone he thinks I want him to be, but I just want him to be him. I get glimpses of him every now and again, and in those moments I really like who I see."

"Mm," Ma nods. "The he whom he is meant to be. And he's quite handsome, too."

Zo smirks. "He is. But," she drifts to her thoughts.

Ma waits patiently.

"Something happened at the peak when he looked in the bright waters. He seemed really confused and hurt. He didn't really want to talk about it, like he only went so far, you know?"

"You know," Ma's voice is calming, "not everyone who travels the path travels at the same pace."

Zo sucks her teeth. "I think I can understand that." She purses her lips. "As long as he's willing to travel, and he's proven that so far."

She picks up a pebble and fidgets with it for a few seconds before eyeing Ma from beneath a raised brow. "So what do Father and Bro think?"

"Ah," Ma smiles. "I'm sure Father feels as well as any father can when his daughter brings a young man home," and she winks. "Broden does seem fond of him, and that's a good sign."

Zo smiles. "I've really missed you."

"My beautiful daughter," she reaches out, "how I've longed for your embrace."

Mahdi shivers again, spraying Zo and Ma. "Humph. I've been leery of that boy right from the very start. And he keeps calling me 'bird.'" He parrots, "'Aye, bird! Aye, bird!' HUMPH. I've a name, boy! A very good one." He returns to preening.

Zo nods with a crooked grin. "Their relationship is kind of hysterical. They're like brothers, but not like Quest and Bro. They patronize each other." She picks up a pebble. "They hold a mutual love, of sorts, hidden deep down beneath lots of competition. Deep down." She covers the pebble with both her hands. "A sort of love." And sits on them. "Hidden."

"Humph." Mahdi shakes.

Ma laughs.

"Aye, bird!" Augur's voice booms throughout the cavern. "We've brought you back some sticks to perch your wet feathers on."

Mahdi cuts a stern eye.

"No one?" Augur pretends to be insulted. "Come now, that was hilarious!"

Father and Bro prepare the campfire, and in no time they're all gathered around happily warming themselves.

"We should discuss our plans," Augur's voice is unusually quiet, as though he's worried the walls are listening. "The Market is no place for path travelers."

Zo scrunches her nose. "What do you mean?"

"Of the few who travel the path," Father speaks, "those who return to the Marketplace commonly harbor resentment for unmet expectations. And unfortunately, those comfortable on the path more often than not settle into it."

"The Market doesn't receive well ones who enter still pursuing the path," Augur continues. "It's Puppeteer territory, and It's no friend to the path."

Zo shifts. "So what should we do? Keep our heads down? Try not to attract attention? How are we going to find Quest if we're too busy watching our own backs?"

"Quietly," Augur insists. "We ought not go about drawing attention."

"Humph," Mahdi shakes his head. "You've no idea what it's like."

"Oh no, bird, there you are wrong. I know exactly what it's—"

"Aye, boy? We have traveled the path. We have lived off the flesh of Maisha Mti and tasted the bright waters of Maisha Maji. We have been immersed—in the very presence of the Three, no less! We've changed, boy. Humph. There's no concealing that."

"Mahdi is right," Father speaks up. "There's no denying what's apparent."

"We're all doomed," Augur mutters.

"And your concern is not ill-placed." Father squeezes Augur's shoulder. "Please, you know the Market well, what do you suggest?"

He considers it for a minute. "We should go to my home. I can make inquiry there."

"But your family," Zo shakes her head, "they—"

"They're my family."

"But—"

"ZO. They're my family."

"Augur." Ma's voice commands dignity and absolution, "We shall try your way."

CHAPTER 43

*T*he next morning the company crosses the great bolder-fallen causeway that spans from the cave's mouth to the wide path, a natural stone dam dividing the fresh waters flowing out of the cavern from those completing their voyage around the great mountain.

The water level on the returning side is higher than the water pouring out of the cave over here, Zo notices as they cross the bridge, *and there's another whirlpool over there*.

"It siphons the waters beneath and back up the great mountain to the source," Father answers her question before she asks. "It's the same process as the small, stone fountain in our garden, just bigger."

She nods, remembering the wall-mounted fountain on the porch outside the kitchen. "That's right, with the lion's head spitting out water. I loved that fountain." She smirks. "Yeah, this is definitely just a bit bigger."

She lifts her head and sighs. "Why is this suddenly depressing? Does anyone else feel depressed?"

A sad note escapes Mahdi. "The traveler grows accustomed to the radiance and beauty along Kubwa Hatima Njia. Aye, it's a simple thing to forget how muted the other side of the river is, humph. The colors we return to seem smeared with a dull brushes.

Even the sway of the trees is subdued in comparison." He stands still, staring at the other side. "Like an invisible netting is wrapped around everything, constricting it from its potential. Humph." His feathers puff, and he continues walking.

"Aye, bird," Augur adds, "these waters are a natural barrier between two very different lands."

The trek back to the Marketplace takes several days and traffic along the wide road grows as they travel it.

Despite Augur's attempts to enforce an embargo, restricting the company's interactions with other travelers, their small party attracts attention. Whispers have gone out ahead of them, and all around they overhear murmurings of, "Three who glow like Maisha Maji." Crowds part before them like oil retreating from water into pockets of gawking spectators, reverent withdraws, and blatant avoidances.

Mahdi whistles. "So much for keeping a low profile, aye, boy?"

"Aye, bird." Augur's mind is reeling. "What do you suppose the chances are we might slip into the Market unnoticed? Perhaps in the early hours when most have passed out—before the temptations arise?"

"Unnoticed? Humph. Unlikely, at best. The Puppeteer knows we're coming. We can be sure of it." Mahdi tilts his head in thought. "The early hours very well may be one of our better options. But we should prepare ourselves. No doubt It already has something prepared."

That evening, the company eats together around a campfire, just half an hour's walk from the Market—close enough to the boarder that no other travelers stop here. In the distance, dancing shadows paint the structures and the faint sounds of music and applause can be heard.

Father passes around his splinter of bark and canteen. They eat quietly together.

Augur finally speaks, "We should enter the Market before dawn. We've less chance of being noticed then."

"But if the rumors are true," Zo shakes her head, "if we do glow, then we're most likely to be seen in the dark. If we enter with daylight there's a chance we can blend in with the mass. That is," she raises an eyebrow, "if you still intend on avoiding attention?"

Augur straightens. "Of course I intend to avoid attention! But we already stick out among those who travel. Why risk it while all eyes are open and likely looking for us anyway?"

Crap! That's a good point. She bites her lip. "If the Puppeteer already knows we're coming—which, can we all agree is likely—we should assume It'll be watching the most when the Market is most vulnerable. Even if arriving with the daytime doesn't help to hide us, it might offer some security to blend in with the crowd. That's not an option if we try to sneak in on our own." Zo can be shrewd when she wants to be.

Augur throws his arms in the air. "Or the throng themselves may turn on us once we're inside the Market." He scratches his head. "We can speculate every possibility and still be wrong." *Why does she alway have to fight me?* "Mahdi, you agree with me?"

"Humph. This wise bird will do best to keep his beak down."

"What?" Augur's mouth hangs agape. Then he purses his lips, nostrils flaring. "Well what do you Three think?"

A pensive hush falls over the company, and all eyes turn.

Father stands. "Daughter, may I speak with you?"

Walking beside Father, Zo looks up at the stars.

Father rests his hand on her shoulder. "Beloved, there's tension with you and Augur."

She bites her lip and looks down. "I don't know," she shakes her head. "I feel like he's hiding something important. The closer we get to the Market, the more anxious and obnoxious he gets, and it's making me anxious and suspicious. Like flags are getting tossed, but no one's making the call, you know?"

His gentle eyes are weighted with concern. "Do you fear he will betray us to the Puppeteer?"

"No," she sighs, "no." She shakes her head again. "No, nothing like that. I just can't place it, but something's not right."

He nods slowly. "Broden likes him."

She rolls her eyes. "Broden likes everyone."

"True enough!" He laughs. "But your brother finds good in him, admittedly amidst flaw."

"That 'flaw' part is what worries me. I've seen it in action. It blinded me, Father—literally, the blind leading the blind, in the desert no less! It would be foolish of me to get caught unawares again. Especially now with you all here with me."

"So better take the wheel? Drive the car so you can kick him out if need be?"

Obviously! She sucks her teeth. *He's digging. His questions are always more than they seem. Think about the question behind his question.* She nibbles on her lip.

"You need to know where you're going before you decide who should drive, Beloved. Is this a short trip, are you just dropping him off? Or are you two going to travel together for the long haul? Because you can't be the only driver if that's the case."

She sighs a heavy sigh and sputters out a raspberry. "I want what you and Ma have. What you two made together is what I want. I want that."

"But that's just it, Daughter, we MADE that. It took effort, hard work and dedication. Commitment and communication. Honesty. It took a decision, faith in the midst of the absolute knowledge that we could each at any moment change our minds. We both always had the freedom of individual choice, and we together were relentlessly determined to that freedom and to that decision again and again and again, even and especially when things are uncertain."

She bites her lip again.

"Decide what you want. Then decide to pursue it, and don't give up. Don't settle." He winks. "You're a fighter, it's one of my favorite things about you. This is how you fight to win. Don't get distracted playing presumptive games of accusation. Time is too precious, Beloved, and so are you." He kisses her forehead and tousles her hair. "I like this, by the way. It's very you."

She smiles and gives him a hug. "Thanks, Father. I'll have to think about all that. But for now, what are we going to do about the Marketplace?"

He smiles. "I have a feeling that's already being worked out."

Returning to the campfire, the sight of Augur's shadowy profile makes Zo's heart skip a beat. She sighs. *Yeah, I want him. Oh man, how is that even fair? But I do, I want him.*

"Welcome back," Broden greets them. "I believe we have come to some resolution." He turns. "Augur?"

Augur nods. "I shall go into the Market tonight. I'll go to my family and get an ear to what's going on so we can make the best decision about how to enter together. I'll return with time to spare should we need to leave before dawn."

Father considers this. "Broden, will you accompany him?"

"No," Augur cuts in, "I should go alone to avoid attention and move quickly."

"Humph," Mahdi mumbles, shaking his head.

"Come now, bird," Augur chews on his thumbnail, "out with it?"

Mahdi's wings are crossed. "I don't think it wise to trust all our quest—and quite possibly our lives—to your hands alone."

Augur's jaw is set and his face is red.

"I agree with Augur," Bro objects.

Ma nods to Father.

Zo keeps quiet.

"Mahdi makes a reasonable point." Father looks at Augur. "You are asking us to put a great deal of trust in you. You will not let us down?"

Augur breathes deeply and stands. "I won't." And he sets out.

"Humph. I still don't trust him," Mahdi mumbles.

"I hear you, bird!" Augur calls back, "May you be solaced anticipating the joy I will savor in proving you wrong!" He covers his head with his hood and picks up his stride.

"Humph." Mahdi mutters a few indiscernible words, then peers one wide eye at Zo. "What DO you see in him?"

Father smiles and crosses his arms while raising his eyebrows. He nods, waiting for her reply.

Feeling up to the challenge, she sits down and leans forward. "For one thing, he's light on his feet."

Mahdi twists around to observe him. "Well, I suppose he is nimble for a blind man."

She smirks and raises an eyebrow. "And he's not put off by you."

"Humph, 'put off'?" Mahdi turns back to her. "By ME? Humph!"

Zo laughs. "Come on, Mahdi. You, dear sir, have proven to be a significant, worthy and dear friend to me. Of course his appreciation for you earns him points."

"'Appreciation,' you say? Humph. Appreciation?" His head bobs side to side. "If that's what you call it, I'd dare say I'd rather prefer not to be appreciated."

"Oh please," she smiles, "I can see you have both rather taken to each other—whether or not you choose to admit it. And that's important to me."

"Humph."

She continues, "He can be extremely loyal."

"'CAN be'?" Mahdi gawks.

"Yes, can be. He's also shown an ugly tendency to put saving face before loyalty, but I think he's working on that. No one's perfect, right?"

"'PERFECT'? Humph."

Zo sighs. "You know what I mean. Obviously not perfect, but we all have our flaws," she tugs on her hair-vine. "And he's goofy and undaunted by the rougher edges of my personality. And there's something about him I can't quite put my finger on. It's like I can see the he that he's intended to be, you know? I know he's not there yet, but I really like that guy," she watches his silhouette shrinking in the distance. "Oh, and well, he's very nice to look at."

"Mm, yes he is," Ma agrees.

"Amma?" Father gapes before laughing.

Ma dismisses him, "Speaking the truth should always be encouraged."

Mahdi tilts his head as his eyes search Zo. "But surely, young one, you recognize there is something not quite right about him? Something is off?"

She hesitates, then soberly admits, "I do…"

Bro sees the conflict etched on his sister's face. "All who travel the path travel in their own time," he assures. "It's our way. The path is always open to any who choose to travel, regardless of what their 'not quite right' and 'something off' is."

Mahdi leans back, thoughtfully bearing those words. "You are quite right. I know it—yes, I know. Humph. I only want the best for my traveling buddy."

Father nods to Mahdi. "We can all agree to that."

Zo smiles. "It's good to be with family."

CHAPTER 44

*A*ugur's heart quickens to the familiar sounds of nightlife drawing nearer.

He stops mid-stride and breathes deep. The fragrances of fried foods and roasting meats, mixed with sweet beers and sweaty bodies make his stomach turn, but he smiles.

Home, at last.

With his hood draped low over his face, he enters the Market.

The combined chaos of movement and sound with the dense smell of it, overloads his senses. *Whoa there. Oh, god, I feel —woah. Pull it together.* He pauses, one hand pressed against his chest and the other covering his mouth. He takes a deep breath and slips between two tents. Leaning heavily on his walking staff, he dry-heaves.

What is wrong with me? This is home. MY home. I know this circuit like it's my own skin! Why is it making me so sick all the sudden? Oh—here it comes—

He retches.

"Augur?"

He freezes, still bent over.

"Aye, Augur-boy! I see ya, yous blind bastard! Come now! Only yous could hear me through this noise. What the hell ya doin`?"

Holding his hood low, Augur straightens and takes a deep breath, then vomits again.

"Aye, Blindman, y`alright?"

His breathing is labored as he returns upright. "Aye, Trey. 'Lo mate."

"Where ya been, Blindman? Night's not the same without ya."

He pinches his nose. "Oh, you know, I—I needed a break."

"Well yous back now, aye? Let me clear a stage, I's 'nounce—"

"No! No, Trey. Not tonight."

"Who's this, aye? Yous never turn down a chance to show. Aye, yous perform even if they wasn't tossin` coins—ya would, an` ya have! Bit o` spews ain'ts hold ya back."

"I know, I know. I took some time off—"

"Aye, and now here yous stand. What's wrong with ya? Yous really sick, boy?"

Augur is hugging his torso. "I do feel ill."

"Best get ya home then, aye. Com`on Blindman, I's walk ya." Trey pulls Augur's long arm around his broad shoulders.

"Thanks, mate." The nausea eases, and he shifts his weight back onto his walking staff. "Tell me, Trey, what news have I missed?"

"Typical devilry, aye, nothin`a brag 'bout. But there's whispers the Puppeteer 'imself's on edge. Word is, the fabled Three's come down the mountain. Travelers been comin` in sayin` a same story, the Three's walking the road—glowin` even, right 'ere beside 'em! And theys headin` this way, is what they say. Got the Puppeteer spooked, can ya believe it? HA! Put out a nice price for informing what'll catch 'em, too! A very nice price, indeed." Trey's eyes glaze over. "Ya see anything like that out 'ere, mate? We's can go in on the pot! Split halfsies?"

Augur laughs. "No, mate, sorry. I don't see much at all."

"HA! No, I don't suppose ya have, aye. Well, still keep those quality ears of yours open. Ya hear a lead, an' we's get it bagged before anyone else, aye?"

"Aye, mate, I'll keep my ears open."

"Good boy, Blindman," he pats Augur's chest. "Good boy."

"So these Three, is there any other word about who they are? Speculation or sorts? Any mention who they're traveling with? An entourage perhaps?"

Trey looks sideways at Augur and leans in close. "Have ya bit o' info yous holdin'? Boy, ya wouldn't be plannin' a keep the Puppeteer's loot all to ya'self, aye?"

Augur pushes him aside. "Shut your face, mate. I said I heard nothing and I meant it. Just asking questions is all."

The tips of Trey's massive fingers massage his chin so that his thin lips press and pull as he stares at Augur through squinted eyes. "Alright, mate, only checkin'. Puppeteer 'imself don't put out price tags often, only once before in ours lifetime, so ya better bet I be searchin'. That's real coin, aye. Kind of coin that'll set us both sweet for a long time comin'. No double-crossin'."

Augur nods. "No double-crossing."

"Alright. Aye, ya mutta goin'a have a fit when she sees ya."

Exhaling, Augur agrees, "Yeah."

"Mum. Mum. Muh, listen… LISTEN!"

Augur's tone snaps his mother out of her rambling suspicions about his disappearance. She turns slowly to him, her head is twisted and her finger is pointed. "What's got into ya, boy? You don't speak to ME like that."

"I just need you to listen—"

"What? You think you gone off and found ya backbone, aye? I's still ya muh."

"I know, Mum—"

"Ya act like yous forgot."

"I haven't forgot, I jus—"

"You leave here without so much as a g'bye, and I's worried sick—worried to death about ya! And now you show up outta nowheres, and I can't have a moment to recover?"

"Mum, I'm sorry, okay? I had to go. And now I'm back."

"Yeah? Well we's been a sorry state since ya up an' disappeared. Sorry state indeed! Not one of ya kin can match ya coin. What coin you bring me, aye?"

Of course, already discussing money, Augur sighs. "I don't have any, Muh."

"What ya mean you don't got nothin'? You take off out there, leave ya family behind like we's some lo plague, like we's didn't raised ya, like you ain't love us! Just leave us to fend on our owns! An' now you come back expecting to just open me arms wide, and you ain't got nothing to show?"

"Mum, I need your help."

"Oh, I see. Now yous wantin' to suck me tit again? What ya need me help for, boy? I done raised you! We alls teach ya how to make coin! And you make enough for us all to live comfy! We's eat together, we's sleep together! Then ya decide to go wandering! Tear us apart, ya did! We's all working to the bone! Struggling for scraps! What ya meaning you need MY help? What else is ya scroungin' to take from me?"

"Mum, I know you're mad and probably hurt, but I had to go. I didn't have a choice."

"What's that supposed to mean?"

"I HAD to go."

She leans close. "You get ya`self caught up again, boy?"

She always interrogates me! If she would just listen. "Listen, I have a few friends and we need a place to lay low—"

Her eye lids pinch as she searches him. "What ya trying to bring in me house, aye? What's you caught up in?"

"Muh, can I bring them here or not?"

"Them's dangerous?"

"No."

"Then how ya caught up?" Her voice softens, "You ought to be back on the street making coin. Ya love making coin! Leave whoever alone to fend. They ain't raise you. I did! You owe no one but ya muh."

"I know, Mum, but I can't. I won't."

Hands on her hips, she glares at him for some time. "You caught up with some girl, boy?"

"Mum—"

"I KNEW it! You ain't denys it—no other explanation! Boy, don't you know the only reason some female wants a blind boy is 'cause ya make coin! She probably watch you for some time, got to following you to figure ya out, how you tick, just to trap ya and get you to take care of her."

"Mum—"

"She lazy."

"Mum—"

"Good for nothing."

"Mum—"

"While we's out here—yous family, Augur—we's working to the bone missing ya. You just going to up and leave ya family, leave me for some twitchy girl?"

"Muh—"

"Probably ugly, too! You wouldn't know!"

"MUH!" His voice is sharp and harsh.

She is silent.

His nostrils are flared and his jaw is tight, *If she would just shut up and let me speak!* He swallows, controlling his tone, "Mum." He sighs. "Yes, there's a lady—a LADY. But it's not just her. And it's not what you think."

Her arms are crossed, but her voice is softer, "What ya bringing her entourage, aye?" She turns away from him. "Her whole family, I suppose? They's all lazy, good for nothin—"

"MUH." As he curls his outstretched fingers, his fists tremble. He takes a deep breath. "Will you help me? We just need a place to lay low for a few. I'll go out and bring home coin while we're here."

Her eyes pierce him.

"You never spoke to me like this before, boy. You IS changed. Yous ain't even taken ya hood off to let me look at you. That girl has changed ya, and I ain't likes what I see."

He crosses his arms. "Can we stay here, Mum?"

"You seen Trey? He been keeping an eye out for ya."

"Yes, I've seen Trey."

Her gaze is still fixed. "Why ain't you show ya face? Been hiding under ya cape."

His breath seizes. *Does she see my glow?* He pulls his hood lower. "I just don't feel well, Mum."

Her stare feels like daggers, it's making me sweat.

"You go bring me some coin tonight, then you an' thems can stay—so long as thems stay low and you bring coin. But ya best bring plenty to cover thems costs, too."

He exhales relief. "Thank you, Mum. I'll go make coin right now. They return with me first thing on 'morrow."

————————

This IS foolish. And I'm the fool. Why do I feel like a fool? I LOVE performing! But this—this is buffoonery! And I'm nothing more than a whorish imbecile. I enjoyed this? I lived for THIS? All the time I've wasted, gone.

"Thank you, ladies and gentlemen! Thank you! Coins and gems, please, thank you!"

Augur is on his knees, gathering his remittance as the crowd departs, when someone yells, "Why ain'ts ya takes off yous hood? Yous much funnier when we can sees ya `pressions!"

Time to go! He hastily finishes his sweep before bowing once more, then slips away.

That scoundrel nearly made me! He weighs his coin purse. *He's right, though. Mum won't be pleased with this light sack.*

As he hurries off, another watches from nearby, silently scrutinizing his performance and his retreat.

And when he loses track of Augur, Trey, too, sets out.

CHAPTER 45

*F*ather and Mahdi are keeping watch when Augur finally returns.

"We've no time," he reports, "We must go into the Market at once. The travelers are all looking for us. The Puppeteer has a high price on our heads. Anything suspicious draws attention. Wearing my hood nearly got me caught, but I didn't dare to remove it. They all say our company glows."

"But leaving now, in the dark, will increase our chance of being spotted if we do glow," Zo returns to her protest.

"Did you not hear me? My hood attracted unwanted attention. It's not raining, no dust storm, not too cold—why is my head covered? If we travel by day with all eyes looking to turn us in for coin, we must still wear our hoods. If we wear our hoods without justifiable reason, we arouse suspicion and are sure to be overtaken. Our best chance is now, when the fewest eyes are open!"

Pursing her lips, she nods in relented agreement. "Fine."

They grab their things, snuff out the fire, and are on their way.

Mahdi glides upfront to Augur. "What took you so long to return, boy?"

"I had to ensure our safety," he shakes his purse.

"Humph. With that small coin? I thought you were returning to your family?"

"I did. But my family expects payment."

"That meager purse is sure to get us turned over. Humph."

"It's all I could do."

Mahdi inspects Augur's slumped posture. "You find yourself less suited to the entertainment business now, boy?"

"Aye bird," his voice is sad.

He crosses his wings and studies him close with one eye. "Here. This should help our plight." Mahdi hands him his own money pouch, filled with precious gems.

Augur smirks. "You're getting sweet on me, aye bird?"

"Humph. I'll gladly turn you over to the Puppeteer myself if I've the chance." His beak smirks and he pats his blind companion on the shoulder. "Anyone ever tell you you're like fungus?"

"Fungus?" Augur squints.

"Yes, boy, fungus. You suck the life out of people and you're terribly difficult to get rid of."

"So I'm growing on you, bird, aye?" Augur laughs.

Mahdi shakes his head, "I suppose, boy, aye."

Augur takes a breath. "We'll need to stay quiet and move together once we arrive," he warns. "Fewer eyes will be looking, but they'll be looking just the same."

CHAPTER 46

pproaching the Market from this direction, Zo is taken by many scattered groups camping just outside the border. It's a community of sorts, made up of makeshift tents, campfires and forlorn vagrants, different from the travelers they've met along the road. *It's like the pics Quest took that summer he was interning in LA. What did he call it— Skid Row?*

Walking among them, she whispers, "Why are all these people out here?"

Augur motions for quiet.

Mahdi ignores him, "We call it 'Lo Zo,' which is short for the Low Zone. It's the nesting grounds for those who cannot stay within the Market."

"Why?" she asks.

"Shh," Augur warns.

Her nostrils flare, and she lowers her voice, "Why can't they stay in the Market?"

"Some haven't the coin," Mahdi shrugs, "some are expelled from their families, some are too sick—"

"'TOO SICK'?"

"SHH." Augur flails his hands like small flags.

"Yes—" Mahdi looks sideways at Augur before lowering his voice "—too sick. The Marketplace doesn't tend to the ill, only the drunk. Humph, there are too many in too close quarters, so the sickly and rejected, the low ones, are sent outside to fend for themselves. It keeps disease from spreading and mitigates crime, more or less."

"But we can help them, Mahdi."

A heavy coughing fit sets off a few groupings away.

Zo turns. "I can help." Her sight is set. "I have to help." She starts toward the cough.

But Augur snatches her arm. His jaw is locked as tight as his grasp. "We have to stick together," he commands.

"Then come with me. I'm going to help." She pulls, but he doesn't release her.

"ZO. We can't stop. We can't risk—"

She snatches her arm back and continues toward the coughing.

The rest of the company follows. Augur, taps his forehead with a clenched fist, his jaw muscles bulge in protest, but he follows, too.

The contrast between these—what did he call them, low ones—and everyone else we've seen is dramatic. It's so dirty here, grimy even, and it stinks like sweat and blood. But even more than that, look at their faces! Even the sleeping ones, it's like turmoil is etched in their faces. No one should live like this.

In an effort to maintain composure, she keeps a hand pressed against her mouth.

Finally reaching the one coughing, she takes out her sap and kneels down. "May I help you?"

He squints up, through septic eyes. "Who's ya? Is yous glow?"

She holds up the sap. "I want to help you."

He coughs into one hand and points with the other. "What's that?"

"It can heal you."

"It hurt?"

"It may."

He takes a moment to consider it, then nods.

She gives him a drop and immediately he reels and gasps, then stares wide-eyed at her. Watching him tenderly, his breathing becomes more normal, and his eyes begin to clear.

He reaches out to her. "I—I can see."

"Okay, Zo," Mahdi whispers, "time to go."

The healed man grabs her wrist. "I see yous."

"Young one," Mahdi insists.

The company carefully retreats.

But the man continues, "Yous is, you are One."

Mahdi takes hold of Zo's hand. "Quickly, young one."

"One of the Three." The healed man now sits up and calls after them as they near the Market, "We've heard the whispers! We've been waitin` for yous return!" He continues yelling, unapologetically waking others, "The Three! The Three's come!"

Crouching behind a wall, Augur yanks a loose sleeve of Zo's tunic and whispers sharply, "I told you not to go."

She jerks herself free. "I couldn't not go. He needed help."

"They ALL need help, Zo. You're just going to throw everything away, risk everything—including all of us—to help some random low one? You don't even know him! He could be after us! His yelling can get us turned over! Have you lost sight of why we've returned?"

He's not wrong, but he's not right, either. She quips through clenched teeth, "I'm not the one who can't see."

Releasing a restrained yell, he punches the clay wall, calling the immediate attention of the entire company.

Somewhere nearby, a groggy voice yells, "SHUT UP, YOUS DRUNK!"

"Control yourself, boy," Mahdi scolds.

Fists clenched, face fixed, Augur takes heavy, short breaths through flared nostrils. *WHAT IS HER PROBLEM? I'M TRYING TO PROTECT HER! WHY IS SHE SO DIFFICULT?*

He forces his words through his locked jaw like meat through a grinder, "Can we at least agree that we can't risk distraction right now? We can save the world later, but we can't save anyone if we get caught."

"Then maybe YOU shouldn't hit walls," Zo snaps back, her own fists are readied.

Muscles tight, Augur forces his composure. "Then we agree?"

She rolls her eyes. *I'm not answering you.*

He exhales sharply and shakes his head. Ignoring Zo, he whispers to the rest of the company, "Keep your hoods pulled low. Stick close and stay quiet."

Augur halts the group before crossing a main way.

"Bird," he sniffs about. "Check 'round the corner for the line."

"'The line'?" Zo asks.

Mahdi moves forward. "Aye boy, humph, their backs are to us."

Augur sighs.

Zo's eyes dart between them, and a scowl curls her lip. "What's 'the line'?"

"The grub line, young one," Mahdi motions with gentle feathers. "The low ones sell their spawn to the grub tent."

Abigail Ortiz

"The low ones… sell their… grub tent?" It sinks in. "You mean they SELL their children— TO BE EATEN?"

Mahdi turns back and nods over his wing. "Humph, only larva."

"But larva ARE their children!" Her mouth hangs open.

Mahdi shrugs. "Well, I suppose if you want to see it that way—"

She throws her arms in the air. "THAT'S WHAT IT IS."

"Young one, the low ones have nothing of value—are nothing of value—except their larva, which they produce in great quantity. Supply and demand. They get paid well enough to survive—"

She shakes her head. "It's disgusting."

"Humph." He twists his neck. "Perhaps to your appetite. Life down here is not like life atop the mountain. You have to accept that—"

"It's wrong."

Seeing tears stream down her face, Mahdi presses his beak.

"It's WRONG," she insists. "Eating the children of the persecuted is WRONG. Selling your children to make money is WRONG. And justifying it is WRONG. It's WRONG. It's ALL WRONG. It's systematic oppression, denying basic rights to groups because they're—what, inconvenient? And training them to murder their offspring by offering financial compensation? It's a complicit genocide. They're literally sacrificing their own children just to survive. It's MORE than wrong, it's sadistic—it's EVIL! You should be ashamed and embarrassed that you would try to defend it, let alone indulge in it!"

Mahdi buries his face in a wing.

Finally breathing, he lifts his head. His beak is still tight. The tension in his face is desperate to hide his emotion. "I am, young one. I am. My old self knew it wrong, humph, but I was content to deceive myself to sate my desires. Humph. No more, young one, no more."

Bro and Ma comfort Mahdi.

Zo remembers Quest's passion for social justice. Unveiling these revelations in the midst of her search for him, her conviction is stirred. She looks up, into the earnest eyes of her Father. "We need to do something."

Augur sighs sharply, restlessly tapping his finger against his walking staff. "Yes. We need to stay quiet and get to safety."

"We need to stop this."

"We NEED to keep our heads—"

"We need to DO something."

"ZO." Augur pauses in painful restraint. He can feel the slow burn of her intensity, and he softens. "Zo, we have to get to safety. We can figure everything out from there. Okay? But right now we HAVE to get off the streets. We're useless if we get caught."

Zo bites her lip. *We're useless if we do nothing.* "Fine, but we're going to do something about this."

"Sure. Yes. Please, just one coup at a time, my lady."

———

"Mum?" Augur whispers, gently opening the door. He pauses to listen before letting the rest in. "Muh, it's just us."

"I didn't think ya be back," she yawns and stretches. She had fallen asleep on the old couch. "You said ya get coin and you ain't came back. I thought ya up and gone, again."

He closes the door behind the company. "No, Mum. Here." He holds out his purse, fattened with Mahdi's help. "I made coin. I had to go get—"

"Trey says ya be back, though." She stands up, staring blankly at the window behind them. "Told me to wait for ya."

"Yes, here we are." He shakes to money sack. "And here, I've brought the coin."

But she ignores him, fixed and walking toward the window. "Says ya sneaking. You know and ya not tellin'. Ya keeping for yaself." She closes the drapes and turns. "I says, 'Not my Augur. Trey, ya wrong.' But I see now." Her eyes stare sadly at the feet of her son, and she nods. "Now I see."

"Mum?"

She pulls off his hood. "Why you glow, Augur?"

"Muh—"

"Why ya glow?"

The door bursts open, and Trey enters with a group of goons. "I's told ya the boy's one of 'em."

Dumbfounded, Augur stumbles back. "Muh?"

"You listen, boy," she pulls her son close and whispers, "Trey's get good coin for thems wanted. Just let him take thems, and we's all set—aye?"

The company is seized by Trey's hired hands. But Trey wraps Augur in his heavy grip.

The coin purse drops.

"You let him go, Trey," Mum protests, "the boy ain't no part of the deal."

"He's glowin'. Look at 'im, woman. He's one of 'em."

"No, Trey—"

"Deal's for three." He motions with his stubble-rough chin. "The bird, the girl, an' atta boy here shiny-like," he pats Augur's shoulder, "makes three. Yous hidin' more?"

"You see clear as me!" she flings her arms wide. "Thems ain't got here but a moment before ya knock me door down!" Then she waves a pointed finger at Trey. "But the boy's not the deal!"

He muscles Augur away from her. "Yous be more than happy once ya gets ya coin, woman. Now BACK OFF!" He jerks Augur by the arm and pushes him out the door with the rest.

A few more shoves and they're on their way.

"Get back here, Trey!" She shrieks from behind, "You get back here!" She throws Augur's coin purse after them, and gems burst out, scattering across the dirt road like colored raindrops.

"Trey, why— How could you?"

"How could me? How could YOUs, boy? Yous 'possed to be me mate. We's agree to go halfsies. An` what? Yous gon` keep the coin yaself? Might respect that after I's bash ya." He scratches his face. "But NO. Yous gone soft for some girl—aye? She be the death of ya, yous wait an` see. Ain't no girl wants nothin` with ol` blind boy 'sept to takes what ya 'as when yous ain't lookin`— HA!" He slaps his beefy hand on Augur's narrow shoulder.

"Yous double-cross dumb Trey, aye? But Trey be thinkin` an` watchin` an` double-cross ya first. Aye boy? HA!"

Augur pleads, "I wasn't double-crossing ya, mate—"

"What? Yous thinks ya love 'er, aye? Ya choose some girl over ya ol` mate? I's tell ya she ain't no good! I's know 'er type. She's take er`thin` ya got an` leave yous scrapin`. Ain't trust a girl ya ain't buy." He picks at his chin again. "An` yous forgot ya errand, boy? Sees what the Puppeteer thinks yous 'fairs, aye! Now stuff it, an` nothin` funny."

"Augur?" Zo whispers, "Augur tell me you didn't know about this?"

Sighing warily, he is defeated. "I didn't."

"Humph. All the riffraff you grew up in, boy," Mahdi whistles. "I feared something of this sort."

"I," Augur's head hangs low, "I didn't know."

"We'll figure it out." Zo looks to Father for reassurance. He smiles kindly and nods.

Augur lifts his head. "At the house, Trey said the bird, the girl and me makes three. They spoke as though WE are the Three, like they don't see Them."

"They cannot," Ma confirms. "One must commit themself to the path to truly see."

Augur can't hide his excitement. "We can use that, right?"

"I's said stuff it, boy!" Trey snatches Augur's walking staff from behind and uses it to hit him between the shoulders.

He falls to the ground.

"Augur!" Zo moves to help.

But Trey stands between them. "Yous done 'is to 'im, aye. He's bet'a off 'ways from ya." He points. "What happens to 'im be on yous."

Feet spread out and knees slightly bent, she stands her ground, daring him to approach. "You don't even know him."

"PSSH, HA! I's done know 'im like we's kin. But yous jus' wait, girl, jus' ya wait. Yous'll see soon 'nough, jus' ya wait." He grins a toothless grin and tosses the staff at her, then spits on the ground before stepping aside.

She helps Augur to his feet and walks with him the rest of the way. "Trey is awful," she whispers.

But Augur keeps his head down and stays silent.

Dawn nears.

The Three have silently kept pace with the group.

I trust your patience, but it would be really nice for you guys to take care of these jerks.

Passing the grub tent again, she sees the last low one in line, her young face wrought in desperation.

She turns to Father. *He's watching her, too.* She looks at their sad parade, *Well, now I've got nothing to lose.*

Unbridled, she calls out, "You don't have to go through with it!"

"AYE! Shut it!" Trey commands from behind.

But catching the eyes of the low one, she continues, "You'll find another way! There's always another way!"

Zo drops to the ground.

Trey stands over her, shoulders hunched, fist in hand. "I's told ya's." His upper lip curls as he raises his gaze to Mahdi. "Who's next?"

CHAPTER 47

*T*he room stinks with the foul odor of lingered moisture, sweat, funk and mold clinging to cold, thick walls. It's a nauseating stench that coats to the roof of your mouth and the back of your throat, settling into your lungs like a layer of dirty film, impossible to get used to.

It's dark, too, but not too dark. Traces of an unsettling shadow lurk in every space as though the shadow itself is intentionally placed, an agent of espionage hiding in plain sight.

Zo has just woken up and is chained to the clammy, stone wall. She gags to accommodate her freshly roused senses. When she settles and finally gives up trying to spit the stink away, she puts her head back down to let her eyes adjust. *Ouch! My neck.* She gently rubs the dull pain. *I remember feeling angry. I remember her eyes,* she thinks back to the low one, *her eyes were so afraid.*

Now she sees the glow of Mahdi and Augur. Each are chained to opposite walls, adjacent to her. And she sees the Three. Bro sits with Augur, Father with Mahdi, and her unconscious head has been lying in Ma's lap.

"You alright there, young one?" Mahdi lets out an unexpected squawk.

"What's wrong?" she asks.

"Humph, aside from being locked up, my wing was broken."

"Broken? —Wait, 'was'?"

"The Three healed me. But I can still feel memories of the pain."

Father smiles. "That's your role in healing, dear friend, choosing to feel the pain."

"Well, I don't WANT to feel it, humph, it just sneaks up on me."

"It may," Father raises an eyebrow, "and?"

"And I control how much and how long, I know, I know. Humph. Sometimes a little sympathy is nice. Especially when I'm the only one who stepped up." Mahdi glares at Augur.

"What happened?" Zo sits up.

"After that meat-headed putz knocked you out, I challenged him. But his goons jumped me and held me back. He had them pin me against a wall, and extend my wing beyond the corner's edge." Mahdi's feathers shake in the memory of it. "Then he stomped it! Completely unfair! Humph."

"But then the Three stepped in, right there," Augur speaks slowly, like still he can't believe what he witnessed. "I saw it. The goons couldn't see, but I saw it. One held Mahdi's wing straight, then Another's hands laid over the First, and the Last's on top, and light radiated from Their hold through Mahdi's wing—"

"And at once I was healed! Humph, it's MY story. Those thugs didn't see it coming—HA! They were thoroughly terrified! The fools thought I healed my own self! Humph, serves them right. Kept their distance from there out, indeed."

"We should have run," Augur is nervous.

"To where, boy? You yourself said the entire Market is looking for us. Your own mum turned us in! Where would we run?"

"Away. Somewhere safe. We could have returned to the path. Or the Wanderland—"

"Not without Quest," Zo interjects. "We're here to find him. We can't go until we do."

"And how do you expect we do that now?" Augur's tone is raw. "I don't suppose he's chained there next to you?"

Zo nibbles her lip as she looks at her family. *I've lost each of them. I had no idea I could find them again. Yet here we are.* She lifts her chin. "We'll find a way. We know they can't see my family, how can we use that?"

"One of you could go get the keys and break us out of here," the scorn in Augur's voice silences the chamber.

"And go to where, boy? Humph. If we are to search the Market for Quest, then we must be free to search without every eye in the Market looking for us. Better we get this over with once and for all. Humph. It can't hold us for long without good reason, the crowds will question. And what reason does It have? Nothing! We've done nothing."

"We will be with you as you face him," Ma reassures. "The Puppeteer will know quickly that you are not the Three, but that doesn't mean he'll let you go. He will recognize that we are with you."

"Ma," Zo looks searches her, "why is It after you?"

Ma sighs, and tears fill her eyes.

Then Father speaks, "He was our second."

"Your second what?" Zo asks.

"He was our child. Stillborn, less than a year after Broden." Father's eyes also mourn. "We created this world to bring him back to us. The path was intended to find him, so that he may find us, but…"

"He polluted it," Bro speaks up. "He was filled with envy, and he raged against this land, dominating it. Corrupting it."

"'Envy'?" Zo shakes her head. "Why?"

The Three exchange silent and withdrawn glances.

Father finally speaks, "He hated us for adopting."

Zo gasps. "It's my fault."

"NO," Father commands her attention. "You are NOT to blame. Despite every opportunity, he has settled for hate. HE chose this. Not you, Beloved. We always knew we would adopt, even before marrying. You were always part of our plan. You did not do this. The Puppeteer did."

For a long time, the company sits in silent contemplation.

"Mahdi," Zo asks, "how did you get out of that dark wood?"

"Humph." His feathers stretch out as he thinks back. "The trees themselves spoke to me. They had not forgotten me."

He pauses, lost in the memory of it, then shivers beneath his down before continuing. "When I did not let their words sway me, they pressed in all around, growing into themselves, an impenetrable wall of contemptible wood."

Zo nods. *Yep. Us, too.*

"I tried to outmaneuver them," he speaks sadly and hangs his head, "but I was not able, and the Others subdued me for some time. Humph. So when I finally came to, I sat and ate and fell asleep again.

"I was tired." He sighs. "It's a difficult thing to endure the path in your own strength. I had not encountered the Three in so long. I simply journeyed assuming I would eventually find Them. But it never happened, and so I was spent. Done. Worn out. Ready to succumb to the darkness again."

Augur's ears tilt toward the bird.

Mahdi leans toward Zo and whispers, "I was wrong. We are not meant to travel alone," he taps the side of his head with one pointed feather, "not as I was." And he winks.

Eyes beaming, he looks up. "That's when I saw Them." A smile cuts through the corners of his beak. "The Three came to me —even as I wallowed in my own sleep and failure. They told me to get up and to fly."

"Fly?" Zo cuts in, "But your wings?"

"Aye, lass, but They are the Three!" His laugh mocks the harsh walls in jovial chorus. "One simply cannot tell Them what They already know! And They know even more! They told me to follow. I wasn't about to believe those dark woods over the Three. So I woke up and I climbed, and when I was perched at the top of the tree, I spread out my wings and laughed."

(He interjects his own story) "—It is after all ludicrous for a bird with clipped wings to try to fly—"

His eyes glaze returning to his tale. "So there I was, finally looking up into the sky, and They were there still before me. 'Follow me,' I heard Them say. So I spread my clipped wings and this time They said, 'Stretch.' So I stretched. And it hurt! But I felt the tips of my feathers tingling, and I stretched farther. And as the pain grew, the sensation increased beyond it! And right there my feathers grew! I'd never believe it if I only heard it, but I lived it, before my very eyes, these right here—" he holds up his wings, "—my own very pinions, my feathers grew! My wings expanded!

"And there I perched, laughing and stretching and growing, until They finally said, 'Fly.' And I flew! HaHA! I flew again!

"And They did not leave me, no! They remained before me. 'Follow me,' They said. And as we elevated, again They told me to stretch even farther, and my very wings grew longer and I was able to fly higher than I've ever flown before!

"'Follow me… Stretch… Follow me…' again and again until I encircled the peak and—OH—what a glorious sight it was!"

Lost in his retelling, everyone startles as a heavy boot pounds the door. "Shut ya beak, aye bird!"

It's Trey.

"Time yous three meet the master."

CHAPTER 48

*M*oaning, wailing, growling, laughter, whips cracking and chains dragging over stone— the echoing sounds grow louder as they march.

They're brought to a large hall, barley lit with a few scattered candles. All kinds of travelers fill this room, lounging on large pillows, and engaging in debaucheries and depravities. A single common thread binds them, iron collars adorn each of their necks like prized jewelry.

The glow of the company's presence draws everyone's attention and an eerie silence sweeps the room.

"Come in, come in," a voice disrupts the standstill.

They slowly walk the crepuscular chamber toward the ever-darkening far side.

"That's enough," It speaks again.

Cloaked in shadow so thick it appears to beat back the very whisper of light, and so deep it may be the very source of darkness itself, the Puppeteer can only be heard.

"Master," Trey bows low. "I's brought ya the Three."

"Have you?—"

Trey drops hard to the ground.

(This was no natural fall.)

Zo strains to see him. *Oh, god, his face is contorted, smushed into the ground! And what is that?* A thin, dirty strand is attached, taut from his iron collar. *That can't be what threw him down, it's way too small. But there's nothing else—is that what's pinning him?*

"—Hm, let us find out." The Puppeteer raises It's voice to address the company, "Are you the Three?"

Silence.

It snickers. "I'll ask only once more. ARE YOU THE THREE?"

Augur tilts his head, his ears desperately search for any indication of his companions' intent to reply. When it's clear none will, he blurts out, "NO! No, we're not!"

"Mmm," It's pleased. "No, I don't suppose you are."

"Master!" Trey begs. "Master, please? Thems most certainly IS the Three. Jus' look at thems glow!"

It sighs. "Unquestionably these have guild with the Three, yes, but unfortunately for you, dear Trey, you have failed me. Again."

"NO!" Spit, sweat and tears mix with the filthy floor, mudding Trey's face. "No! Please? Master, I's brought thems to ya. Thems the Three, no doubt!"

The Puppeteer's voice is unconvinced, "You may leave, Trey."

His head is released, and he hops to his feet. "Please, Master! Please? I's done as yous asked. Please, me reward?"

"LEAVE MY PRESENCE BEFORE I REWARD YOUR INSUBORDINATION BY PEELING YOUR SOILED SKIN FROM YOUR SNIVELING FACE, AND COMMAND THE PROCESSOR TO BEAT IT CLEAN LIKE A SULLIED RUG."

Whimpering, Trey covers his face and stumbles backward before turning and running away.

It scoffs. "There's no such thing as 'good help.'" And It redirects back to the company, "Now, two of you I know…

"Bird, something's different about you. You're brighter, obviously, but there's something— OH, yes, it's your tips! They appear to have," It snickers, "filled in?"

Mahdi's eyes narrow, but he holds his silent protest.

"Hm," It continues, "and you, blind boy, well you look rather the same. But you could see that, now couldn't you?" Its mocking laugh bounces throughout the chamber, rousing cackles and insults from the spectators. "It's about time you returned, boy. Why, I nearly entertained the notion of your betrayal."

Augur is dropped to his hands and knees. The force throws his oversized hood back, midway down his backside, revealing his iron collar.

Stunned, Zo stares. *What?* She gasps. "No."

Overcome with shame giving way to rage, Augur turns his low head away and pounds his fists on the ground. "AAAAAAARRRGHH!"

"Hm," the voice sneers, "it would appear I've outed you, blind boy. Don't tell me you didn't see that coming?"

Angry veins protrude from Augur's forehead, and he locks his jaw. Sweat and tears smear down his face, casting dire shadows from the ill-lit room.

Staring at him, broken on the floor, Zo's eyes flood with burning tears. *The whole time? And I didn't see it? The WHOLE time. And I overlooked it? All the signs I ignored, the things I excused— I defended him, I BELIEVED him. Even after I should have known better. He LET me believe him. The whole time…*

Augur turns toward her. "Zo, I—"

"Oh yes! Do explain yourself, boy," It taunts.

"—I," he turns his face back into the floor. "I'm so sorry."

"Zo?" A new voice softly speaks through the dark, "Zo?"

"Zo, I'm sorry, I—" Augur continues, but he no longer has her attention.

"Zo," the voice is raspy and weak, "it can't be?"

Eyes wide, mouth agape, she takes one step and turns her ear. "Quest? Quest, is that you?"

"Zo." There's movement in the dark.

She steps closer, too.

"Hm," the Puppeteer chuckles. "This just gets more and more delicious."

As her glow nears, melancholy eyes pierce through the darkness. Memories of those eyes seize her, and overcome with emotion she crouches into a full squat, covers her face, and cries.

"Quest!"

CHAPTER 49

S he wipes her eyes, but her hands stay fixed to her face as she studies him. *He's bigger than I remember, stronger perhaps? But he doesn't look healthy.*

His dark eyes are sunken and girdled with weary rings. His always clean-shaven face now wears a scruffy beard with sprouts twisted in. His hair is overgrown, matted and woven with shoots and leaves. His skin is paler than usual and appears stiff like the not-yet-barked skin of a young tree. The family crest he once proudly wore is gone, replaced by an iron collar weighing so heavy on his neck that he bends slightly forward, bound to an invisible pillory.

Zo reaches out, but he recoils, shielding his eyes in pain. It's been a long time since he's been in the light.

"Quest?" She pauses. "What are you doing here?"

He doesn't look up. "Where have you been, Sis?"

"I've been looking for you. Searching—"

He twitches strangely, like he's yanked from behind. He strains himself forward, still covering his eyes. "You…left me?"

"What?" She tilts her head. "No. Never. That's not—"

"I needed you," he continues, "and you left me."

"Quest, I—"

"You left me."

"No," she's firm.

There's a long pause.

"Quest," her voice trembles, "I've been—"

"Go." He starts to turn.

"What?"

"Go away."

She steps forward. "I've been searching for you!"

He turns back and looks around her, then points at Mahdi and Augur. "Looks like you found replacements."

"What?"

Rage blinds him. His eyes peer dead into hers. "Deny them."

"WHAT?" She scoffs.

"Deny them. You've spent all this time searching for me? Prove it. Reject your companions." He twitches again. "Or are they more important than me?"

"What? Why would you even think that?"

He lifts his head. "Prove your loyalty, Zo."

"Why are you doing this, Brother? These are my friends. They've helped me. We've all been searching—"

"Them or me?"

"—for you."

His eyes haven't softened.

Mouth open, she lowers her gaze. "This isn't you." She turns toward the enshrouded Puppeteer. "You're doing this!"

"Hm." Quest drops his head. "I knew you wouldn't."

She turns back. "Please, Brother! I—I've found our family!"

"WE are supposed to be family, Zo. YOU and ME. But you left me. And now—hm, now you've denied me." He turns again and shuffles back into the thick darkness.

"Please, Quest, you MUST listen!"

"Go away, Zo. I've found myself here. And you've gone and found your own."

Cold sweat crawls over her skin like a million spiders. Her eyes burn. Her stomach wrenches, buckling her over. She lifts her head, glaring with malice toward the deep dark of the Puppeteer, and points. "You did this."

A thick chuckle echoes through the silence of the hall.

"Me?" It taunts. "Hm, my Fin made it very clear who is at fault, girl. Though I do find the drama delightfully succulent! Mmhmhm."

"'Fin'?" The new name makes her skin hot. "His name is Quest."

"Was, child," Its tone belittles. "Do try to keep up, hm? Now, I already know the bird and the boy, but you, girl... I suppose I would have caught up on the details from my little blind errand boy, but now, now you have unveiled yourself as sister to my dear émigré in thrall. And you wear the glow of the Three, which leads me to wonder if in fact my blind boy finally accomplished a task with some semblance of success? So pardon my informality but I must plainly ask, Who are you?"

She stares down the darkness with fire burning in her eyes and holds her silence.

"Hm, not going to talk? Well, it would seem you've taken to my blind boy, so perhaps you can be persuaded."

Augur's face slams into the floor with a squishy thud.

Another iron-collared slave steps out of the darkness, fists clenched around a bullwhip. He's built like a defensive wall, thick and wide, and despite his large humpback, he towers over Zo.

"Tell me exactly who you are," the Puppeteer demands, "or the Processor gives the boy his long overdue reward."

Zo stands still, frozen in shock and defiance.

The Processor lets the whip snap right next to Augur, and a plume of dust makes him gag.

"Speak, girl!" It commands.

The whip raises again.

Her eyes narrow on her cowering companion.

We met in that dense forest, I was all alone for so long, and you seemed kind. My truest friend warned me about you, but I ignored him because I took your kindness for honesty.

Then you leapt into the unknown at the cliff, and again, twice down the narrow ridge, where you said you loved me. And you sought me out when I was lost in those twisted tunnels.

And you admitted you'd been lying to me in the desert, and I forgave you and taught you how to climb, even though your weight was killing me. You shared so much atop the mountain, and you chose to come with me beneath the waters to return to the Marketplace.

I continued to follow you, even though I continued to wrestle with uncertainty. And all of it has brought us here. I've finally found my brother, but he's under the influence of this deranged sociopath! And you, Augur, I finally see what you've been hiding all along.

You submit to It.

Everything you've done has been tainted by the taut thread of the Puppeteer.

Her stomach turns over and adrenaline surges.

This changes everything.

She cinches her jaw.

The whip hurls forward, and as fleeting moments seem to stretch through slowed time, her fury shifts to horror as Broden throws himself over Augur, and the lash splits into her brother's back.

He winces.

Gasps fill the room.

All the others see is that the whip has had no effect on Augur. Not so much as a stitch of his garment moved.

Zo stands frozen, but her eyes are now wide and her mouth gapes.

The Puppeteer breaks the silence, "I WILL LOOSE YOUR TONGUE!"

The Processor begins flogging Augur, but Augur is never touched.

Broden takes his thrashing in silence.

Augur's hands cover his head, and he flinches at every startling crack of the whip. In between, he marvels at the long-suffering of his covering.

Murmurings are circulating.

Father holds Ma and watches, eyes brimming.

A burning rage overtakes Mahdi. He rushes the Processor like a dark bolt of lightning and side-tackles him. Grabbing the loose end of the whip, the black bird of light wraps it around the Processor's neck before the brute even realizes what's happened.

"NO!" Broden's command echoes throughout the hall, followed by deafening silence.

Mahdi freezes, confused, before dropping the makeshift noose. The raised feathers on his shoulders heave as he calms. He gets off the trebling Processor, and moves away.

Whispers again flood the hush.

The Puppeteer's voice tears through the awe, "Now, now, hm. It would appear we have One among us. And where there is One, there are Three."

Its attention turns back to Zo. "You have proven yourself rather useful indeed, hm." It sneers. "Processor! Place these three in solitary quarters. Perhaps time apart will give them the opportunity to consider a fresh perspective."

But the Processor doesn't obey. His eyes are fixed on Mahdi.

"I said REMOVE THEM!"

It jerks him forward, but for a long moment he still hesitates.

He finally clacks his tongue inside his open mouth and slowly rises to his shaky feet, before cautiously nearing the company. Standing before them, it's obvious he's too afraid to try to force them to do anything.

Father and Ma get Bro on his feet.

Mahdi helps Augur up.

Zo waits to catch Father's attention. *I see your eyes, Father. I see you burning, a raging wildfire! And yet, somehow you remain controlled. How are you so controlled?*

She turns to the witless Processor. "We will come with you."

CHAPTER 50

Zo sits in silence.

Eyes wide open, she sees nothing but the memories of her journey together with Augur.

How could he be so selfish? How could I be so stupid...

———————

Augur wallows about the ground, angrily beating his fists and unwittingly digging his nails into his own skin.

The Three sit with him.

"I'm sorry," he tortures himself, "I'm so, so sorry. I'M SUCH A FOOL! I'm so sorry!"

"Augur," Father gently speaks.

Lifting toward his voice, Augur imagines Bro's ripped and blood-stained clothes. He drops his head again and hits himself. "I'm so, so sorry."

———————

Mahdi's wings are bound.

He watches the shadows with scrupulous suspicion. *Either they're moving or I'm going crazy. Whichever the case, I'll not be taking any chances!*

"HUMPH," he jerks, catching himself dozing. He is exhausted, but settles back and stares wide-eyed into the darkness. *It would appear that you have grown around me.*

"Maaaahdi," the whisper sounds like a distant call, "Maaaahdi."

"Humph. Keep back, you wretched darkness. I have no part with you. Not anymore."

"Maaaahdi! Maaaahdi!"

"I'll have none of your taunts, thank you. Humph." The feathers on his chest puff. "Leave me be."

"Oh, Mahdi, you look tired. Hungry? Let me get you something to eat. I'll send for a grub, one or two?"

He reflexively sniffs about. *Oh, I can smell it even over the stench of this rank air. That sweet, delectable—*

He stops.

"NO. I said I'll no longer have any part in your darkness, and I mean it! My collar is off. My feathers regrown—overgrown even—HA! This bird is free of you. Humph. I may wrestle with my temptations, but you will keep your atrocious delicacies. I was bound by your iron once, I'm not going back."

He preens his pinions, distracting his beak from tempestuous fantasies. "Before, I never dared to imagine the possibility of existence apart. I simply didn't know there could be another way. Until I witnessed one execution in particular—surely you must recall—the traveler wore no collar. He was like no one who had ever walked the Market before. Humph, he glowed.

"So I asked questions. I traced his path as best I could, only I didn't know," his voice travels back with his thoughts.

Then he whistles a sharp note. "But now, humph! Now I know! Humph. So tempt me with your delicacies, beat me till I mulch, or hang me up before the mass and drain my warm blood from my cold body—none of it matters now, because now I know!

"I know freedom from your iron. I know what it is to live! To FLY! I know life without your darkness. And I'll never go back to your leash. HUMPH."

His feathers soften as he begins to sweetly sing the tune, "This Little Light."

The darkness creeps away.

———————

The bird's gentle song fills the prison block and breaks through Augur's tormented sleep, and it soothes him.

Finally easing, a familiar voice beckons him, "Augur."

Swallowing hard, he tenses again.

"Augur."

"I—I'm so sorry."

"Are you, Augur? Are you sorry enough to change?"

"I want to. I've tried! I—I can't."

"Augur."

"I traveled the narrow path! And what changed? Nothing! Nothing. I'm nothing." A sob consumes him.

"Augur, do you want to change?"

"Yes, yes I want to. But I can't."

"Do you want to change, Augur?"

"Yes, but—"

"Do you WANT to change?"

"'Do I want to change?' Yes! YES, I want to change! BUT I CAN'T! I can't. I tried and I can't! I can't do it on my own. I want to. Of course, I want to be rid of this heavy iron! I want to be free! I didn't want to hurt Zo! I did my best, I tried to convince her not to come back! I—I, I DON'T WANT TO HURT HER.

"I want to be with her. I WANT to change. But I can't, I can't change! I need help. Please! PLEASE, I NEED HELP. I need help."

Lifting his weary his head, he looks at Father. "I can't do it. I need help."

Father nods. He takes Ma's hand, and she takes Broden's. Immense light emanates as Bro reaches out to him.

Again overwhelmed by the sacrifice, Augur hides his face.

"Look at me," Bro commands.

But seeing his torn and blood-stained clothes, he recoils again.

"Look at ME." Broden leans close.

Augur turns and gazes beyond the garment, and sees Broden is healed. His eyes widen, and Broden reaches out again.

Augur leans forward.

…Then he wakes.

"OUCH."

Surprised by the vision, he startles, stubbing his fingers against something that wasn't there before. Reaching for it, he finds the object is cold, hard and heavy.

Allowing himself a moment to comprehend it, he freezes. Then slowly, stretching his head forward, he feels his neck.

"It's gone," he whispers in admonishment. "It's off. It's off! I, I'm free?"

He covers his mouth, fearing his hushed words might be heard by the shadows.

A few moments pacify his caution, and he picks up the iron collar and rubs his fingertips along the inside. *So this is freedom? I will not forget what It did to me. I will never go back.* And he shoves the collar in his bag.

A soft scuffling comes from somewhere in the cell.

Remembering the Three, he perks his ears, but only hears silence thereon. He braces against the cold wall. "Show yourself."

"Hm, whatever for, blind boy? Hmhm."

"I am your slave no longer. You are not my master!"

"Yes, boy, I can see. Your iron is removed, but time will prove the rest. Tell me, whispers have informed that your own mother turned you in?"

Augur bows his head. "Trey tricked her."

"Mmm, so then it's true," Its smile can be heard. "How delicious."

"You leave her be!"

"Or what? Do you wish to save her, boy? Despite her betrayal? Despite her using you? Don't you want to see her squirm?"

"You touch so much as a hair—"

"I don't have to, boy. Mmm, she already wears my iron. I simply need pull my string and—"

"Stop!" Augur lunges forward.

"Why ever should I? It satisfies me, fills my belly with titillating indulgences," and It drops to a deep whisper, "gratifications you couldn't dream about in your wildest imaginings. Mmhm. 'Stop,' you say? You'll need to give just reason to restrain myself, boy. What have you?"

How can I save her? Come on, Augur, think! What can I do? How can I? I can't. It wants me to compromise the Three. I would betray Zo, again. What can I do?

Despite his new freedom, he feels defeated.

Then the light cuts through his blindness, and he sees the Three standing over the Puppeteer. For the first time, Its form is revealed. It is small and huddled, like a parasitic plant, no more than an insect among the mighty postures that preeminent and expose It.

Emboldened, Augur speaks, "I am free of you, Puppeteer. I've no need of your deals any longer."

"So you say, hm? And we shall see."

Augur reaches in his bag, unwraps his lightning pipe and begins to follow Mahdi's tune.

———————

As his music reaches Zo, her convictions about his betrayal bolster and her attitude sours. *This Little Light of Mine? What does he know about light? He won't shine! He's only ever served darkness.*

Rubbing her balled fists into her eyes, she doesn't notice the presence of light.

"Zo, may I come in?" The safety of Ma's familiar voice is enough to defuse her.

"Ma." She sighs, snuggling into her embrace. "I'm such a fool."

"No," she shakes her head, "not my daughter."

"I believed him, Ma. I forgave him and I trusted him. I wanted him so much that I stifled my gut, and even Mahdi's warnings. I put my faith in him, and he played me, again and again and again. And it's affected all of us! I let him into our family, and he's ruined us!"

"My darling, listen to yourself." Ma squeezes her. "This isn't like you!"

Zo's voice is small and set, "He's ruined me."

Ma straightens. "Now you listen, forgiveness is NEVER a sign of weakness. It takes great strength to forgive. Releasing one from their righteous dues demands that you lay aside both pride AND justice. It's sacrificial love, and THAT is the greatest power in the universe." She squeezes Zo close. "And it's always in your own self-interest because—even more than the one pardoned—forgiveness frees YOU from the weight of their actions, and the responsibility of sentencing, and the obligation of executing, and the unending burdens thereafter."

She holds Zo back and looks into her eyes. "Never, NEVER regret forgiveness. No, no, my Love. Forgive freely and often."

"But, Ma, he—look at us! We're actual prisoners locked in dungeon all beca—"

"We're here because we forgive, every one of us. And we'd do it again. You don't believe this is surprising to any of us, do you? We knew, my Love. And your gut speaks loudly, if my memory serves well, and you've always had the wisdom to listen. Mahdi has grumbled all along, but still he came. And Augur, well, Augur made it quite clear what he anticipated, but even he came willingly because—"

"I don't want to hear it, Ma." Zo pulls away.

But she persists, "—because he loves you."

She sucks her teeth. "He has a crappy way of showing it."

Ma shrugs. "And that's the only way he knows."

"That doesn't excuse it."

"No. It simply explains it. Tell me, why do you think he follows you?"

"Apparently because he was ordered to."

"Yes, well, why would he go out of his way to save you—twice? Why would he jump off a cliff for you, three times! Why he's so convinced he loves you that he left the mountaintop to follow you right back to the Puppeteer? He loves you, darling, he only doesn't quite know how to be true."

"He's a fool, and I'm worse than a fool for believing him."

"No, Love, you're a fool's salvation. A proper Salvador. And we couldn't be more proud of you."

They hold each other tight.

Zo sighs. "None of that changes that we're still stuck here."

"No, dear. But we are here together."

She breathes deep again and a tingling relief wraps around her body like a soft throw. She snuggles closer. "Thanks, Ma."

A faint and mocking applause echoes in the cell as a shadow grows from the door. "Family reunions are," It gags for effect, "just lovely, hm?"

Zo rolls her eyes. "How would you know?"

"Touché, girl." It sneers. "Hmhm, I like her. She's got spunk. You know, I could give you great wealth, girl. Whatever your desires fancy may be at your disposal to do with as you please. You need only wear my iron. I offer you a world for the taking."

Zo scoffs and she shakes her head. "I've seen how you reward your slaves. You know nothing about me. My family is my world, puppet-man. Not interested."

"Mmm. Because you gave me such a delicious show today, I'll pardon your impudence—but only once, girl. Now if it's merely family you desire, then family I provide." It snaps. "Come forward, Fin."

Her ears perk as the sound of shuffled steps near. *Quest!*

"Zo."

"Brother?"

"Deny them, Sis."

"Quest, they're OUR family."

"WE are our family—YOU and ME. Everyone else is dead! They're gone. Stop living in your fantasies, Sis. Deny them and be done with it. We're family. We can still be family."

"Come with us, Brother?"

"WE are family. Sis, look," he holds out his foliage laced hair and points. "We're the same. You're just like me, you can't hide it. I see your vine, we're the same. Stay with me."

"No, Quest, I won't settle. Listen, I'll show you. You just have to come with—"

"STOP." He hangs his head and scoffs. "'Settle'? Just stop, Zo."

"Quest, they're here! Ma is right here!" She looks at Ma. "Say something."

But Ma is silent.

Biting her lib, Zo tilts her head. "Ma?"

"See, Zo? It's in your head. It's your wild imagination! You're a dreamer. But this is no dream. You need to stop holding onto them. They're DEAD. But I'm right here."

Zo pleads, "Ma?"

"Deny them, Sis."

She tugs at Ma's arm. "Say something."

"Deny them!"

"Why won't you speak to him?"

"DENY THEM!"

Ma reaches to wipe the tears rolling down Zo's face, and Zo sees that she, too, is crying.

She turns back to the door. "Quest, you can't see or hear them because you have to travel the path. You must get to the path, it's the only way. Please, Brother? Please join us. Travel the path!"

"THAT'S QUITE ENOUGH," the Puppeteer cuts in.

After a long silence, Quest speaks, "I'm not your brother, not anymore."

"What? What does that mean? You can't change—"

"My sis is dead to me. Dead. Along with everyone else. I have no family left. My place is here." And he shuffles away.

Her breath leaves her lungs like a battering ram driven through her torso. As the words of her beloved brother sink in, she can't breathe.

The Puppeteer's laughter echoes throughout the chamber.

But Zo only hears the replaying her brother's words. Her eyes glaze over and her face flushes red. Tears tread cool trails down her warm cheeks.

My sis is dead to me. Dead... I have no family left.

Finally, breathlessly and full of sorrow, she whispers, "Quest."

ABOUT THE AUTHOR

Abigail Ortiz began writing *Zo's Quest* to provide context for a dream that left a resounding impression. Creating the characters and backstory, and journeying with Zo through *Zo's Quest* became an outlet for Abigail to process her own experiences of family and interpersonal trauma, church hurt, and self-discovery. The *Zo's Quest* series began as a parallel world for Abigail to reflect on and engage with her own path, and has emerged as a transformative parable, providing the reader with the hope, inspiration and confidence to pursue their own actualization.

Abigail was born and raised in a small, hilly town in the beautiful San Francisco Bay Area. She and her family now live just south of Nashville, TN, but she still daydreams about snuggling in a heavy sweatshirt on dense, foggy days, and the sweet scents of eucalyptus and grassfire carried on a summer breeze.

AbigailOrtiz.com